Norah and Emma

Verity Short

ISBN 978 0 9929542 5 3

Print Edition

For Olive, Christine and Cynthia

who came through for me

Table of Contents

CHAPTER 1

Remembrance

Gothic Cottage – 1957

HEAD RESTING AGAINST the wing of the armchair, Norah surveyed the room. The empty bookshelves lost their shadows after the maid drew the curtains, but that served to let the greyness flood the room faster. Had there ever been a time before life became a cycle of restless days followed by endless nights, punctuated by pain and discomfort from her hip? The bliss of unconsciousness – even at the cost of a few unsettling dreams – would be a welcome exchange for hours of pain-free existence. Instead she had to lie and contemplate the dawn force itself into the room, the leaden drabness creeping with agonising slowness through the chinks and cracks, until at last Florence opened them and allowed the dull, flaccid grey-suffused light to fill and envelop the room. Despite the gloom, Florence was putting on her bright and cheerful act. Didn't she realise the wheedling gave her away? Not like servants in the old days. They had a proper sense of duty and were glad of the work.

"Back in a jiffy to light the fire, ma'am. Soon get you warm and snug."

"Perhaps you might get on with it. The quicker the fire is going, the sooner you can fetch my breakfast."

Florence bustled out to collect the necessary wherewithal to light the fire. *Thinks I'm taken in by that fixed grin,* thought Norah, turning her attention to the garments Florence had laid out next to the washstand. How tedious it was having to get dressed in the cold, head fuzzy from lack of sleep, brain exhausted by tortuous insistent ramblings through a twilight world it refused to relinquish for oblivion. Why wouldn't it shut down and rest sometimes? Norah stared at the outfit she was about to don. Clothes might have lost much of their fussiness since the long skirts and petticoats of suffragette days, but she'd give anything to swap the ease of dressing now for the clothes and energy she'd had then, when her vitality and commitment would never allow undergarments to hamper her.

Florence burst into the room with the coal bucket on one arm and a basket with fire-lighting paraphernalia on the other. Annoyed by the fuss she was making, Norah glared at her from the armchair where she'd sat down again after dressing herself. *Thinks she can get one over on me, pretending it's too much for her these days.*

"Why didn't you bring it in two lots, Florence? That way it wouldn't be so exhausting for you."

"And leave you sittin' in the cold a moment longer than necessary? For sure, couldn't live with meself.

There now, I'll get the fire lit in no time, and you'll be lovely and warm. Max too – how is he today?"

"I decided not to disturb him until you got the fire alight. He's nice and cosy under the bedclothes; thought I'd let him enjoy it a bit longer."

"Sure, he's such a comfort, don't know what we'd do without him."

"You're so helpful, Florence. How would I manage without you?"

"We've seen many years together, good and bad, more good than bad. Wouldn't want it any other way."

Watching Florence struggle with the fire, Norah became alerted to the unmistakable click of the garden gate. Using her walking stick, she leaned forward, stretched out and pushed the lace curtain aside. It was getting more difficult to move surreptitiously so that the caller was unaware she was watching. The chair had to be moved nearer the window. She'd get Tony to help next time he returned from one of his trips. Trouble was, he was away so often she didn't know how long she'd have to wait. Some son he turned out to be – never there when she needed him. Maybe Florence might do it. On the other hand, Florence would grumble so much, it would be worth waiting for Tony. The only one she could rely on these days was Max. He never questioned, always did what she asked and gave nothing but love in return.

As she scrutinised the young man approaching the front door, Norah noticed he was carrying a briefcase.

His companion hovered outside the gate. *They'll be Jehovah's Witnesses. You can always tell. They call in twos and have fresh faces, full of hope and enthusiasm. Politicians put on their serious face and carry flyers and pamphlets.* Ambition mixed with nervousness reflected on the boy's face, which reminded her of her own canvassing days.

"There's a caller about to knock, Florence."

"I heer'd the gate. D'ya want me to get it, Mrs Elam?"

"I'll see to it. You concentrate on the fire. Help me out of this chair first."

"Very well, ma'am."

The smile didn't fool Norah. The eyes gave it away. Florence might be annoyed and irritated but she'd deal with her later. For now she was going to have fun with the gullible young idiot at the front door. She hadn't lost her appetite for verbal sparring. This would be gratifying.

"Well, young man?" Norah snatched the door open.

Larry stepped back. Surely not. That commanding voice couldn't belong to the small, plump, grey-haired old lady, standing in front of him wielding a walking stick.

'Dumbstruck, are we? Have you walked up my garden path to stand there? You must have started with a purpose. What is it? What do you want?'

Larry looked round and called to Bill, waving at him to come over, but Bill was examining roses by the gate.

"Seems Bill has gone deaf," said Norah. She'd seen Bill before despite his being some distance away. *Interested in my hedge and flowers – honestly, Bill, that trick is as old as forever.*

"Come on, then, I've asked you what you want once already. I won't ask a third time."

"Did you know we are in the end times, and that Jehovah is coming to judge you?"

Norah shoved Larry aside with her stick, hurting his arm. Alarm registered on Larry's face as he watched her hobble a short way along the path, glance about, then return to the doorstep before turning to face him.

"I'm looking, can't see him, when's he expected? Is it in the next hour, because I've other engagements then, so he better hurry up if he wants to judge me."

"I didn't mean right now. The end times began in October 1914, and Jehovah will decide when to complete them, so don't know the exact time or date. It's explained here in *The Watchtower*. Would you like to buy one?"

"Give me a copy, then. You are correct about October 1914, something did end, but not what you imagine."

"If you want to talk about it, I'm sure I can explain everything."

"I doubt that. Let's take the issue of the Bible and your claim that it's historically and scientifically accurate."

Larry gulped. Norah observed the blush spread

across his face as he looked towards Bill, still studiously ignoring Larry's attempts to attract his attention. Good job she read up her notes on JWs yesterday. Her intuition hadn't let her down. *Now let's see...*

An hour later, Larry, mind numb with the barrage, was relieved to realise he was dismissed.

"I believe I made the points I wanted. That will be all for now, young man. When you can come back and assure me that it will be a hundred and forty-four thousand women ruling earth from heaven, with no men included, I might consider joining you. I'd like to create a men-free zone in paradise, where women decide the fate of everyone resurrected and living on earth."

Larry picked up his briefcase and scurried down the path to where Bill was still undertaking an intense study of plant taxonomy near the gate. As he did so, Larry was horrified to feel teeth sink into his ankle. He looked down to see a dachshund yelping and pulling at his trousers, growling through clenched jaws as he tugged and tugged and wouldn't let go. Larry's howl of pain gratified Max as much as it did his mistress.

"Max, come away and leave that young man alone. I suspect we've left enough impressions on him for one day."

With that she ordered Max inside and followed him in, slamming the door. Larry went to meet Bill.

"How did I do?"

"Did she pay for the *Watchtower*?"

ೞ ೞ ೞ

NORAH STOMPED INTO her room, exhilarated and pleased with her achievement. She hadn't lost it – could still best an opponent in a good argument. It was easy if you stuck to logical, unarguable fact. The pain from her hip was excruciating, made worse by getting up and down from the chair. Perhaps she shouldn't have spent an hour lambasting that young man on her cold doorstep, but it was fun. Made her feel young again. Her brain could still do it, why couldn't her body? *Damn this hip.*

"Come and help me get comfortable, Florence."

"Thought you were never gonna finish. Been in twice t'see t'fire. Didn't eat your breakfast. I'd to take it away, your tea cold an' all. Can't have you taking a chill, though. Here, let me wrap a blanket 'round your legs."

"Go and get some fresh tea now. I need to warm myself inside out."

That shut her up for a while, she thought, as Florence left to do as bid. Needed to get her tactics ready before Florence got back. As she gazed about the room, she was reminded of Dudley. It was a shame she'd been forced to sell his books, some priceless first editions amongst them, but she needed the money – hunger for food overcame hunger for words. She also got the satisfaction of annoying Tony, who claimed they were his; that his father left them to him. Florence should be grateful she'd empty shelves to clean, haunted though they were by the myriad words used to mould sentences and ideas that once filled the volumes that stood on them – row after ordered row. Now abandoned, they were a playground for the dust that evaded capture by Florence's occasional foray with a duster, the motes dancing in the air for a while, then settling down again to await her next assault.

There wasn't even a picture of Dudley, just those two portraits above the fireplace of Julie and Désirée. They were beautiful. Norah fancied herself looking graceful in a deep blue gown like Julie's. Her own fingers weren't quite so long and elegant, but she'd have looked as imposing.

Florence arrived with the tea tray.

"Put it down on the desk and pour me a cup."

"Are you warm and comfortable ma'am? I was going to ask …"

"I say, Florence, did you ever notice how Julie and Désirée's hair is fashioned the same in those pictures?"

"You did mention it once or twice. Wonder if …"

"See how their tresses are dressed with those delicate flat curls framing their faces."

"Must a' been style then, ma'am. Wanted to …"

"How sad their eyes are – have you noticed how they seem to stare at you with amazing directness?"

"I do. Been meaning …"

"Perhaps they reflect their burden of duty, and that's what troubles them."

"Could be right, Mrs Elam. Can I ask …?"

"Well, Florence, I'm keeping you from your duties. Better let you get on. As it's your afternoon off, leave my lunch tray in the dining room. I'll help myself."

ᛦᔆ ᛦᔆ ᛦᔆ

FLORENCE CLOSED THE door behind her. Norah turned her attention to the leather-tooled desk, where she and Dudley had worked together on her articles and pamphlets. She'd been good at writing speeches and propaganda. Emmeline and Christabel never failed to appreciate her efforts. Christabel said her speeches were emotionally expressive – one word or a theme was all it took for her to produce a masterpiece of prose.

Then there was The Leader. Norah looked at the signed portrait from his wife, Diana. The greatest politician she'd known – a man before his time, his ideas never fully appreciated. His vision for the role of women in society was revolutionary. What a tragedy it was never realised.

Norah heard her granddaughters in the hall, moaning. When would they learn? Couldn't speak quietly; didn't they realise she could hear them through the door?

"But why do we have to come every week, Mummy?"

"Shhhhh. She'll hear you," said Olive.

"But, Mummy, we hate that room. It smells horrible."

"Shhhhh. She'll hear you, then you'll be made to stay longer. Best get it over with."

"But, Mummy, why does Max get to sleep under the sheets at the bottom of her bed? Daddy says it's what makes the smell."

"Shhhh. I keep telling you, she'll hear you, and it'll make it worse."

"Can't you come in with me and Mary? If you're there she may let us go quicker."

"No, I can't. You know she likes to see you on her own."

"Mummy, please don't make us go. Grandmamma is always so cross."

"For the last time. Shhhhhh. Knock on the door and get on with it."

Norah flinched. She must not betray irritation with their childish disobedience. She must concentrate; make them understand the importance of what she had to tell them. They'd inherited their mother's stupidity – she couldn't even teach them discretion. Norah's only recourse was to make sure they listened.

"Come in," Norah shouted. "Hurry up, and close the door behind you to keep the draft out."

"Good morning, Grandmamma. We hope you're feeling better."

"Don't say what you don't mean."

"We're sorry, Grandmamma."

"You better be. You're here for your own good. Pay attention. Now study the portraits. Do you remember what I told you?"

"Yes."

"So tell me again, then I'll be sure you haven't forgotten – Carina – who are the ladies in the portraits?"

"The Clary sisters."

"Mary – pay attention – whom did Julie marry?"

"Julie married Joseph Bonaparte, Napoleon's brother, and became Queen Consort of Naples and Italy."

"Good – and Désirée – who was she engaged to?"

"Désirée got engaged to Napoleon, but he decided to marry Josephine. Then Napoleon's General, Jean-Baptiste Bernadotte, asked her to marry him. Bernadotte and Désirée became King and Queen of Sweden."

"These ladies are your direct ancestors. Your grandfather, Dudley, was the great-grandson of Bernadotte. Being related to Napoleon and Swedish royalty means we have aristocratic credentials and social standing that carries obligations. These require you to behave properly and observe correct decorum and habits. It is important you don't forget. This is why it is necessary that I remind you regularly."

CHAPTER 2
Holloway

"**M**RS DACRE FOX got 'ere with Mrs Drummond. Come from Marlborough Street Police Court couple a hours ago," said Emma delivering her report to the senior wardress on the new arrivals at evening changeover.

"Ah yes, '*General*' Flora Drummond," said the senior wardress. "She's been our guest before."

"Aye. First time for Mrs DF though," said Emma. "Police in Black Maria said she yelled and shrieked at magistrate right through 'er 'earin. Took four men to drag 'er from court into van. That's 'ow she got 'ere all untidy."

"Why haven't you completed the admission procedures?"

"Wardress on duty when they got 'ere said as we should leave Mrs DF to calm down a bit."

"And she hasn't calmed down yet?"

"No. When we eye her through peephole and see 'er lying down, we try an' go in. But she lays on bed screeching. Won't let us to touch 'er. Shouts she don't want no food nor water."

"If she's lying on the bed, how did the cell windows get broken?"

"We saw 'er through peephole. She got up, took off 'er shoes, climbed on't bed and smashed windows with 'eels."

"Very well, I'll talk to my colleagues and tell you what's to happen."

Next morning, Emma waited outside the senior wardress's office for orders. As usual, she arrived first. She brushed down her skirt then ran her fingers round her cap to check no stray hairs had escaped. Fiddlesticks, some had. No mirror anywhere here to check she'd recaptured them. No wonder, all them endless flights of stairs and heavy metal doors to be locked and unlocked to get here. Always made her feel shackled like the prisoners. The clinking of the keys hanging from her waist jangled every nerve with every step, reminding her that they was each one 'em inmates, everyone 'ad to follow the rules. Wardresses and prisoners coupled together like links in the chain the key was 'ung on. Even at the top of the chain they'd to keep to the rules. Here came the others; they better stop whispering or they'd be getting a tongue-lashing before they got the day's orders. The senior staff member arrived and summoned them into her office.

"Mrs Dacre Fox will submit to admission procedures this morning, whether she likes or not. She'll be told that her disorderly, hysterical behaviour yesterday and wilful damage of cell windows, has earned her three days in solitary confinement on bread and water."

Emma and the other wardresses went straight to Norah's cell to await the senior wardress. When she arrived they got ready to enter.

"Remember, avoid eye contact. It's an essential part of controlling the prisoner. Do you understand?

"Aye," all four answered, in tune.

The prisoner lay on the bed with her back to them. In keeping with prison etiquette, the senior wardress kept her voice to a low monotone. No inflection of her voice allowed betrayal of inner thoughts. She didn't have to avoid eye contact; the prisoner didn't look at her, not yet.

"Mrs Dacre Fox, I've come to tell you that your defiant behaviour in breaking cell windows and refusing to submit to admission procedures is to be punished by three days' solitary confinement on bread and water."

"Oh yes?" Norah snorted with all the contempt she could muster, then turned and stood up. "I'm sure it makes you believe you have power over me by attempting to punish me. The fact is, I'm on hunger and thirst strike anyway, so trying to frighten me with bread and water for three days is futile." Norah looked at the three junior staff and sniggered. "I suppose you've come with her to try and force me to comply with admission procedures. Well carry on, do your worst, we'll see who comes out of it with their principles intact. You'll not break my militant spirit. I'm right in seeking to bring the issue of votes for women to public attention, having been forced into militancy by intransigent politicians and hypocritical church leaders. You should be ashamed of making yourselves lackeys supporting them in their attempts to silence us through questionable laws that advocate the torture and imprisonment of innocent women. None of you can even look me in the eye. Cowards."

Cʒ CʒCʒCʒ

EMMA SAT DOWN in the wardresses' recreation room. At last, a chance to think and rest her weary, aching legs. Did she want to think, though? Would she ever understand why these suffrigitt women was so willing to be force-fed? They was different from the other prisoners with their slogans and stomach to fight. Where did they get their 'unger for the vote from? Why'd they want it? Was it gonna make any difference to the lives of the other prisoners – the women in prison for debt, the dollymops, the women who stole to feed their kids? Most of 'em wouldn't get a vote anyways. Those suffrigitts were the 'ardest to understand. They was working girls like herself, who wouldn't get a vote 'cause they was under thirty and didn't own no property. But they was as greedy to get a vote as Mrs Pankhurst and them middle-class professional women who must find prison life 'orrible. The rule never to look in their eyes was a good'n, but she weren't able to resist sneakin' one once or twice. Whenever she done it, she was careful not to stare too long in case the prisoner noticed and stared back. She knew from the glimpses she'd taken she couldn't stand their gaze for long, frightened of being trapped by it, 'ypnotised and unable to break away. If she got caught by the senior staff she'd 'ave been in trouble. But those obstinate stares wed with pain had begun to 'aunt her dreams, and every night as she drifted off to sleep she prayed to be free of dreams full of accusin' eyes followin' her everywhere.

Two of the wardresses involved that morning sat down.

"That Mrs DF's a right one. Never seen 'er afore, she new? Do we ken much 'bout her?"

"She's General Secretary of the WSPU," said Emma, " 'as been a couple of years. Not 'eard of afore then. Knows Emmeline and Christabel Pankhurst and Grace Roe."

"How d'you ken?"

"Fiddlesticks. Don't you read? It's impossible to ignore 'em, 'specially since they bin in 'ere to 'ave tea, or, should I say, refuse to 'ave tea."

"Aye, but where'd you find out so much 'bout her?"

"I buy their newspaper sometimes."

"You oughta be careful, girl."

Emma moved to a quieter corner of the room. She wanted peace to contemplate, couldn't stop herself. It was always the same, so much 'ad changed since she took this job – slow – but it 'ad changed. It 'ad always bin difficult, the rules was strict and most days she never got a chance to sit down. The guv'nors ran 'Olloway by a strict code that wardresses and prisoners never crossed, or wasn't meant to. Spiders and webs, spiders and webs. Invisible barriers spun through the place, 'ard to see 'til you looked, but strong and bindin', with no escape. They said as women what found themselves in 'Olloway deserved to be 'ere, whatever the reason. Like everyone else, she never questioned why or 'ow. But now she did, and couldn't understand.

Emma shook her head and smiled to herself at the idea that the locals called this place 'Camden Castle' and set off to report that she was going off duty.

CB CB CB

NORAH LAY IN her cell too angry to relax or sleep. She wasn't thirsty or hungry, although her body tried to remind her that she was both. Couldn't get her thoughts in order. Kept repeating her slogan, 'No Compromise, Bully Back'. Flashbacks from incidents during the last two days kept springing up, together with thoughts of what she hoped to achieve. She ached to know whether or not she'd succeeded. But the success or failure of what she'd done would be determined in the future. What a pity hindsight would be the judge. Like the supply of food or drink, which her body craved, she could count on no immediate gratification on either count.

Norah pondered how she got here; reciting to herself the speech she gave to the press while camped on Lord Lansdowne's doorstep with a suitcase of nightclothes and a stool. She pictured the scene, the press hanging on her every word... 'I have been summoned to appear this afternoon for making inciting speeches, and as Lord Lansdowne has also been making inciting speeches, yet seems to be perfectly safe from interference, I thought I had better be with him so that if they take me they can take him as well'.

Looking around in the semi-darkness, she imagined how justice would see Lord Lansdowne and Sir Edward Carson in cells facing punishment for inciting Ulster militants to violent uprising. Norah remembered her conversation with the Archbishop of York, whom she interviewed about the issue of force-feeding. The bile rose as she remembered his response to her question as to why male militancy was tolerated, but not female. His ignorant reply must have sounded stupid even to him. How he delivered it with a solemn face she found hard to imagine, '......the WSPU position was different...' he said '... the Ulster rebels had created a situation which the government had to accept'. Quick as a flash she responded to his ridiculous suggestion. 'This is a direct incitement to militancy. We are to create a situation which is such a terrible menace that the government must yield, then you will support us?'

She was more infuriated with the Archbishop of Canterbury and his fatuous responses when she saw him. He tried to suggest the women had brought the problem of force-feeding on themselves, militancy causing them to fail in their Christian duties as women, by opposing the will of God. Norah had reported her thoughts on that bit of nonsense during one of her speeches. 'As I sat looking at that old man, the feeling which was uppermost in my mind was that of contempt … I wondered if Calvary had almost been in vain'.

Norah scrutinized her cell walls. It may be summer out there, but in here it was permanent winter, empty of proper warmth, human or inhuman. Motes did not dance in the few rays of light that penetrated these dank walls. They hung grey and suspended, miserable to be trapped, wanting to escape and hide in any corner they could find. The name of this place, Holloway, stood for and embodied the hypocrisy of the government and the authorities who condemned her to this cell for her principles. The literal meaning of the words 'hollow' and 'way' aptly described their actions, and the walls lent credence to it; cold, damp, grey, fusty, stony, dimly lit, confining and miserable. She reflected on the torture to come, how she might play a game in her mind conjuring up a list of words that applied to her tormentors and her cell. It might help take her mind off it and get her through it.

Despite the hard bed and the pains gnawing at her stomach and throat, Norah dozed in fits. Her clothes were uncomfortable. She'd been wearing them since she dressed to go to Lord Lansdowne's house a couple of days ago, although in her befuddled state she wasn't sure how long ago that was now. Because she refused to make her bed and tidy her cell in defiance of the rules, they took her bedding away, which made the bed harder and the cell colder. Startled, Norah sat up as she experienced a searing pain across her face. It took a moment to realise that she'd been dreaming. The nightmare faded, but in her mind she saw the dogs and then the whip as it lashed her face, the whip on the end of a monstrous arm out of proportion to the body it was attached to.

Norah struggled to concentrate, she must stay strong. She chanted under her breath 'Never Compromise, Bully Back' and remembered her unapologetic, defiant speech made at the magistrates' court. She'd written it, perfected it and practised until she got it word perfect.

"If I am charged with making inciting speeches, why are not Sir Edward Carson and Lord Lansdowne and Mr Bonar Law standing beside me – these men who are guilty of incitement to take human life? I was arrested on the doorstep of a man who has made worse incitements than I have made. I shall do exactly what my conscience tells me to do; if I want to go to prison I shall go; if I want to stay outside prison, I shall stay outside. It is an impossibility to make me give my consent to those things with which I do not agree."

The memory of the first part of the speech came strong and clear, she'd rehearsed it many times. She was proud of several more phrases and brooded over them.

"Why should you prosecute us women, whose only

crime is that we stand for the downtrodden, sexually, economically and politically? The whole thing is a travesty and a farce; it has become a public scandal. You are the laughing-stock of the world."

Norah was most proud of the bit where she could visualise the magistrate trying to interject and say something, but she'd spoken over his weak efforts to interrupt. "I don't want to hear anything you have to say. Be quiet." That told him, the mean, snivelling little man, carrying out orders and incapable of seeing what an idiot and hypocrite he was.

Norah dozed. Her disturbed sleep lasted until roused by the sound of a key clanking in her cell door.

CB CB CB

EMMA CAME ON duty three days later and waited outside the senior wardress's room on the landing she was assigned to that day. The senior wardress arrived and reported that the prison doctor had decided that Mrs Dacre Fox would be force-fed today. She, Emma and two other wardresses would accompany the doctor to her cell. The Cat and Mouse Act had been introduced the year before. Did it 'elp or 'inder her work? She weren't sure. She tried to discuss it with her Da, who said, without stopping to draw breath –

"Suffrigitts deserve force-feedin', they's deranged and unbalanced." Emma wondered where he got those words from. What did they mean, did he know? She didn't, but thought she might.

"They don't be'ave like nat'rul women. Nat'rul women watch after their menfolk and children; they don't go shoutin' in streets bein' violent. They 'ave to be punished. Force-feedin' teaches 'em. Lettin' 'em out on licence when they can't stand no more, forces 'em to fink twice afore they do it again."

Fiddlesticks. Da hadn't let her get a word in; so convinced he was right she didn't dare contradict him. She doubted 'e would 'ear anythin' she might say anyway, 'is mind was made up.

Emma tried to discuss it with her Ma, who gave her a haunted, fearful stare and said –

"Never dwelled on't, don't 'ave any idea."

"You sure?" Emma asked. "You 'eard me asking Da 'bout it. 'Aven't you ever wondered?"

"What your Da says is right. Anyway, I've too many other things to worry 'bout. Can't waste me time on stuff like that. Thinkin' don't put food on't table."

Disappointed, Emma felt sorry for Ma. Watching her prepare porridge, Emma thought Ma's ideas was a bit like the lumpy, watery stuff they made in 'Olloway, prepared in an 'urry and 'orrid to eat. Her Ma 'ad spent so many years strugglin' with everyday problems she ignored anythin' that wanted too much thinkin' 'bout, concentratin' on what she needed to do to get by.

Emma tried to speak to other wardresses. These chats took place in whispered exchanges. It was impossible to talk out of earshot of senior staff, whose vigilance made them ready to intervene to stop unsuitable topics being discussed. Opinion was divided. Some wardresses 'ad sympathy with the suffrigitts. Others followed the official line, unbendin' in their determination to ensure the women followed prison rules. The attempt by some suffrigitt prisoners to be made First Division political prisoners got laughed at by prison guv'nors. Through the senior wardresses they sent the message down the line – 'Who do these women reckon they is? Politics ain't no concern of theirs, they should be'ave proper in accordance with the role given women in society and for which they's physically and mentally suited. If we let 'em get away with this, who knows what might 'appen.'

Emma was in a quandary. She knew she 'ad to follow orders and ignore her growin' unease that the suffrigitt prisoners was right to call force-feedin' torture. The prison guv'nors 'ad law, doctors and everyone on their side. Why then did force-feedin' make 'er feel so uncomfortable? With some prisoners it weren't so difficult. Mrs Dacre Fox was one of 'em coz of 'er defiant attitude, inviting 'em to do their worst. But other suffrigitt prisoners put up with it very dignified. The motives of the silent ones was more unnervin' than the ones she called 'shouters' 'cause you never knew what went on be'ind their eyes. Was they offrin' the least line of resistance to get it over with quick? Or was they tryin' to undermine the authority of them doin' the feedin'? Her sneaky looks showed the pain, misery and fear. She 'eard the women describe force-feedin' as oral rape. Was they exaggeratin'? She didn't know; she 'elped do it, but 'ad never experienced it 'erself. She wondered if she would ever 'ave the courage to face some'at like that for some'at she believed in.

Lost in these thoughts, before she became aware of it, Emma found herself stood outside Mrs Dacre Fox's cell. She forced herself to forget her meanderings and concentrate. She drew breath, straightened her shoulders and followed the others into the cell.

ଔ ଔ ଔ

THE MOMENT NORAH was alerted by the key in the lock, inner strength pulled her to her feet. *Here they come... Five of 'em... Ha... frightened of me struggling, are they?... Mustn't disappoint then... A curse on you, wardress! This is oral rape! Be ashamed, foul woman...* She took her stand in the corner of her cell, fingers of one hand up her nostrils, her other arm drawn defensively across her chest. They wouldn't take her, she'd struggle to the end.

"My, so many of you. All come to take part in the pantomime?" she mocked, although the effect was diminished by the echoing nasal sound that replaced her usual commanding voice.

"If you know what's good for you, you'll submit with no struggle," intoned the doctor.

Norah saw the senior wardress nod in agreement. *Never, you hateful obnoxious little man...* Four wardresses descended on her. They dislodged her arms, grabbing them, then they dragged and stretched her out on a plank with one wardress either side, one at her head and another holding her feet. The doctor lent on her knees to get access to her mouth. Norah clenched her teeth, forcing the doctor to try inserting the tube through her nose. *Ahhh... the pain... How much longer... Ha... He can't get it down that way... wretched fool...* She remembered being a little girl and the time when her father raised his arm bringing a whip down on her face, but this pain was worse than the searing pain she remembered then. *Ahhhhh... he's trying my mouth again.* She came round realising she must have lost consciousness. *Ahhh... he's got a steel gag in. Brute, he's broken at least one tooth... more dentist bills... but he won't get that disgusting filthy tube down that easy... Bet he didn't clean it after his last torture session... Abominable wretches... each one of you... paid torturers... Close your throat, Norah, close it... Don't retch... Control yourself... He's pushing so hard... Ignore the pain, Norah... No taxation without representation... Votes for Women... Incompetent fool... Look, his eyes betray him... Torturer... Compassionless fool... What a vile, filthy ....* She could feel the tube was too wide. The pain was excruciating. *Look at me, wardress, don't turn your eyes away... Look at me!... Coward!... How much more tube does he think will go down?... It's in my stomach... Stop pushing, Can't take any more... For goodness sake get on... pour that filthy muck down the tube...*

After days without sustenance, her body tried to force the food back up. Her stomach and legs curled in extreme pain. She felt the wardress tighten the grip on her head to hold it still while the others kept forcing her legs down so that the doctor was able to lean on them. It seemed interminable, but in the end the tube got dragged back out of her mouth. *Now you can retch Norah... Good aim, down his front and shoes... vile, evil torturer... How satisfying...*

The doctor stepped back, slapped her on the cheek and muttered, "Well, she may think that a small victory, but I shall have the last laugh."

Norah, glared at him acidly and with a contemptuous expression retorted, "You may think you have the last laugh, Sir, but I will definitely have the last word!"

The hollow sound of the huge door slamming behind her tormentors was branded on her memory and connected forever with a cacophonous surge of emotions.

Norah lay in her cell a few hours later, going over what happened. In her weakened state her mixed feelings were hard to untangle. In the woolly place that was her brain, the different strands wove together and split apart, but were dominated by the physical pain from the violence done to her and the craving of her body for water and food. The nourishment poured down the tube may have done some good, but not much, since most of it got vomited up. When she reflected on it later, Norah remembered, apart from her anger at the barbaric torture meted out to her, her satisfaction at what she achieved. "Now my friends can see that I'm one of them. I've endured what they have;

I've made the ultimate sacrifice and earned my place amongst them. I've followed Emmeline's exhortation to the full; I've shown my true calibre through Deeds not Words. I can hold my head high."

CB CB CB

EMMA STOOD BEHIND the senior wardress five days after Mrs Dacre Fox arrived at Holloway. The senior wardress handed Mrs Dacre Fox her Cat and Mouse licence and told her she was to be released.

"Let's hope you see sense and return on a voluntary basis when you've got your strength back. You still have most of your one month sentence to serve. It would be silly to go into hiding and take part in more militant activity, forcing us to arrest you again. That will go worse for you. We'll see you again once you've recovered."

Norah took the licence out of the senior wardress's hand and turned to be escorted out of Holloway. Although weak and exhausted, she was acutely aware of her footsteps echoing along the corridors together with the jangle of Wardress Baxter's keys. She lost count of how many gates were opened, closed and locked behind her on the way out. Her hands ached from being balled into fists, and she muttered and cursed at staff under her breath. Finally the big entrance gate opened, she stepped out and listened to it slam shut behind her. She unclenched her hands, smoothed out her licence as best she could, tore it to pieces and threw it into the air.

CHAPTER 3

The Journey to Holloway

EMMA STOOD BESIDE her Da and looked up, eyes flitting from one to the other of the winged griffins that brooded over the gates in front of them. She wondered what story book they copied the statues from. Must've been a scary one 'cause both creatures 'eld a key and shackles. The words 'Olloway Prison always set alarms ringing in her head. Now she stood before the inner gatehouse, every nerve-end in her body at attention. Everyone told her she'd nothing to be frightened of, but she couldn't stop biting her lips. Ma told her off 'bout it, but she couldn't 'elp it. She sensed her lip swell as she licked the wound. Didn't know metal and salt mixed, but that was how it tasted. What was she doing 'ere? Why did she fink as she could be a wardress? She was only sixteen, she wouldn't be able to do it.

She craned her neck to see how high the wall went and almost fell over backwards. Fiddlesticks. Thank goodness Da held on to her. She'd tried to imagine what it might be like behind them walls, tried to picture how life would be, but now, faced with goin' through them gates, she was scared. A small door to one side of the massive studded gate opened and for the first time she glimpsed inside. She was nervous, overpowered with a sense of bleakness. Her hands shook, while her mind registered a loud echo from her heartbeat. The rhythmic thump sounded so loud it reminded her of one of those military drums she'd seen many times on the parade ground, like the time when Da's regiment marched off to the Boer War when she were little. Da whispered in her ear.

"You've no need for nerves, girl. You're doin' what's right. It'll be good."

"Aye, Da, but this place scares me."

"Once you've 'ad trainin' and get workin' reg'lar, won't be so bad. You'll see. You'll be as useful 'ere as you was to Ma at 'ome."

"I 'ope so. Gonna miss ya."

"Wouldn't be bringin' ya 'ere if I didn't fink it weren't for best."

"Aye, Da."

With that he squeezed her arm and guided her through the open gate. Emma looked down. She stumbled over an uneven cobblestone. Da caught her again. If only her 'ands would stop shakin'. Fiddlesticks. Ma always said as her 'ands was large, bony and clumsy, not like a young lady's. What wiv 'em bein' so big folks always noticed 'em, impossible to 'ide 'em. Right now she wished Da hadn't been a warder here till he moved to another prison when 'Olloway got changed to a prison for women. If he hadn't been, if he weren't a warder, he might not 'ave 'eard about the wardress jobs and made 'er apply. She remembered the day he told 'er. Never one to waste words, was Da.

"I fink you should take a wardress job at 'Olloway."

"Why, Da? Don't wanna be a wardress. Rather stay 'ome with you and Ma. What if I ain't any good?"

"It t'aint an easy billet, but you'll get respect."

Emma gave way. Was she bothered about respect? What did it mean anyway, getting respect? Did she want to be respected? What she needed was work. Da said so. Bein' a wardress was one of the only jobs she might get. Da said so. Either that, or become a wife like Ma 'cause she had now't else to do. Havin' seen Ma battle to bring up 'er and 'er brothers on 'er own – 'cause Da went away fightin' – Emma decided she'd prefer to escape that endless struggle. There was other reasons not to get married. She'd feelin's inside 'er she didn't understand. Fiddlesticks. Just 'cause she weren't interested in boys. Once, she tried to tell Ma she didn't want to go out wiv lads, but Ma said that weren't natural, and she'd soon grow up and be wantin' to 'cause that was natural. That was the way it was. Girls liked boys and boys liked girls in the end. Emma longed to grow up and like boys, 'oping as 'er feelings that told 'er she didn't would disappear.

CB CB CB

ON A SPRING day two years later, Norah sat next to her father, John, in a carriage on the way to her wedding. Both kept silent, absorbed in their own thoughts. From under her veil Norah stole a glance at Papa, then looked away. She didn't want to talk to him, but did wonder what he might be contemplating, sitting there as inscrutable as ever. Perhaps he was lost for words for once. She hoped he was ashamed at the fuss he made about riding to the church, even proposing at one point that he walk and she ride in the carriage on her own. Imagine if he got his way and it rained.

To distract herself she looked at the passing houses and trees, thinking how different they seemed today. Why? A carpet of spring blossom lay beneath them – although some petals clung with stubbornness to the branches – underneath which the last of the daffodils and bluebells enjoyed the shade. The trees appeared like old intimate friends, that she didn't have time to stop and greet. Some of her neighbours along here would be waiting at the church. Then she realised what troubled her – she was riding past them when Papa's usual rule forced everyone to walk. It was one of his rituals. Would never get in a car, hated them. She'd be able to make her own decisions on how to get to church from now on. Had told Charles she didn't want her household run in the dictatorial way Papa ran his. She was sure he listened because he promised that he wouldn't insist on unreasonable rules. In fact, ever since she met him he'd been obliging and pliable on most matters, so she hoped it would work out.

It was a short ride to the church. The sky was cloudless. What a relief to have a beautiful warm day – meant no fussing with umbrellas or things. Look at this dress, too much silk and lace. It looked pretty, but what a fuss Mama and Dorothy made. She must pull herself together; concentrate on getting through the ceremony. She looked at Papa again, convinced he was glad to get rid of her – had said he thought he would never marry her off. Excited at the idea of the new life in front of her, she was frustrated that the way to achieve it involved being married. She reflected on her conversation with Mama yesterday.

"I'm so pleased you and Charles will wed," said Charlotte. "I did wonder if you'd ever find someone to share your life with, you're so headstrong and stubborn."

"Mama, I know you insist you've been happy with Papa, but I resent his strict discipline – the way he treats you like a chattel and the way the law allows him to do it."

"Life is not about law, Norah. You must work together and make a partnership that suits you, as we did."

"But you paid a heavy price, Mama. You always deferred and were never allowed to think for yourself."

"That may be how you see it, but there are ways a woman can exert influence without having law on her side."

"That may be right for you, Mama, but the law

supports men against women. When you married, everything you had became his. You couldn't divorce him if he was unfaithful or cruel, but he could divorce you on the flimsiest of grounds; we were your children, but legally we belonged to Papa. He could send us to another country if he wished, and you couldn't do anything about it. If he decided to leave you and not give you money to look after us, he didn't have to, and on top of that the law gave him the right to beat you with a stick as long as it was no thicker than his thumb. It's always been the way, you know – 'a woman, a spaniel and a walnut tree, the more they're beaten the better they be'."

"Papa never beat me."

"No. But he beat us when we were children."

"Have you talked to Charles? Does he accept your feelings?"

"Charles knows I want to be treated as equal inside our marriage, even though the law gives him power over me."

"It sounds as if you know what you're doing, but I'm afraid. My dearest wish is that you'll be happy and fulfilled. Perhaps you'll understand when you have babies. My children have brought my life meaning and great joy. I hope it will be the same for you."

The carriage arrived at the church. Norah accepted her father's hand as he helped her out. They walked to the vestry door. Was she dreaming? No – it was real. The heady smell from the flowers in her bouquet and the sudden silence where there had been loud chattering a moment before told her she was awake. The bridal march sounded out its first chords. Papa gave her arm a gentle tug. She repeated the mantra that she decided had been composed for her – *aisle, altar, hymn, aisle, altar, hymn.* It worked to keep a smile on her face. Chanting it in her head with every step, she let Papa lead her past the guests, anxiously scanning the faces in the pews. *Where is Mama?* There she stood with Dorothy and her brothers near the front. She should have remembered from the rehearsal. How wonderful having Dorothy and Augustus here. She'd miss her when she went back to South Africa.

Mama faded from sight as she concentrated on Charles. As she arrived at the altar she watched Papa, relieved of his chore, sit next to Mama. She wondered if his smile indicated happiness or relief. Then she turned her attention to Charles. Stood beside him all she could envisage were 'wifely duties', beatings and sticks the size of thumbs. What was she doing here? What madness brought her to this altar? Why did she agree?

CB CB CB

CHARLOTTE WATCHED JOHN and Norah process down the aisle, reminded of her own wedding day by the scent of the flower arrangements drifting around her. It was a shame the flowers competed with the guests' perfumes, but she was sure the fresh roses would win. Norah looked pleasing in her high-waisted calf-length silk and lace dress, with small, loose-flowing, lace sleeves covering the tops of her arms. Her waist-length veil, when lifted, framed her face, highlighting her eyes. Physically, John and Norah shared the same characteristics – small, wiry and energetic – but burdened by personalities so large that people who only heard them speak would have imagined tall imposing bodies to go with them. John's face was precious to Charlotte with its oval-shaped open features, penetrating deep-set eyes, turned-up nose and small, set lips. Norah had the same features but hers weren't, as yet, lined or creased with evidence of suffering. Charlotte blamed their constant arguing on their similarities; two stubborn individuals who weren't able to admit that underneath, they grudgingly admired each other.

Charlotte shuddered as the image flashed into her mind of the day that determined the course of Norah and John's relationship. Dorothy and Norah had been outside feeding the dogs. They both adored animals, always finding wounded birds or other creatures to nurse. Charlotte became aware of a commotion, and rushed to meet Dorothy in the doorway.

"Mama, Mama, come quick." Dorothy shouted and sobbed as panic reverberated through her tears.

"What is it, Dorothy? What's the matter?"

"Papa slashed Norah across the face with his whip."

"What? What do you mean? Surely not, you must be exaggerating." Charlotte threw her arms around Dorothy and kissed her head, trying to calm her.

"No, come quick. I'm frightened. Papa is very angry."

"But why? Why would he do that? Did Norah provoke him?"

"The dogs barked, Papa went to whip them and Norah jumped in to stop him."

Charlotte remembered how Norah clammed up afterwards, betraying her inner feelings through the anger and fury in her eyes consistent with the fierce red weal on her face. It took a long time for Norah to find someone she wanted to marry. Now she hoped Norah would find happiness, although afraid because she believed her daughter's impulsive, stubborn nature would test Charles to the limit.

○③ ○③ ○③

NOT LONG AFTER her interview, Emma heard her application for wardress training had been successful. She reluctantly collected her stuff together, ready to move to her new home. With so little to take; she wasn't sure why she bothered. What she needed was 'er memories of 'ome, 'er bruvvers and Ma and Da, and she 'ad those, locked away in her 'ead where no one could steal 'em. She was goin' to live in quarters at the back of the prison with the other wardresses. Her prison uniform would be given 'er when she started work, but she got hold of a picture to show Ma. It was plain, grey, and ankle length, gathered at the waist with petticoats underneath. The top half had a high simple neckline with long sleeves gathered at the wrist. The only adornment was a long key chain that hung from the waist. It reminded 'er of when she'd been at school. She saw an illustration in an 'istory book of a grand lady with a key-chain 'anging from her waist. She asked the teacher what it were, it was so 'andsome. The teacher called it a chatelaine. The grand lady's 'ad keys on, but she also 'ad nice, useful things like scissors, a thimble or a watch, perhaps a small purse or comb as well. Emma's wouldn't be pleasin' being for prison keys an' all – 'eavy jangling ones at that.

"Practical, but tain't pretty," Ma commented as she shrugged her shoulders.

"It 'as to be, practical that is. There's lots of stairs and walkways. I'm sure the bare brick walls make it cold, even in summer."

"Aye. Anyways, you was never pretty wiv your broad shoulders, small bubs and tiny hips. Bein' lanky, wiv your 'air pulled back and tied, I sometimes wonder folks don't mistake you for a boy with your mannish face. That uniform won't 'elp."

"Please, Ma. I never wanted curly 'air nor pretty frocks."

"Just as well you was a tomboy. We never 'ad money for dresses, pretty nor t'otherwise."

"See the key chain, Ma. Noticed 'em when I went with Da, 'eard the keys clanking the 'ole time the wardresses was walkin'. Ev'ry time they lock and unlock doors there's an 'ollow echo. Creepy, it bein' called

'Olloway an all."

"You'll get used to it."

"I 'ope so coz I'll 'ave to, won't I."

Emma couldn't stop thinking about it. She'd miss 'er family. Da 'ad been a blacksmith when 'e and Ma wed. She remembered being little, remembered 'is solid arms, the smell of smoke and 'ot metal as 'e pounded things like 'orseshoes into shape. Those same arms, strong but gentle, lifted 'er up in play with her bruvvers. Then there'd been that long, terrible time when 'e joined the army and the family moved to married quarters at Aldershot. They'd gone to school, but poverty never stopped knockin'. Thems was the years when Da went to South Africa to fight in the second Boer War. He got wounded at the siege of Kimberley. She recalled Ma frettin' and the long months waitin' for news. The time it took 'im to come 'ome after 'is injury seemed endless. In the end 'e got shipped home, but 'e took forever to get better. Then when 'is six year enlistment ended 'e got work as a prison warder, with quarters, at 'Olloway in 1901. They'd to move again in 1903 when 'Olloway got changed to a women's prison, but life with Da at 'ome gave them security. It was that what she'd miss, being on 'er own now. Wouldn't be able to get an 'ug from Ma if she felt sad or upset. She'd 'ave to make decisions for 'erself, without 'elp. Hard, this growing up business.

CB CB CB

NORAH AND CHARLES moved into a small flat above a shop premises. Norah was delighted to be in charge of her home, although hoped they would soon move to better accommodation. The rooms were small but adequate, as long as you didn't want to entertain too often. It would have to do for now. She was pleased with her efforts to make the place presentable, except that the maid took too long to get used to the way she wanted things. She had plans, though, and they would eventually have to move to lodgings more suited to the station in life she was sure she was bound to fill. But nothing was ever achieved in a moment, it took planning. How to get Charles to realise this? After considerable thought, she believed she knew where to start.

"I've been considering the name we should put on our writing paper and invitation cards."

"Won't that be Mr and Mrs Fox."

"Although you're a stationery clerk, your father is a doctor. It would make more impression to use the Dacre as well and call ourselves Dacre Fox."

"That sounds pretentious, don't you think?"

"I most certainly do not. We need people to associate us with the Establishment; give them cause to show us respect. Dacre is a well-known name running through English history, held by barons and earls – it will bring us to attention."

"You might be right. It can't do any harm. Although I suggest we don't use a hyphen and make it double-barrelled."

"Good. Decision made. From now on we'll be known as Mr and Mrs Charles Dacre Fox."

Life settled into a routine, but peace and harmony were not to be long-term residents. Norah was forever irritated by the way Charles's complained that he was unhappy with the amount of time her animal welfare work took up. Fool. He'd been aware of it since before they married. Hadn't he understood how much time she gave to it, or had he ignored it, thinking love would overcome? She dreaded the scenes that became a regular feature of their lives.

"Will you be spending most of the week on your anti-vivisection work?"

"Why?"

"It takes a lot time. It's almost the sole subject of our conversations. I hoped we might do something different together instead."

"Have you been talking to your father?"

"What makes you ask that?"

"Because every time you adopt this tone, it turns out he's been complaining to you about me."

"He's a doctor. He believes animal experiments are vital to advancing cures and improving medicine."

"And you know that animal experiments disgust me. The way they use dirty tubes and implements to carry out their abominable experiments; passing infections between animals and causing them dreadful pain."

"Norah, please – I've a great deal of sympathy with

what you say, but my father has a point."

"Charles," she responded with all the mockery she could summon, "I despise you and your father for showing sympathy with animal cruelty. If you don't want to argue about it, don't talk to him about what I do. I am your wife; show some loyalty to me, for goodness sake."

It didn't help when Charles walked away from her after such exchanges. She was suspicious when he retreated to his study and shut the door. She never felt she got her point across. Did he do it to annoy or was he too frightened to stand his ground? She could never get to his reasoning. Sometimes when he agreed with her, she wondered if he did so to shut her up. What infuriated her was his disappointment over her failure to get pregnant. He went so far as to suggest that if she conceived, that would force her to give up campaigning, and that would solve their problems. Little did he know.

Then one day Mama came to tea. The moment they sat down, before the maid brought the tea tray, Norah became aware Charles had asked Mama to speak to her.

"It's clear you and Charles are having difficulty starting a family."

"Charles blames me."

"No one is to blame. But you spend so much time working for your causes you aren't giving yourself a chance. I've noticed how tired and irritable you are when campaigning. It can't help."

"Why is there always an automatic assumption that

if I'm not pregnant it must be my fault?"

"No one is suggesting that. I'm trying to get you to consider what might help. Have you visited the doctor?"

"You've been talking to Charles. No I haven't seen a doctor. I don't like doctors – don't trust them."

"I want to see you both happy and fulfilled."

"And you believe the only way to achieve that is to have babies every year like you did?"

"I realise my way is old-fashioned. But I loved having babies. If I had a choice, I'd still have wanted to be a mother."

"We benefited from your devotion. I'll always be grateful. But I've enjoyed my public career – limited as it is – and the longer I can pursue it without children interfering, the longer I intend to make the most of it."

"That stubborn streak of yours hasn't been restrained by marriage. If anything it's got worse."

ଔ ଔ ଔ

WORKING AT HER desk, Norah was immersed in the letter column of *The Times*. She read it every day, together with the other journals she subscribed to. It was important to complete all reading before proceeding to deal with her correspondence. Such a routine kept on top of the animal welfare debate. From the beginning it had been a point of contention between her and Charles as to who should get the paper first when it was delivered each morning. She solved the problem by the simple expedient of suggesting that they get two copies brought to the house. Although annoyed at the expense, Charles gave way. She found it easy to convince him that she needed her own copy because of her anti-vivisection work.

It was annual report time again. She must finalise her General Secretary's report today. It had to go to the printer. Ah. How timely. *Look – here he is – at it again – that repugnant bacteriologist quack, Sir Almroth Wright.* How long would he be allowed to torture animals in the name of developing vaccines? Monkeys were monkeys, humans were humans. How could a vaccine tested on a monkey be fit to be used on a human? It was so pointless and disgusting. What was he spouting now to justify his work? Hold on a minute, he wasn't jabbering his usual rubbish about the appropriateness of animal testing vaccines this time, he was attacking women. Why? She read on. How could he write such virulent and awful things? She paced the room, her breathing getting faster. She sat down and read it again. Perhaps she read it too fast, perhaps she misunderstood, perhaps she had dreamt it. No, the words were there in black and white with his title at the bottom. This so called 'gentleman' and 'pillar' of the medical establishment claimed that women – because of their hysterical natures – should be confined to the home. His diatribe was inaccurate, illogical and distorted, and anyway what right did he have to comment on women's mental health? He wasn't a specialist in that subject. He'd no remit to give opinion outside his area of expertise. More than that, how could he claim to have medical evidence supporting his allegations? If he did, it was quackery, like his animal experiments. Of course – *The Times* published this gibberish because the Third Conciliation Bill was about to be debated. *Let's hope Parliamentarians voting on the bill aren't as narrow minded and partisan as this idiot.* She cut out the letter and put it to one side of her desk. She needed to get on with her report. Perhaps in a few days' time when women had got a vote, she might look at it and laugh at his preposterous drivel.

Her pile of letters from *The Times* kept growing. How frustrating that the Bill got defeated by the usual jiggery-pokery that went on between politicians, horse trading votes for vested interests. She debated this effrontery to democracy time and again with Papa when he'd been the agent for that Liberal politician who stood in their area. More irritating were some of the replies published in *The Times* in response to that cretin's original letter, correspondence from women who supported him. Why did *The Times* give them space to air their distorted notions? How did they have the gall? *How dare they betray their sex that way? Why are they so stupid as to believe that because Sir Almroth Wright claims to have medical evidence, he is right? What are they trying to hide from?* She yearned to be able to get these women to see how they were mistaken to postulate that women had no role in public life; that they didn't need to be dependent on men's indulgence, they could be independent and self-supporting on their own merits. Mama didn't help, suggesting that everyone was entitled to their opinion.

Not long after this Norah found herself sitting on a tram making her way home. She looked out of the window, attracted by a commotion on the street. Two policemen had accosted a young girl. *Why should two burly policemen be needed to restrain her? She's a thin little thing. Quite a fight she's putting up. There's a piece of chalk in her hand. What's she written on the pavement? 'Votes for Women'.* The girl needed help, the fight was too unequal. Norah alighted at the next stop, speculating that the girl must be pleased at the size of the crowd she drew, although it made it difficult to push through them. At last.

"Excuse me, officers, you should desist in handling your prisoner so roughly."

"Keep out the way, ma'am. This girl is bein' arrested for committin' an offence."

"What offence?"

"Incitin' folks to support a militant organisation."

"It seems to me you're the militants. Why are two of you are needed to overpower her? It's hardly an equal conflict."

More women arrived and joined in the jostling. In the tumult one of the policemen lost his grip on the girl's arm. Norah watched her take her chance. Not wasting a second, she struggled with the other policeman and succeeded in shrugging herself free of his grasp. Small and lithe, she dodged beneath the cordon formed by the women who closed behind her to help her run away. Norah observed her disappear around a corner. She wondered if the policemen had noticed where the girl went, and decided to follow to offer help if needed. She looked round to see one policeman had followed her. The other one must be in a struggle to get away from the crowd. She saw the girl slip into an alleyway a little ahead. Norah turned and faced the policeman.

"What is your rank and serial number, officer?"

"Why?"

"I'm going to report you for unnecessary violence inflicted on that girl."

"Now listen, ma'am, you're obstructin' me carryin' out me duty."

"We can't have that, can we? If you'll excuse me, I'll be on my way so you can pursue your victim."

Norah turned to walk away while the policeman searched the street and alley. His quarry was nowhere to be seen. Norah walked back towards the crowd and waited for the policeman to pass her. When she was sure he'd lost interest she retraced her steps and found the girl, who emerged from a doorway in a side street.

"He's gone. You can come out."

"Thank you. Need to get to my next pavement to chalk."

"What militant organisation are you supposed to belong to then?"

"The Women's Social and Political Union – WSPU for short."

So Norah's attention became concentrated on the WSPU. The image of the two policemen and the young girl haunted her. Such a brave young thing, no more than a thin scrap, but quite prepared to tackle those uncouth men. She started buying *The Suffragette*. The slogans jumped out at her – 'No taxation without representation'. That's a good one. She wondered if she might adapt it for one of her animal welfare campaigns – 'No experimentation without representation'. It might work. Women and animals had a lot in common – weak and defenceless, subjected to arbitrary laws without the chance to fight back. Laws coded and imposed by men. If women got the vote they could stop men passing measures to legitimise horrible experiments or beat their wives with impunity. Was this the answer? Violent men understand violence. Mrs Pankhurst was right. Men were so intransigent, women had to carry the fight to them and retaliate to change the unjust, biased way in which they dominated democracy.

She joined the local branch and became Honourable Secretary of the local Division. Her appetite for the work was insatiable. She enjoyed every facet of it. She felt she could do anything; fundraising through jumble sales, Dutch markets, street collections, writing reports on branch activities for *The Suffragette*, arranging street sales, organising women to attend demonstrations in London, the list went on. Nothing daunted her. Except for Charles. Even then he didn't intimidate, just irritate.

ଔ ଔ ଔ

WHILE NORAH WENT out to deliver speeches several days a week, Charles would return home to interminable empty evenings. He felt abandoned. Meal times, when they should share sustenance, nurture their partnership, turned into vigils filled with longing for her company. He tried to talk to her, tried to stay calm and non-confrontational, but she flew into rages, questioning his manhood and right to criticise her work. Month after month he waited to hear she'd fallen pregnant. He longed for a child. Why didn't she crave to hold a baby in her arms? He did. He felt convinced she would enjoy being a mother. Women did, didn't they? Wasn't that why God created them? To nurture and love. It was their destiny. He wondered if the problem arose because she wasn't concentrating on supervising her home and looking after him. Instead, she took on more and more work for her causes, like an insatiable glutton. Running around speechifying and organising meetings about women getting a vote must be why she couldn't conceive. Why did she feel no shame about her neglect of him or her apparent infertility? It didn't bother her because she told him so, with loud, unapologetic declarations every chance she got, but most often at breakfast.

"I'll be out tonight. I've to chair a gathering at Kingston."

"When will you be back?"

"I'm out this afternoon to organise a fund-raising fête, take in donations and set out the Assembly Rooms.

Then I'll go straight to the meeting so won't be home for dinner".

"Haven't seen you the whole week except one evening."

"So?"

"It would be good if we could find time for each other."

"Are you questioning the value of my work?"

"No. But I'd like to spend time with you, and for us to have dinner together."

"What? A nice quiet evening in while you read and fall asleep by the fire, while I dance attendance and do as I'm told – so as not to upset your well ordered life?"

"I didn't mean it like that. I want to spend time with my wife. Is that so unreasonable?"

"Say what you mean. You think what I do is 'unwomanly', that I'm not carrying out my Christian duty to care for my husband. Lord save his miserable, dictatorial little soul."

"Please don't get angry."

"Angry? ANGRY? I haven't started yet. You men treat us like chattels you can order about, throw crumbs of respect to when you fancy or when we do what you want. Let me tell you, our day will come. We won't be pushed around by you, the government, their lackeys, or anyone. We can do it for ourselves. We demand the right to a proper say in society to influence and improve it. Look what a mess you've made of it so far."

That's how it always ended; Norah angry because

she forgot that she was talking to him and not a huge crowd at a rally. Charles wondered why he wanted to share anything with her, let alone dinner. Mealtimes, when they did share them, was where she rehearsed speeches, unaware of his presence. She practised lines she wanted to deliver to convey maximum effect, adjusted them when she thought of something better, and then scribbled it down. It was a surprise that the door was still on its hinges, she slammed it so often as she went out. What must the housemaid make of it?

ᘓ ᘓ ᘓ

EMMA FOUND TRAINING difficult. It was hard work and she felt homesick the whole time. But she made new friends and life settled into a routine. Every day presented a challenge. She learned about the prisoners and what brought them to Holloway. From training, she knew this was discouraged. They said it would make it harder to maintain discipline if she showed interest in the women's lives, but Emma believed she could do her job better if she understood how and why the women had got there.

The suffrigitts caused special problems. The first time she got duties to do with Mrs Pankhurst, she'd been working about eighteen months. Christabel Pankhurst, her daughter, had served a short sentence the year before. Although Emma had nothing to do with Christabel she heard about her from the other wardresses. These women broke the rules, the whole time. Da had a rule that said you never broke rules. You followed orders – accepted your betters knew best. Da said that not following rules put other soldiers in danger, and it was the same in civilian life.

Them suffrigitts didn't accept that inside 'Olloway. They said 'Olloway's rules didn't apply to them because they was political prisoners. Christabel and Mrs Pankhurst was professional women – Christabel 'ad a law degree – was clever and could do anythin' she wanted. But here they was believin' so strong in women 'avin' a vote, that they broke the law – on purpose. They was prepared to come to 'Olloway, and be shut up with debtors, drunks, dollymops and drug addicts. Ma and Da were never well off, but they managed to keep body and soul together. It was a matter of pride, no matter what happened you didn't risk goin' to prison. Women who ended up in 'Olloway deserved to be there, no matter 'ow 'ard it got you never stole or sold yourself. The law and the prison guv'nor said the suffrigitts should be 'ere, but the law breakin' they did was different to the other women. They did it deliberate. They said women needed a vote to make life better for everyone, not just men. It was confusin', 'specially when Mrs Pankhurst stayed so dignified. Emma wouldn't want to wear that prison uniform, them stained underclothes, coarse brown woollen stockings with red stripes, that shapeless prison dress stamped with broad arrows and mismatched old shoes. Mrs Pankhurst must've 'ated it. What did clothes and uniforms mean anyway? Herself, she often got mistook for a nurse because their outfits was similar. Anyways, putting Mrs Pankhurst in prison garb didn't make her a criminal the same as prostitutes an' their like.

"Did ya see commotion in exercise yard today?" asked Emma's colleague relaxing over tea in the wardresses' quarters after coming off duty.

"Just 'eard 'bout it."

"They say Mrs Pankhurst insisted on walkin' next to Christabel and talkin'. Warned she'd get solitary if she didn't stop."

"I 'eard she said as the silence rule is cruel and un-fair, that she wouldn't take 'eed of it."

"Aye. Said rules was 'specially wicked stopping her talkin' to her daughter."

"Maybe she's right. Why can't we go easy with rules? Prisoners talk anyway. Might be better if we 'eard what they was sayin'. With 'em whispering an all, we never know what theys thinkin' or plannin'.."

"Maybe, but thems the rules. Now Mrs Pankhurst is in solitary. Govn'r put a note on her file that says as she's a dangerous criminal."

"That's silly. 'Ow can wantin' to talk to ya daughter be a crime? How can 'e say that's the same as stealin' or prostitutin? Don't make no sense."

Emma expected trouble, there always was. Sure enough a few days later she heard a brass band playing a suffrigitt march outside the walls. She was gettin' to know their tunes, she 'eard 'em so often. It was her afternoon off. She was going to visit Ma. As she came out into the street, she saw it. A long procession headed by the woman they called General Drummond. Emma knew her. She had to deal with her when she was a prisoner. Small woman she was, but you'd never credit it the antics she got up to. The suffrigitts circled the prison as they sang their marching song and shouted through megaphones. Quite a parade it was. Some marched with banners, while others rode high on wagonettes dressed up in homemade prison uniforms, shoutin' as 'ow unfair it was that Mrs Pankhurst couldn't see her daughter what was ill.

How did Emma manage to get caught up in their marches? There was that time she came back to the prison when she had to struggle through a police cordon. That day she heard 'The March of the Women' for the first time. It had been made up by Ethyl Smyth what was servin' two months for smashin' shop windows. Miss Smyth's supporters demonstrated outside while she sang the song inside her cell with the other suffrigitt prisoners joinin' in. The wardresses hadn't been able to shut them up despite threatnin' all sorts. It had been a real shock to Da when she told him, what with Miss Smyth being the daughter of a Major-General an' all. At first he'd been speechless with anger. Then, when he started talkin', no one could get a word in edgeways coz of his questions. 'Ow could a woman like that, a professional woman, daughter of an 'igh ranking orficer, throw stones and break windows to get women a vote? It went against everything 'e believed in. 'Adn't her Da b'ought 'er up proper? Didn't she 'ave no pride in 'erself? If she'd been a soldier she'd 'ave been drummed out the ranks.

The wardresses' living quarters at the back of the prison were a place of much chatter and gaiety when staff came off duty.

"Is anyone gonna 'elp me get ready for me date this weekend?" said one girl.

"Who're you goin' wiv?" sang several voices at once.

"My sweetheart. 'Ope to wed soon."

"You wanna leave? Ain't ya comfy 'ere?"

"I wanna get me own 'ome, 'ave kids. Don't wanna work like this forever."

"What 'bout you, Emma? Ain't ya got no boy to walk out wiv?"

"No. I ain't pretty like you. Boys ain't interested in me."

"You don't try an' make yourself pretty," came the chorus.

"Fiddlesticks. Anyways, maybe I don' wanna. Maybe I is 'appy like I am."

"Ya can't wanna stay 'ere your 'ole life like a dried up old prune?"

"Don't know. Do know I don' wanna get wed for the 'ell of it."

"Strange thing to say. Since when we gotta choice? Ain't it what we 'ave to do in the end?"

"I'm 'appy the way I am at the moment, ta."

It wasn't as if Emma didn't think about it. Her Ma, aunts, girlfriends from when she was little, the other wardresses was sure they'd fall in love, marry and have kids. Anythin' else was unnatural. But she couldn't see 'erself doing that. At the same time, she didn't want to think about 'aving feelings for other women. She knew about inverts, seen 'em in 'Olloway. They was perverse. Ma and Da said so. She tried to go out with a boy once, the other wardresses persuaded her, but she 'adn't enjoyed it, and 'ated it when he tried to kiss her.

Was something wrong with 'er? Per'aps she'd no right to be loved, per'aps she was strange, a freak. It didn't 'elp when she saw lesbian inmates treated bad by staff and fellow prisoners. She watched the lesbian women fight back by formin' a gang and doing things that made the other inmates 'fraid of 'em. 'Oped they'd be left alone if they earned a reputation not to be tangled wiv. At any rate, it was too upsettin'. Best not to think about it too much. Best to ignore 'er feelins in case they got 'er in trouble and then turned 'er family 'gainst her. She couldn't cope if she disappointed Ma and Da so they didn't love 'er no more.

CB CB CB

NORAH WORKED HARD at her image within the WSPU. She was determined to be thought of as a respectable 'Society Woman', benefactor and good administrator. Pavement chalking, stone throwing and direct action were not for her, she was the general directing the troops, their militant unapologetic spokeswoman. Large demonstrations and storming Parliament were good. Emmeline and Christabel took part in those, so Norah gave herself permission to do so as well. What she enjoyed most were the 'At Homes' always publicised in *The Suffragette* and *The Times*. These attracted wealthy supporters. Norah felt comfortable at these gatherings, and was persuasive in getting guests to donate.

In contemplative moments she acknowledged she learned her networking skills from Papa. She watched him many times work a room full of people, using that natural charm the Irish were said to be endowed with. Despite being small, he never got overlooked – his reputation preceded him – and he always left a profound impression. No one realised that while he had a lot to say, there was more significance in what he didn't. Norah used this sophistry herself. When hosting At Homes, guests assumed her to be a woman with important professional connections who gave with generosity to the cause. In reality she donated little except time. The rule was never deny, verify or challenge personal information in the public domain if it achieved the reaction you wanted.

It worked. She'd been promoted to General Secretary of the WSPU and was an accepted member of the inner circle. Emmeline and Christabel, were personal friends along with Grace Roe, Flora Drummond and Annie Kenney.

"Were you followed?" asked Grace.

"Managed to elude them," said Norah, throwing off her coat as she arrived at the safe flat where Grace hid from the police while out on licence.

"We've got a lot to do to finish putting up next week's middle pages for *The Suffragette*. We best get on. The printer needs our copy."

"Lucky I finished my speech for Knightsbridge Hall this week, together with the summary for the printer. Christabel gave me her theme and I completed it today."

"Christabel relies on you for speeches, appreciates your ability to write them. Says they are full of fire – rousing, defiant and theatrical.

"I like to write them."

"I know we say it often, but it's amazing how much you look like Christabel."

"It's kind of you to say so, Grace, I'm younger than her, but it's so flattering. I hope she doesn't mind. She may not find it a compliment to be compared with me.

"I'm sure it's not a problem."

"As you might not get there this week, except in disguise, I've brought you a full copy of my speech, not the edited highlights that get handed to the press. You see I pay you a well deserved tribute."

"That's kind."

Norah enjoyed theatrical displays. She hoped Emmeline and Christabel would like the one she planned for the next occasion someone was released on licence. Annie Kenney had been in Holloway and was due to be freed. It presented an opportunity not to be missed, so she put her proposition to Christabel, pleased when she agreed. It wasn't long until the weekly Knightsbridge gathering, and they accepted that would be the perfect place and time.

The day came and Norah chaired the meeting with her usual panache, but anyone who knew her well, could tell she struggled to control her excitement. She was going to enjoy this. Needed to curb her nerves. The crowd inspired her, and she sensed the tension build as she got towards the end of her speech. *Right, it's now or never.* She turned and waved forward a stretcher from the back of the platform, while she urged the crowd to silence with a grin.

"Fellow militants, we have a visitor tonight. Please welcome her. It's Miss Annie Kenney, lately released from Holloway on licence after facing torture by force-feeding."

Norah supervised the placing of the stretcher between two chairs, while Annie raised her right hand and fluttered a handkerchief, then lay back, limp, to stare at the crowd.

"You can see the results of Miss Kenney's terrible ordeal. I have here her Cat and Mouse Licence. Who is going to bid for this licence and see their donation swell our coffers?"

"I'll give fifteen quid," someone shouted.

"Is that all Miss Kenney's ordeal is worth? Come on. You can do better than that."

"Twenty, then."

"I still say that's not enough, considering her suffering. Come on, make it twenty-five and we'll settle for that."

"Twenty-five it is, then."

"While we're at it, I've got two broken hats and a walking stick from the last time the police tried to arrest one of us."

"I'll give seven quid," came a shout from the back of the hall.

"Sold."

Grace, Emmeline and Christabel loved these antics. Now she looked forward to the after meeting, when they would discuss how it went, sure they would have a good laugh about it. She couldn't wait.

CB CB CB

CHARLOTTE'S UNHAPPINESS GREW as she watched Norah's growing commitment to the WSPU and the breakdown of her marriage. Knowing Norah's impulsiveness and dislike of being confronted with uncomfortable truths – a reflection of her father's stubbornness – Charlotte decided it was time for a mother/daughter chat over tea. Perhaps she might tempt her to bite off a chunk of common sense alongside the tea and cakes.

"Norah. I'm aware you're committed to this campaign to get women the vote, but have you considered what you're fighting for?"

"Yes, Mama."

"And what do you believe that is?"

"The slogans say it, 'Votes for Women' and 'No taxation without representation'."

"Yes, but what do you propose those ideas mean in reality?"

"That women will be granted recognition as full citizens, able to enjoy the same rights as men on equal terms in every aspect of life."

"Is that what you hope will happen if women get the vote?"

"Yes. Not at once, but it's the first step."

"It's a wonderful idea. But have you considered what you'll do if you don't achieve those things you anticipate go with a vote?"

"Those who don't want us to vote argue that women have no right to meddle in politics. They will continue to contest the point when we do. The vote is the beginning, the key. I am not so stupid as to believe we will achieve everything we want in one go. It has taken many years to get this far, but if we don't make a start, our situation will never change. Besides, I want to prove to Papa and those osseous, self important old politicians he campaigns with and for, that they aren't the only ones who can do it."

CHAPTER 4

Holloway and its Aftermath

C HARLES THREW THE newspaper down on the table, blushing with shame and confusion. Why did Norah do it? What drove her? Where on earth did she get these ideas from? Why couldn't she be satisfied being his wife? The questions raced round his brain. He hoped that this report hadn't appeared in the Manchester press, in particular the Guardian, which his father took. The article would provoke him, and Charles was anxious because he knew it must get to his father's ears in the end. Norah was reported to say, '… that if Dr Forward, the Holloway medical officer, was prepared to carry out the torture of women – i.e. forcible feeding – by order of Secretary McKenna, he must be prepared to take the consequences'. The reason for the press statement was that some suffragettes decided that the 'consequence' for Dr Forward should be a beating, which they administered outside the walls of Holloway when the doctor was on his way to work.

Charles knew that, as a medical practitioner, his father accepted that patients take against you, but this was quite different. Norah's statement called into question Dr Forward's ethics, and suggested that he colluded in the punishment and torture of women within Holloway. His father had been involved in baby farming cases in Manchester and believed that women in prison deserved to be there. How could a prison physician be wrong, whatever his duties entailed?

Charles was conscious of previous occasions when Norah had come to his father's attention as a result of WSPU activities. His father had worried about the marriage from the start, and their last conversation proved difficult.

"Charles, I read the newspaper reports about Norah. Wasn't altogether comfortable when you married her. Why you did marry her?"

"I don't know now. Believed I was in love. Then she became a suffragette."

"For goodness sake, these are excuses not answers. You need to control her. How will you prevent her bringing shame on the family? Manchester is not so far from London that her antics don't get noticed up here."

"How can I stop her? I can't lock her in the house and refuse to let her out."

"What about that silly affectation, using 'Dacre Fox' as your married name? Your middle name is Dacre, your surname Fox – no hyphen – they are meant to be separate."

"Can't remember how that happened, although suspect I know why. Anyway, we haven't hyphenated it."

"Stop trying to justify yourself. She runs you ragged. Have you no backbone left?"

"I'm as unhappy as you and Mother. Don't know what to do about it."

"You better decide on something. Find a way to stop her bringing shame on the family."

When he told his father that he didn't know why he married her, Charles told the truth. His own predilections for a wife were formed by the quiet, comfortable and ordered home he grew up in. He wanted children, and believed that like most married couples, he and Norah would become parents. He hadn't counted on Norah, who stunned him. She whirled into his life in an energetic frenzy, and Charles had been impressed with her commitment to animal welfare and the zeal and energy she devoted to it. Norah was different from other women he met. He became entranced, and convinced himself that her caring side, demonstrated in her love of animals, would augur good mothering skills. After their wedding, although her animal work took up some of her time, it wasn't excessive. But then came the WSPU. Since then she'd been consumed and driven, her relish for the campaign insatiable.

Now he found himself, a few years after they wed, alone, desperate and ashamed. He wanted to rush out, find as many copies of the newspaper as possible, and then destroy the evidence of his terrible marriage. Attitudes towards him were mixed. While mortified when his father and father-in-law asked why he didn't control her, his embarrassment at work troubled him more. It started when he overheard a conversation.

"Hey, chaps, have you seen this latest report about Mrs DF's activities in the papers?"

"No, let's see." Charles hesitated outside the room at the sound of Norah's name. He observed three men crowded around a newspaper. They hadn't noticed him, being absorbed by what they read.

"What a woman. How unlucky can a chap get, fancy being married to an hysterical harridan like that," said one.

"If she has the time to do that sort of thing, it might be because he ain't sufficient or giving her enough in the bedroom. They haven't got kids. If they did have, she mightn't rampage the streets."

Embarrassed silence descended as Charles stopped listening and made them aware of his presence. He walked into the room as the newspaper was stuffed into a desk drawer.

The stunt on Lord Lansdowne's doorstep forced him to find the courage to do something. He found out a warrant had been issued for her to appear before the magistrate for making inciting speeches. He questioned the maid about Norah's plans, humiliated that he'd to resort to interrogating a servant. From her he learned about the theatrical spectacle Norah had planned for the benefit of the press. He confronted Norah. He told her that if she went ahead and got arrested and imprisoned – instead of appearing in court and agreeing to be bound over – she needn't bother to return home.

"Fine, if that's what you want. You are a coward and aren't informed enough to see the justice of the cause I fight for. You accept what your father tells you is scientific evidence, that women who want to vote are unbalanced, hysterical creatures, who have no business in politics."

Too late he found the courage to respond. He realised afterwards that it was the only time he'd responded with corresponding venom. "Well, your behaviour confirms medical opinion and has never given me reason to doubt it."

C3 C3 C3

AS THE TORN pieces of her licence fluttered to the ground, Norah noticed her mother standing with outstretched arms waiting to embrace her. She may be exhausted, weak and dizzy, but she hadn't betrayed that to those despicable prison staff, those ruffians and hypocrites. She walked out of Holloway, head raised high, dignity intact. They hadn't changed her beliefs or had the slightest effect on her thirst for justice. She'd have to return, but for the moment her body was as free as her mind. They'd never succeed in incarcerating her thoughts; those would roam unbound, never confined within her physical being. Her surroundings would not constrain her ability to reason.

"Is that what I suspect?" asked Charlotte.

"Yes, Mama."

"Such stubbornness. I've come to travel with you to the coast where Grace Roe has arranged a short stay while you recuperate."

"That will be wonderful. But how did you persuade Papa to spare you?"

"He expressed his unhappiness, but agreed I can stay a couple of days."

"Generous – I'm sure."

Norah knew it was coming – the real reason for Charlotte being here – the conversation they must have. Norah couldn't put it off; guessed Papa imposed it as a condition when he gave Mama permission to stay while she recovered her strength. His words echoed in her head – "Make sure you tell her what I reckon to her behaviour and the way she's treated Charles."

"Are you going to tell me why you married Charles, then?"

"I wonder myself. He's turned out such a whining ninny."

"That's harsh."

"Is it? I was under pressure and it seemed a good idea. I got my own home to run without interference or having to put up with Papa's rigid routines. The independence on offer was too tempting."

"Did you discuss this with Charles? Did he understand?"

"Charles is pliable and said it wouldn't worry him as long as the household ran smoothly. At least that's what he said to start with."

"Did you ever love him?

"Love? I suppose I loved him, but now I'm not sure. When I remember those earnest conversations, I cringe. I told him I wouldn't be treated by him the way Papa did you."

"You insist Papa behaved towards me as if I was a servant, but you don't take into account that I was content."

"You say that, but did you never get fed up with Papa's strict rule that only men were allowed to talk and debate at the dinner table? Women weren't allowed to be heard. Had to remain silent."

"It didn't seem worth the bother to argue over it."

"Don't you see, Mama – that's the problem."

"What did Charles say when you told him that?"

"Said it would never do. If he must wait until he'd sons to talk to at mealtimes, we'd be silent a long time. He agreed that, despite the law, ours would be an equal partnership – that he wanted to share everything – hopes, joys, sorrows. Said I'd be good for him because of my ideas and energy."

"He's unhappy now. Has told me he regrets there are no children."

"Well, the way things are, I am relieved I never achieved a pregnancy. Felt that for a long time, although won't admit it to him. We still don't have any idea which of us is responsible, but it doesn't matter. I'm happy with the situation; I'm in control and it means I can get on with what I want to do without being saddled with a baby. I've no idea how you put up with eight children."

CB CB CB

NORAH'S RECOVERY WENT well. At any time she might be summoned back to Holloway under her licence, but managed to escape police surveillance and slip back to London. She met with Grace, and with Emmeline and Christabel's approval instigated a plan to embarrass the Bishop of London. Now here she stood, disguised, with her Votes for Women sash hidden beneath her outer garment, sneaking into Westminster Abbey. Thank goodness the Abbey had more than one entrance. She was pleased they agreed to let her volunteer for this stunt. She must remain calm and find an inconspicuous hiding place until the right moment. Damn – the muscles in her leg tightened – she was getting cramp. She saw a convenient pillar and slipped behind it. She leant over to try and massage the pain out of her calf. Having written to the Bishop and told him she would be at his service and seek sanctuary, she was anxious not to be caught too soon by officials on the lookout for her. She hoped the press and everyone who read the copy letter printed in the newspaper today would turn up to play their part. She'd to keep out of sight until the worship commenced. She experienced relief as the organ sounded out the first notes of the Bishop's processional music. At last. She guessed they'd reached the altar, the signal for her to take a pew. She joined in the hymns but wanted to get on with it. The preliminaries seemed to take forever. Finally the moment arrived – as the Bishop mounted the lectern she tore off her coat, exposed her sash and walked down the aisle towards him. In her mind she echoed the chant from her wedding day – aisle, altar, hymn. *Calm yourself,* she thought – *you've got to shout your message out before they can prevent you.*

"My Lord. In the name of God, stop forcible feeding. I myself am a prisoner under the Cat and Mouse Act and will be arrested on leaving the Abbey".

So they'd appropriated a nun to deal with her. An attempt to play it down and not attract criticism at what goes on inside the Abbey. *Why on earth did she need to cover my mouth with a handkerchief? I'm going quietly. Stupid puppet.* She pitied the poor woman, unable to decide for herself, a rule follower. She hoped the policemen that the nun handed her over to weren't too rough, but that might be a hope too far. She was glad she managed not to dwell on Holloway and what was to come; otherwise her courage might have failed. They bundled her into the Black Maria. *Curse 'em, they've torn my dress. Drat, more dressmakers' bills. At least my sash is intact.*

The five days in Holloway seemed interminable. On release Norah wondered whether her second episode of force-feeding was worse than the first. The jury remained undecided. Anticipation increased fear, but torture was evil however prepared you might be. What troubled her more were dreams; or were they visions?

She was never sure if she was asleep or awake, they seemed so real.

"How terrible it is, Grace. Despite excruciating pain from thirst and hunger and the physical struggle during feeding, I manage to snooze."

"I know what you mean," said Grace. "You doze from exhaustion. But though I nap, I'm still conscious, and it never refreshes me."

"My experience is the same, especially when I have dreams or visions of my father. Not sure which they are."

"That hasn't happened to me," said Grace. "What's your latest dream?"

"I told you before about the nightmare when my father raises his arm to slash me with a whip. The one where I wake with a sensation of pain across my face."

"I remember."

"This one troubles me more. My father stands in a muddy patch of ground covered in rotten potatoes, pointing at me as I stand on the field margin, saying 'Briollán' over and over. It's Irish Gaelic for a senseless or stupid person."

"What do you suppose it means?"

"He's goading me, implying I don't understand real hunger. That what I do is irresponsible self-punishment?"

"What does that do to you?"

"Makes me angry. Then I wake with a foetid stench in my nostrils like rotten potatoes and realise the smell comes from inside the cell. I guess I'm most upset because my father attributes questionable motives to our Votes for Women campaign."

"I suspect you have the dreams because you're exhausted after your second incarceration and force-feeding. You'll cope better when you've regained your strength."

"I hope so."

"I meant to congratulate you on your performance the night of your release before you came away."

"You appreciated my performance? I enjoyed it, despite feeling weak. The crowd buoyed me up."

"You held the whole of Knightsbridge Hall captive. I've never experienced a silence like it."

"I chose the white dress, with a full veil the same colour, to accentuate my pale complexion. The slow walk from the back to the front of the platform as I revealed myself made the silence more profound."

"You had them in complete control, and the applause when they realised it was you showed how they appreciated it."

"Policemen waited to snatch me away, but they got caught out a bit too."

"You hit the target with the theme of your speech."

"If 'No surrender even unto death' is appropriate for Ulster militants it is pertinent to us, even more so."

It would be her third arrest for defying her licence in as many months. Never mind, as long as it was planned well, and someone got the message through if she was arrested, it should still make an impact. She spotted the plain clothes detectives ahead of her. Prayed they wouldn't recognise her until she got closer to Buckingham Palace. She was determined to deliver Emmeline's demand to see the King's Secretary then hand him the letter from Emmeline for the King. Good job she briefed the young volunteer that morning.

"Now you're certain you understand what you've to do?"

"I am, Mrs Dacre Fox."

"So have you got your handcuffs ready to chain yourself to the railings?"

"I have."

"And the copy letter? Have you memorised your speech? Tell me what you'll say."

"I'm to tell the press and anyone within earshot, that Mrs Dacre Fox came to deliver a letter to the King, highlighting the nonsense that allows Sir Edward Carson, who has encouraged and incited murder, to be received at the Palace, while women found of guilty only of destroying property, are taken away to face hunger and thirst strikes and force-feeding."

The last thing Norah saw before being dragged away by the police was that the young girl succeeded in chaining herself to the railings and was surrounded by the press, proclaiming her message.

C365 C365 C365

JOHN WAS UNHAPPY. The things Charlotte and Norah

expected him to do. How did he get inveigled into it? He'd been cajoled into an agreement to let Norah move home after her imprisonment and marriage breakdown. What should he have done, she'd nowhere else to go? He supposed he should be grateful her militant campaign had ceased, even though it coincided with the declaration and outbreak of war. That liaison of hers with the Pankhursts caused him untold embarrassment. Norah never ceased to frustrate him. Now she was on the campaign trail with Mrs Pankhurst on the issue of national unity, support for the war effort and the Anti-Alien thing, which he supported. Was it possible to experience anger and admiration at the same time? It must be. That was his experience. Perhaps he hadn't heard correctly due to the background noise of the printing machines. But his ears didn't deceive him; Norah had asked him to support her campaign.

"Papa, I need eight thousand leaflets printed for this Albert Hall rally. Will you do it?"

"What for this time? Don't use that wheedling voice, it annoys me."

"Another Anti-Alien demonstration. I have a rough mock up. Here," said Norah handing him a copy.

<u>A Clean Sweep!</u>
<u>Demonstration</u>
Royal Albert Hall
On Tuesday, Nov 5th
At 7.30pm

To demand the Unconditional Surrender of the
Enemy in our midst, and the Immediate
Evacuation of Great Britain

Speakers:
The Right Hon. W. M.

Hughes

(Prime Minister of Australia)

Dr. Ellis Powell (Editor of the Financial News)
Major Harford Hawkins, V.D. (Alderman of the City of London)

Chair – Mrs Dacre Fox

For particulars of admission write: Mrs Dacre Fox, 3, Eastwood House, Emperor's Gate, S.W.7

"Why should I support this rally?" John looked up from his perusal of the leaflet.

"Because you share my outrage with our government's failure to act on the issue. You stepped in to chair the Trafalgar Square in July, so assume you're happy to sponsor this rally."

"Never assume anything, I've told you often enough. You know what I say. To assume makes an ass of you and me. My contacts tell me the war is almost over."

"But women have the vote now. An election is to be announced for December. Mrs Pankhurst has been promised that before then a Qualification of Women Act will pass, allowing us to stand as candidates. I'll stand as an Independent on an Anti-Alien ticket. This is part of my campaign plan."

"So you want me to fund your election campaign as well?"

"Yes. Although I've some funding in place, I'll need your support."

"Have you no shame, Norah? You're aware of my ambivalence. Yet you come here asking as if it's your right. Your behaviour the last few years has been selfish. As for poor Charles. The way you've treated him is disgraceful."

"The past is over. I'm moving forward. Will you support me?

"As I've a strong commitment to the Anti-Alien issue, I'll print your leaflets and endorse this campaign, but don't expect to exploit my support for other causes. I'm not going soft; I shan't give way every time."

The trouble was, he couldn't refuse. As Norah pointed out, he'd already supported her at the Trafalgar Square rally. Norah organised that almost single-handed, canvassed prominent politicians and public figures and got their backing. The list included the Bishop of Birmingham, Rudyard Kipling, Harry Lauder and Mr Massey, the Prime Minister of New Zealand. The Lord Mayor of London was to chair, but pulled out at the last minute and John stepped in. He wondered then how calculated her request to him had been. There must have been others to ask. He was conscious that she manipulated him through issues he had strong commitments to. When had he ever passed up the chance to air his views on a public platform? He had a duty to contribute to the public debate. That didn't stop him being irritated, though, and in a quandary because he knew she knew. He was a vehement supporter of the Anti-Alien issue despite its being against Liberal principles. The issue cut across political loyalties. His problem arose because of sensitivity over Norah's political bedfellows, so much so that he avoided enquiring after them. Why then, did she provoke him?

"Papa, will you be at the Hyde Park rally next week?" Norah glanced at her mother as Charlotte drew breath.

"No," came the curt response. "This is not the time or place to discuss it."

"You're aware of the petition calling on the government to intern enemy aliens. I've been collecting signatures. We've gathered one million, two hundred and fifty thousand, and will march to Downing Street with it after the rally. You've given generous support for the campaign so far."

"Yes, but you'll share a platform with General Page Croft and Leo Maxse." John tried to keep calm and not be provoked, but was conscious that his voice betrayed irritation.

"Why is that a problem?"

"Because those gentlemen are politicians opposed to Home Rule for Ireland. While I agree with the Anti-Alien campaign, I won't be connected with them in public. Your political affiliations compromise me."

"Do they, Papa? What about your political affiliations? You're supposed to be a liberal, but your alliances ensured a delay in women getting the vote. The Third Conciliation Bill in 1912 was defeated by the shenanigans of the Irish Parliamentary Party who wanted preference given to the Home Rule Bill, and didn't want time wasted debating Votes for Women."

"Asquith wasn't to blame for that," John shouted. Out of the corner of his eye he sensed Charlotte attempt to intervene.

"Yes he was. His failure and pusillanimous behaviour led to me, and women like me, being tortured and force-fed."

"Norah, you are being provocative."

"And you, Papa, are being hypocritical. Is that because you aren't convinced women deserve a vote, despite your liberal principles? Or is it because you compromise those principles when it's convenient?"

"Don't push me, Norah, or I'll ask you to leave the dinner table. I won't face provocation in my own home."

He threw down his napkin then left the table and

the room, infuriated to see a smile on Norah's face.

"Was that necessary, Norah?" asked Charlotte.

Norah noticed tears in her mother's eyes and was overcome with guilt. "I'm sorry, Mama, I didn't mean to upset you. I wish Papa would accept that I'm as good at politics as he is."

"You fail to acknowledge that Papa has accepted that. If not, why would he support you or even allow you to discuss it at dinner?"

"He tolerates my views. Doesn't accept I have a right to them, which is a different thing."

"You're wrong, Norah. Respect is something to be earned as well as demanded. You seem to be under the impression you need only demand it."

CB CB CB

JOHN READ THE press reports of the rally. He was angry. The picture printed alongside the report showed Norah at the head of the procession to Downing Street in front of the lorry transporting the petition. The vehicle, decorated with the Union Jack, the Stars and Stripes, the French Tricolour and the flags of other allied nations, was accompanied by bands and banners. How did she manage to catch him off guard? He supported the petition. He agreed with the Anti-Alien campaign. He wished she hadn't aligned herself with those far right politicians. If they hadn't been so prominent in raising the petition and securing signatures, if it'd been more cross-party, he would've marched with pride at her side.

He'd always been ambitious when it came to politics, but liked to believe his pragmatism counted most. The trouble with Norah was that she turned anger at injustice into a ruthless ambition to win with no thought for the cost. Time and again he tried to get her to understand.

"Norah, when are you going to learn to temper ambition with restraint?"

"I find that an amazing statement coming from you," said Norah. "I don't remember you taking that approach when we were young, although I'll admit you have mellowed."

"That's because I've learned to pick my battles. I don't take on challenges because they're there. Confrontations cost. I would've thought you realised that by now."

"If you refer to the Votes for Women campaign, that battle would never have been won by peaceful means. We tried long enough. In that regard you spout rubbish."

"I suppose you'll learn," said John.

Over time, his disappointment that she had not been born a boy grew. She had the qualities his sons lacked, none of whom ever challenged him. They would argue, but then back away, and Norah infuriated him when she defended them.

John convinced himself that Norah never concerned herself with the effects of her behaviour on family or his public career. Like the time she got involved in fistfighting and stone-throwing on Plumstead Common near Woolwich. It was another incident connected to her Anti-Alien campaign that he was obliged to read about in the local press. She'd mounted a speaker's platform at a rally shouting, "Are you out to win the war? Are you a friend or enemy of Germany? Are you wishing for peace at Germany's price?" Further abuse got hurled and it degenerated into a street fight. Norah never tried to hit or punch him, but reading the report of this foray made him wonder whether there were times when she might have. He had administered discipline to her as a child, but that had been necessary for her own good. That gave her no reason to retaliate now, did it? That wasn't something women indulged in. Or did they?

On the matter of women's voting rights, he was ambivalent. It was the principle of getting the last word with Norah that counted. When Parliament passed the 1917 Act giving women qualified suffrage, he accepted it in public. Norah had been anything but gracious and used it to provoke another argument with him, making cutting comments on the triumph of 'justified militancy' over 'hypocrisy'. She wanted to irritate him, and he always fell into her trap. He wondered why she couldn't be pleased that her aim had been achieved and leave it at that.

೮೮ ೮೮ ೮೮

EMMA STARED AT her mother in disbelief.

"This is terrible, Ma. When did letter come?"

"Yesterday. Da and me argued. Can't believe it 'as 'appened. Da says he's proud his sons 'ave died in a war so we don't 'ave to face a wicked enemy again."

"It's cruel, Ma. Will and Tom already dead in them trenches. Now Walter injured."

The tears stung her eyes as her Ma's thoughts tumbled out like a waterfall.

"Da says as I should be strong. Not be sad. That 'avin soldier sons I should 'ave expected it. 'Ow can my boys be taken? Surely the good Lord can spare one of 'em? Why must I be so 'elpless? Why can't I protect my bairns? Why didn't I 'ave girls? 'Ow can Da be so sure this'll be the war to end all wars?"

"It's cruel, Ma, but this says as Walter is alive and coming 'ome. Does it mean 'is injuries ain't too bad? When will 'e get 'ere, when can we see 'im?"

"They 'aven't said. Soon as they do, you'll come wiv me?"

"Course, Ma."

While Emma waited, anxious for news of Walter, life in Holloway stuck to rigid routines. The silence rule caused problems, as always, and, as always, prisoners resisted it.

"It's amazing 'ow women get round the silence rule," said Emma one evening, relaxing with fellow wardresses after work.

"Aye. Some'ow they get to pass notes or whisper. It's

a struggle to keep 'em in order."

"Always said it were silly," said Emma, "and today showed it."

"What 'appened?"

"T'was one of them women what 'ad been suffrigitts 'fore the war. Clever they is, always findin' ways to get round rules."

"Seems they can't keep away, must like it 'ere. What's she in for?"

"Being a conchie. 'anding out anti-war pamphlets, she were. They said as she drove an ambulance in France. Who'd 'ave thunk it? Never would 'ave 'appened afore war. Got trained as a mechanic so as to fix the thing if it wouldn't go."

"Amazin' how women are useful now, what wiv men away at the front. Seems we can work in munitions factories, join the land army, be doctors or nurses. There's even some women as 'ave bin made police orficers."

"Been trying to understand what police wimmin are about," said Emma. "Been looking at stuff on 'ow they reckon as they can 'elp women. You remember Mary Allen. One of them suffrigitts in 'ere. Now she's one of 'em, 'igh up in the organisation she is."

"Get you, Emma. Why d'you wanna learn more than what you need to do your job 'ere?"

"Dunno, can't help it."

"Did you see Mrs Pankhurst and that lot are pro-war? That Christabel 'as bin round the country 'anding out white fevvers to men as they call cowards?"

Emma ended the conversation. She needed to be alone, to wonder. Fiddlesticks. Once she'd 'ave agreed with Da, would've supported what them Pankhursts was doin' to support the war effort. But what with Will and Tom dead, didn't them conchies 'ave a point? Sad was how she felt most days. That was when she weren't angry. Angry was 'ow she was when she thought about Ma and 'ow un'appy she was. Other families 'ad lost boys, but this was 'er family. At unexpected moments grief would swallow her. Would the pain ever go? Why did she feel so empty the whole time? Why did 'er bruvvers' faces haunt 'er dreams? She felt tired and couldn't understand. Was anythin' worth this price? Fiddlesticks, it all seemed senseless. Every day brought news of death and families torn apart. When would it end? Thank goodness she 'ad 'er work. The 'Olloway routines kept her going. Didn't give 'er time to ponder. Now there was Walter. Some of 'er feelings of misery over Will and Tom 'ad gone away, but 'earin 'bout Walter crushed her spirit. The questions kept runnin' in her 'ead; How could it 'appen? How could so many men be dying? How many more would die? Guilt overwhelmed her. She 'oped that Walter's injuries would be serious enough that 'e didn't have to go back to the trenches, but not so bad as 'e would recover with arms, legs, eyes and 'earin. Emma waited in suspense for news. At last the day came and she and Ma set off to the hospital to see Walter.

A nurse led them to Walter's bedside. Said 'er name was Ruth. Emma thought Ruth 'ad a lovely face, cheerful and gentle with eyes that smiled, a small nose and thin, smiling lips; her soft, blonde, curly hair tucked tight under her cap. Ruth seemed so sweet natured, shy and sensitive. How did she cope with this misery? Emma's anxiety grew with each bed they passed on the way to Walter's. She tried not to look at the men lying in them with terrible injuries. Some would never see or walk again. The smell of antiseptic mixed with odours she couldn't recognise. 'Olloway had smells, lots of 'em, some foul, but this were different. Were it possible to 'ave worse niffs than 'Olloway? They found Walter's bed at the far end of the ward. She'd to hold back the tears when she saw he'd no bandages on his 'ead, but did 'ave some around his chest and left arm. At least 'e wouldn't be blind. It was selfish, but she couldn't stop feeling pleased. Found it difficult to take in. How did the nurses manage? Ruth was brave to face it every day, must 'ave real pluck. She'd seen terrible things in 'Olloway, but now't like this.

By the time they reached Walter's bedside, Ruth's calmness had communicated itself to Emma and she greeted her brother composed. Ruth explained that Walter had shrapnel wounds to his chest and arm, and that the doctors had considered amputation because of worry about infection. They were waiting to see if some treatment they tried would stop it so they might operate to save use of the arm. Ruth stayed by the bedside while

Emma and her mother spoke to Walter. Emma noticed Walter and Ruth looking at each other.

"Did you see them two exchanging looks, Ma?" asked Emma on their way home.

"Didn't notice nothin'. Too worried 'bout Walter."

"They was so taken wiv each other."

"Walter 'as to keep 'is mind on gettin' better, an' not on some girl, pretty as she might be. I 'ear them trenches is like an 'ell 'ole. Thank goodness my boy ain't in 'em just now, even if 'e is poorly."

ALMOST A YEAR later, Walter and Ruth got married. Although her conscience nagged, Emma was thankful when Walter's injuries meant he didn't have to go back to the Front. She got her wish. After the wedding the couple settled in Northchapel, close enough for Emma to visit on occasion. Emma enjoyed going to stay. Ruth always welcomed her with affection, and many times Emma rejoiced over how it turned out that he and Ruth met and began to build a life together. Ruth was patient with him, attending to every need before he asked. Emma would watch them and envied Walter, wondering if she would ever have such a relationship. Emma tried not to think about it. Knew she weren't the same as other women, that she could never love a man the way Ruth loved Walter. She was confused. Fiddlesticks. Was it possible she might love another woman that way? How did she know that was what she wanted? How did women set about having caring relationships with other women? The questions kept coming. Emma didn't have any idea 'ow to find answers.

Walter was unable to work. His recuperation took forever. His arm never recovered enough strength to let him do manual work, but it was spared. Emma was pleased that Ruth's family lived nearby; it was a nice quiet village where Walter seemed happy. The memory of the trenches was written on his face, but neither Emma nor Ruth ever got him to speak about it.

C3 C3 C3

POLLING DAY FOR the 1918 General Election was the fourteenth of December, although votes weren't counted until the twenty-eighth of December. Norah and Charlotte were at breakfast – Norah seethed, tired after a rotten night's sleep.

"What will you do now you've lost Richmond?" asked Charlotte.

"No idea. I'm furious that one woman won a seat; a woman who won't take it up as she's an Irish Nationalist serving a prison sentence in Ireland for her part in the Uprising. I don't understand why it was simple for her to win election to a Parliament, which she boasts she wants to destroy, disintegrate and discredit?"

"I understand your anger, Norah. Why don't you take a short holiday? I'm sure Papa will agree I go with you for a few days. You can then stay on if you want."

That was why Norah was sitting in a window seat, in winter, staring, her mind as grey as the sea and the gloomy, heavy clouds outside. The last four years had been difficult. Despite the initial optimism of a short conflict, a terrible fog had descended and insinuated itself into everyone's consciousness. It penetrated every aspect of life, never lifted, but deepened with time, touching everyone in wretched and personal ways. One of her clearest memories was of frontline bombardments that were heard in England notwithstanding the width of the English Channel. The nation held their collective breath and listened, wondered which family might be next to get bad news, while they hoped and prayed it wouldn't be them. She couldn't remember enjoying seasonal changes, although registered they came and went. The fighting and misery never ended, and when spring came round each year, the promise that it carried evaporated quickly. Summers served to remind the populace of what they'd lost, while autumn and winter disappeared in gloom. Her own pursuits kept her busy and focused, and she used that to bolster her better moments, grateful for the distraction. Although getting the vote had been an appropriate reward for the hard work and suffering women endured, the joy was tempered by it being achieved on the back of this terrible war. Her hopes that women would influence events and be able to help prevent future wars smashed in one short day of voting.

Her family was lucky, if that was a term your personal predilections recognised or delegated to the idea of fate. Despite her brothers serving in the forces, none died. Although the family were dispersed she wasn't sure it made a difference, except to Mama. There was irony in that, although she felt sure none of those who lost loved ones would see it.

Despite the difficulties Norah enjoyed the challenges. She took on and pursued personal and political objectives where she could develop her talents. Mrs Pankhurst believed that if the Kaiser won the war, women's rights would be set back irreparably, and this increased Norah's determination. Norah didn't want to see women's efforts and the suffering they endured, destroyed by a victorious German Kaiser. As a result of her countrywide tours with the Pankhursts, she found the confidence to pursue her own political career independent of them. By the time of the Women's Victory Celebration, organised by Emmeline at the Albert Hall to coincide with the female suffrage bill passing through Parliament, she no longer saw much of them.

But Norah did remember accepting with pride her medal with three bars from Emmeline's hand, pleased her mother came to witness it.

"Did you enjoy the day, Mama?"

"You must've been proud to receive your medal from Emmeline. Pity Papa didn't come."

"It was his decision, although it pleased me that he chose not to. Didn't want him there. He never supported our campaign. Accepted the outcome because he'd no choice."

Thinking of her father reminded her of persistent troubling dreams. The current one replaced the nightmares of the arm with the whip and the muddy potato field. Norah dreamed it again the night before the Victory Celebration. She was in a forest, dense with mature trees, trying to find her way. Then a clearing opened, and she could see the branches had formed an arch above it, their upper boughs imitating a cathedral roof. In the middle was an altar, surrounded by people. At first she didn't recognise anyone, but then saw her father beckon. Lying on the altar was her purple, white and green WSPU sash, emblazoned with the slogan 'Votes for Woman', the one she'd worn when she pleaded for asylum from the Bishop of London at Westminster Abbey. Her father asked her to sacrifice this before he'd give his support. Her father asked her to sacrifice this before he'd give his support. Norah stood undecided, tormented by the idea of what that meant. Her father seemed content that he was in control, and while she struggled with her fears, he called forward a large horse and cart and helped the driver load her independence onto it, to be carried away into the forest. Norah attempted to stop the cart disappearing, then woke, straining and shouting, "No, don't take it, don't take my independence!"

Norah described the dream to Charlotte.

"What do you suppose it means, Mama?"

"You are troubled asking Papa to support your campaigning, and resent having to do so."

"That's one interpretation. My own is that the dream confirms what a bully he is. He has to control everyone, but now that we are older he cannot exert the same strict discipline he did when we were children."

"Do you think so? I thought he'd relaxed and become more approachable."

"He can still be controlling and hostile, although I do agree he has realised that more can be achieved if he listens and follows your advice."

"Norah, you are always ready to judge him as harsh and unreasonable. You are like him, and as difficult."

"You may be right, but I know one thing, I won't allow these dreams to trouble me. He won't dictate what I do. I'll follow my conscience. He gives grudging respect to what I do, but won't admit it."

Norah dragged her mind back from thoughts of her father to concentrate on the immediate future. Her hope of a parliamentary seat gone, she must put her anger about that to use. If she didn't she'd allow it to make a mockery of the whole election process, and raise questions about the validity of what she and her WSPU colleagues achieved at great personal cost. Women had a lot of work to do to shape and fashion their mark on society.

CB CB CB

THE CLOSE OF war brought more sadness for Emma. Not long after peace was declared, she'd to go to Northchapel to attend Walter's funeral. He never recovered his strength. Emma was glad that he had Ruth to see him through. Ruth nursed him with love and dedication to the end, always hopeful that he would recover. As she stood with Ruth, Da and Ma at his graveside, she contemplated what a terrible price her family had paid. She hoped that she would never witness another war, and thought that if she did she'd want her vote to be for peace. But there was the catch. Although women had been granted a vote at the end of the war, it was confined to women over thirty. Emma couldn't vote. All she could hope for was that it wouldn't be necessary.

After Walter's funeral she went to the seaside for a day. As she strolled along the beach and watched the breakers lap the shore, she knew she couldn't ignore it. She was different. The waves broke on the sand, left tide marks, filled up holes or knocked down sandcastles the children built. They couldn't be stopped. She couldn't change what she was, didn't know what to do. Who could she talk to? She longed for someone to share her secret, and felt alone. If she spoke to others about it she would be laughed at, despised and shut out of normal life. Ma and Da would by no means forgive her, they wouldn't understand. They'd say she brought shame on them. She'd watched the inverts in 'Olloway. She couldn't ask them, although she tried to listen to their whispered conversations. They defied everyone, didn't try to hide what the guv'nor and other wardresses called their 'sick perversion'. By sticking close they appeared strong. But as an example it was clear that what they were would never be accepted – they'd always be thought of as ugly and bad, unnatural in some way. Most of them were in for drugs and prostitution, and having to give themselves to men to get money to buy drugs or drink, or buy food for their youngsters, must be miserable if her own feelings were anything to go by. No wonder drugs and prostitution went together. Perhaps with women doing men's jobs, people might start to think different, but not soon enough for her.

CHAPTER 5
Pollarded Ambitions

ANOTHER SLEEPLESS NIGHT. Why couldn't she let it go? Why did she feel so angry with herself? It was the system, it had to be. She hadn't failed. So why blame herself? Perhaps she'd not done enough, spoken to sufficient numbers of people, hadn't put her message across. All those dreams of achieving what she worked so hard for – gone in a puff of smoke or the wave of a magician's wand. It reminded her of her wedding; except this time she'd been dumped at the altar. All her hopes and plans, the anticipation, the excitement of the day, and then – nothing. Now she'd to plan for a future she hadn't anticipated. Norah Dacre Fox wouldn't take a seat in Parliament, take part in debates, use her skills to better the lives of women or have her voice heard on animal welfare. She felt impotent, cheated. It was as if, despite being removed, the metal grilles that hid the Ladies' Gallery in the House of Commons chamber were reinstated. Women remained locked out of deliberations; they had a vote, but continued to be excluded. Male politicians weren't going to be distracted by the sight of Norah Dacre Fox offering insight into how things should be bettered for everyone. She'd been patted on the head and told it wasn't the fault of democracy if the public didn't vote for her. She fought for so long to have the thing she prized most snatched away from her.

So she must keep working for her causes from outside Parliament. There were pressure groups to form, MPs to be lobbied, town councils to be appealed to. She would keep campaigning on animal welfare, and that still unresolved issue – the threat posed by foreigners who brought the nation to the brink of a deep chasm during the war. No one understood what saved the country from falling into it, some believed it had. Who knew? The press mithered on about it. The whole population seemed to be in the grip a painful hangover; everyone suffered so much from the war.

Papa supported her on the Anti-Alien issue, but she was aware it rankled when she insisted on discussing her campaign each evening at dinner. It was something she never forgave him for, that stupid rule of his that only men had the right to talk at the meal table, that women must remain silent. Now she would get her own back. With the family gone she was the last one living at home. She had a victory in forcing him to relax his rule. He had to, otherwise he would be sat there in stately silence as only Mama and herself shared his meals now. Still, he stood firm on his right to choose topics for discussion. Why? Women had the vote, history had moved on. She wanted Papa to recognise that and not dictate what she might talk about and where. Mama pleaded with her to let Papa have his way, but she persisted in her determination to have the last word.

"I am giving a speech next week, Papa. Are you coming?"

"Not next week. Other commitments preclude my attendance."

"You won't mind if I rehearse now, then. If you aren't coming you won't need to listen twice."

"Is it the usual one about persons of '…enemy blood… gaining ascendency in our national life….' etc.?" said John, rolling his eyes upwards.

Norah saw the eye roll. She had him. His irritation got the better of him.

"Of course. It's part of my 'Defence of British Rights in Britain' campaign and the way… '…enemy penetration poses a grave threat to the whole fabric of our constitution and the foundations of our Empire….'."

"Norah, we wish to enjoy a quiet dinner. I'd prefer to do this later."

"But Papa, I know how you are concerned that… '…Germans in particular proved themselves to be the enemy not just of mankind, but of the whole of civilization…'"

"Norah, you've recited these phrases so many times I'm able repeat them in my sleep. I helped you prepare your election address, remember? Can we please enjoy our dinner in quiet and do this later?"

"Very well, Papa, if you are losing interest I shall find someone who is interested and wants to help me."

Someone – perhaps it was Mama – tried to suggest that her frenetic campaigning fulfilled some kind of bereavement process. She rose to the jibe, agreeing she was bitter about her election defeat, but insisted that she carry on her campaign so that the wrong would be righted. Anyway, if you repeat something over and over, someone is bound to believe it in the end.

ᚙ ᚙ ᚙ

AT THE END of the war Dorothy and Augustus returned home from South Africa. Norah's delight at this news spilled over. They shared many interests. Norah looked forward to the comfort of having her sister near enough to visit and gossip with.

"So update me on the anti-vivisection campaigning?" said Dorothy one afternoon at tea.

"We're organising our campaign on the Dogs' Bill."

"I read about that at the RSPCA meetings. What are your plans?"

"I am writing to MPs and other prominent figures, asking them to vote for the bill when it comes before Parliament. We'll book a hall, hold a rally and read out the letters of support. Always gets a good response."

"Let's hope so. I suppose you're stressing the usual stuff. How animal experiments cause misery, deny dignity etc. How animals have no voice to express pain and anguish, relying on us to do it for them."

"That's right. The letter gives descriptions of how they use dirty tubes to carry out abominable experiments, spread infection, and make things worse."

"I suppose you question the unreliable evidence that comes from it."

"In no uncertain terms."

"I get upset about monkeys. Got to love them in Africa. London Zoo lets me help in the monkey house. They're so like us. I can't bear to imagine their suffering."

"I've received an invitation to stand for election as Honorary Secretary of the London and Provincial Antivivisection Society," said Norah. "I'm planning to write a few papers for them, which might get published."

During the Dogs' Bill campaign Norah met Edward. He introduced himself at the end of a gathering she chaired. Their friendship blossomed and she decided to call him Dudley (his third given name), in part as a form of endearment, in part to hide his identity. After her failed marriage, Norah didn't want to get involved with anyone, especially as Charles refused to divorce. She was aware Charles lived with another woman, but couldn't be bothered to do anything about it. Divorce was difficult and expensive. She found Dudley attractive and likeable but wasn't sure why. It'd been easy to engineer a meeting between Dudley and Dorothy as she and Augustus attended every rally and meeting Norah organised.

"Dorothy, now you've met Dudley, what do you

think of him?"

"Seems nice, very sincere, although struck me as nervous, the sort that might jump at his own shadow."

"You may be right. But he has lots of contacts I can use."

"You're after his network then?"

"Not sure. He might be good for a bit of fun as well."

"But you said you didn't want to get involved with anyone, didn't want responsibilities. Happy being a free agent. Anyway, you're still married."

"So's he, so it won't go anywhere."

"Might still lead to disaster. Be careful."

Dudley's sincerity struck Norah most; she found herself drawn to him, despite reservations. They went for tea after campaign meetings to discuss tactics.

"Wonderful to enjoy tea with you again," said Dudley.

"Same for me, I couldn't wait either. There are lots of ideas I need your opinion on."

"Happy to be involved. Although, if I may say so, you work so hard and have done a lot of campaigning before, so not sure what I can add."

"Your contribution is invaluable. Besides, I look forward to our chats."

"It's the same for me. Great to slip my leash sometimes, if you'll forgive the pun."

"How loose is the leash? Would it extend to tea at my flat sometime?"

"What an outrageous suggestion, Mrs Fox," said Dudley, laughing. "Still, I suggest we explore it anyway."

"I am sure we can manage it. Needs planning, but as you know that is my forte. I keep a small library of anti-vivisection material at home for people to borrow. There must be some stuff of interest to you. I shall arrange a private browse."

"A private browse. How intriguing," said Dudley, raising his eyebrows and tilting his head to one side.

And so the affair commenced with Dudley borrowing from her library. She found it exciting and fulfilling, the way she had as a young woman. She had no memory of her emotions responding this way when Charles courted her. As a pregnancy was impossible, there was no worry there. Why not enjoy a fling? So much changed since the war. What difference did it make now? It was nothing more than sex and he was committed to a marriage, so they were able to enjoy the pleasure and none of the pain.

Some eight months later, the kaleidoscope of life turned, her certainties shifted and a radically different pattern for her life emerged.

"You've been unwell for a while. You must consult a doctor," Dorothy pleaded.

"Dorothy," Norah responded with impatience, "we both agree that doctors are idiots, with vile treatments based on animal experiments. I'll not put myself at their mercy. If I rest and eat properly, I'll get better. I know my body, and will handle it myself."

"But we must be able to find a doctor you approve of. Please let's try. If it's something serious, we need to make plans."

Norah gave in. Dorothy went with her to the appointment. They found themselves astonished by what the doctor told them, although Norah exhibited more fury than astonishment.

"You're pregnant, Mrs Dacre Fox, about four months on."

Norah's temper got the better of her. "Don't be preposterous, I said coming here was a waste of time. I can't conceive children. You're wrong, but then what else is to be expected from a bumbling idiot of a doctor. You'll arrange a second opinion and be proved wrong."

"Norah, calm down," pleaded Dorothy. "I realise you are shocked, but you must allow that the doctor has some idea of what he's talking about."

"No, why should he? It doesn't follow. Doctors are fools. They never have any idea what they are pontificating on, and this idiot is worse than most. I can't get pregnant, I am forty-three, for God's sake, and never got pregnant with Charles. So what is the cretin suggesting, a miracle?"

"Mrs Dacre Fox," interjected the doctor, "You don't want to be pregnant, which is obvious from the way you responded to my diagnosis. That doesn't change the facts. No matter how much abuse you hurl, it won't change them. I'll arrange a second opinion, but that won't alter anything either."

Norah continued to reject the idea, but her body said he was right. It wasn't her fault, it had to be someone's, but it wasn't hers. Why would it be? First there were those stupid doctors who told her when she never conceived with Charles that it'd been her fault; that her insides were defective. She got angry when the blame fell at her door, so angry that she wouldn't agree to any examinations, internal or otherwise, to confirm it. Then there was that idiot Charles. He was responsible for this, he insisted she was infertile and unable to bear children. Charles and the doctors arrived at their conclusions based on inbuilt prejudice against women, and she would never give them the satisfaction of disproving them. Why should she? Next she raged against her useless body that let her down. Her self-loathing became intense. She would not accept she lost control and allowed this to happen, it had to be some kind of fluke.

Norah remembered Emmeline's campaign in 1915 urging WSPU women to adopt illegitimate children to save them from the 'moral degeneracy inherited from their parents'. The number of war babies being born while husbands were away at the front was the reason for the campaign being launched. It focused on the 'particular sin on the part of the mother' and she supported it. Now she'd become a morally degenerate mother herself. She was in no doubt she'd lose their friendship and wouldn't hear from them anymore. She was sad about Grace with whom she shared so much joy and friendship in the midst of their struggle. Why had she been so stupid? Even though she no longer saw them, she kept in touch and couldn't bear the idea of forever being banished from the circle of friends she worked so hard and sacrificed so much to join.

The last person to blame was Dudley.

"How could you do this to me? You let your lust get the better of you, you selfish man? Why couldn't you control yourself? Sex has always been exploitation of women by men. You are no different."

"Norah, please can we leave aside how we got here and try to concentrate on what will be best for the baby?"

"So you want to ignore that you satisfied your disgusting lusts, betrayed your wife and children, and get away with it? The sex wasn't that good anyway. You are such a weak man and your love-making pathetic and unsatisfying."

"Norah, because you now disparage what at the time you claimed to be enjoyable, doesn't change the fact that we must decide on what to do for the baby. Getting upset like this is not helping."

"Upset? UPSET? You can't even begin to imagine what I am. Now, for the next however many months, I must endure carrying this child inside me. How dare you, why weren't you more careful, why didn't you exercise self-control?"

Norah carried on shouting, repeating herself over

and over. When she did calm down, having exhausted her blame vocabulary, which was extensive, she demanded he provide for her and the baby. Her anger flared when he hesitated and said that he would be unable to provide anything more than financial support at first, pleading that he found himself torn by loyalty and responsibility to his existing family.

Norah made arrangements to undergo the delivery with Dorothy's help. This was the best arrangement she could get as Mama would not defy Papa, who became angry when he discovered Norah's pregnancy. Augustus was not happy either, but Norah was grateful that Dorothy stood up to him.

Norah remembered the day she went to register the baby. Dudley didn't go with her to the registrar's office. They rowed about it, so she went alone.

"I came to record a birth."

"Certainly, madam," said the registrar, "if you will complete the certificate in my presence, then I will sign to seal the formalities."

Norah set about filling in the form.

When and where born – Twenty ninth May 1922 – 17 Scarsdale Terrace

Name of baby – Evelyn Anthony Christopher Fox

Sex – Boy

Name and surname of father – Norah left this blank and proceeded to the next box.

Name and occupation of mother – Norah Fox formerly Doherty – No occupation

When registered – 4 July 1922

At this point the registrar's attention became diverted, so Norah decided to write a name in the column reserved for the name and surname of father. But she got no further than the word 'George' because the registrar, returning his scrutiny to her, saw what she had done and insisted she stop.

"Madam. You are aware of the rules. I cannot permit you to enter a father's name on the certificate as no father is present to attest to his status."

"Another stupid male rule. Why did this one get invented? I know who the father is. Why do you need to? I suppose as usual it is because you regard women as unreliable and not able to remember who they got pregnant with. Or else that they would lie about it."

"Madam. It's not as simple as you suggest and I don't have time to debate it. Anyway, I don't make the rules. I simply follow them."

Norah struggled to hide her annoyance as the registrar crossed out the 'George' and made a note to that effect on the side of the certificate. He signed it and gave her the copy.

"Why did you start to scribble George under the father's name?" asked Dorothy.

"I intended to write George V for the hell of it, but didn't manage to finish it."

Dorothy burst out laughing. "I'm not sure the Queen would approve."

℘ ℘ ℘

NANNY RUTH REGISTERED Tony's high-pitched screaming as she opened the gate. Mr Elam must be out, or tried to intervene and retreated. She threw off her coat, hat and bag, and ran to the nursery. On entering the room she witnessed Norah leaning over the baby, shouting, with her back to the door.

"Where the hell did you go? Sloped off to your library?"

"It was my afternoon off, Mrs Elam," said Ruth. Tony lay close to the edge of the nappy changing area, screaming, in danger of falling off, with a long drop straight to the floor. *I must keep calm,* thought Ruth.

Norah straightened up, then turned on Ruth with an acid glare. "Oh, I thought you were Mr Elam. Well as you're here, take the brat. I can't stand the yelling. I tried to change this disgusting nappy, but it screamed and wriggled so much I don't know how to fold or fasten the clean one. The pin slipped into the brat's tummy. Serves it right, stupid thing. Then it had the audacity to pee over me."

"Here, let me take him," said Ruth.

With Tony safe in her arms she wrapped him in a towel and cradled him close. "Did he get his two o'clock feed?"

"Feed, what feed? Mr Elam tried to say it might be crying from hunger. I'm sure you didn't tell me to give it a bottle. Fools, both of you. I've more important things to do than worry about this brat's routine. Get on with your job and for heaven's sake stop it making that excruciating yelling. It's giving me a headache."

Norah stomped out of the nursery, relieved to be absolved of responsibility. Tony's crying annoyed her, but hadn't upset her. It wasn't her fault. It was Dudley and Nanny; idiots who left her alone with the baby. They should know better.

Cuddling Tony, Ruth went to find the kitchen maid, who prepared a feed. Once comforted with the bottle and less distressed, Ruth bathed and dressed him, sitting with him in the nursery rocking chair, humming until he fell asleep.

When he settled, she went in search of Mr Elam, who she found hiding in his study surrounded by his beloved books, staring distractedly at his *memento mori*. He was a small, slight man, his face creased with worry, but with eyes that showed understanding acquired through pain. Always immaculately turned out, he was soft spoken, in keeping with his words that were ever gentle and considered. Ruth was never sure whether the hesitations in his speech came from nervousness, or a deliberate slowness to cover his quest for the right word. He apologised to Ruth and agreed they needed to talk.

"Nanny, I am sorry about today. Is Tony settled?" he asked.

"Tony is settled, but was distressed. It isn't good for him to be upset like that."

"What can we do, Nanny? I hoped when you went off this afternoon that Mrs Elam might cope. I'm usually here, but today I had business in the village. You can guess what I found when I got back. My attempts to help rejected."

"I've been wondering about it," said Ruth, "and believe I have the answer."

"Nanny, please don't say you are going to leave us. Tony and I would miss you."

"Don't worry, Mr Elam, I've no intention of deserting Tony. I've decided from now on I won't take afternoons off, or, if I do, will take Tony with me. Do you agree?"

Dudley let out an immense sigh. "Thank you, Nanny, we are so grateful."

Later in the nursery, watching Tony sleep, Ruth reflected on their conversation. Mr and Mrs Elam came to live in Northchapel from London when Tony was a few months old. She learned through village gossip they needed a nanny, and applied for the job. Although married, she hadn't been blessed with her own child – a great sadness, especially with what happened to Walter. After he died from his injuries last year she'd been left wondering what to do.

She'd no training as a nanny, but Mr Elam interviewed her because she'd been a nurse.

"I am going to be frank with you, Mrs Baxter, although what I need to say is embarrassing."

"I understand," said Ruth. "You can rely on me."

"I hope so, and I trust that will remain the case whether I offer you the job or not."

"I don't gossip."

"Our previous partners refused to divorce. Mrs Elam's real name is Mrs Dacre Fox."

"I won't tell anyone," said Ruth.

"Good. I'm more concerned, however, about Mrs Elam's inability to adapt to motherhood. She was under the impression she couldn't bear children. It shocked us both when she fell pregnant."

"I can understand that," said Ruth.

"She's found it hard to adjust and has struggled ever since the birth."

"I understand. I'd be pleased to take the position."

"Very well. I am delighted to offer it to you."

"Thank you, Mr Elam, you won't be disappointed."

Ruth was overjoyed. Even more satisfying, she had the baby to herself as his mother showed no interest. She hated taking afternoons off but today gave her the perfect excuse not to do so any more. She was happy to give up time off on the pretext that Tony should not be left with Mrs Elam. The state she found them in today provided the proof she needed.

CB CB CB

EMMA AND ANOTHER wardress made their way to The Shed – that large, purpose built, two storey, brick building at the end of B wing. It was twenty years since it had seen use for hanging the baby farmers, long before Emma arrived at Holloway. Now here she was in January 1923, charged with making sure that everything was ready for tomorrow. Emma shivered, looking at the cold grey winter skies. How appropriate. The Shed and the area around it attracted an eerie atmosphere, everyone avoided it, said it smelled of death and was haunted.

"I 'ear Ellis and Pierrepoint Jnr, the 'angmen, 'ave bin in. Checked the lever and workin's. Made sure they bin oiled and won't stick."

"Aye," said Emma, "we've to make sure everythin' else is clean and spruced up. I 'ear as the drains in the pit 'ave bin examined, so we don't 'ave to do that. Never been in 'ere, 'ave you?"

"No. It's 'orrible an' gruesome. There's been demonstrators outside for days – jeered the 'angmen when they came to check it were going right – probably 'ave bigger crowds tomorro' morning."

"It 'as bin suspect. No one thinks the evidence 'gainst Mrs Thompson is quite right."

"Aye, no reprieve nor no mercy there."

"Will you be there when it's done?" asked Emma, "I've to 'elp remove the body after. I ain't 'appy 'bout it."

"No, it'll only be Miss Cronen, the Superintendent, even tho' I bin guardin' Mrs Thompson, supervisin' her solitary walks in yard. I've to take 'er to gallows, but then 'ave to leave. All of us what 'ave been guardin' her are un'appy. Can't believe there 'aint no mercy. It's a real 'orrible, sad story."

"Let's start upstairs," said Emma.

They climbed the stairs. Emma became conscious of the cold steel handrail under her fingers, and looked up at the vaulted roof and whitewashed walls, trying to avoid looking at the gallows. The dim grey winter afternoon gloom seeping through the windows high up near the ceiling enhanced her unease. No other light source penetrated the bleakness. She examined the silver-plated Christian cross on the wall to one side of the gallows, to make sure it had been polished. The wooden floor had been swept, although to get a room like this dust-free proved impossible. She gave a final cursory glance at the trap door and lever, shuddered and turned away. Was this how death smelt? Dusty and chilled?

The execution took place at nine o'clock the next morning. Emma wasn't sure whether to be grateful to be spared the hanging. Could anything be more awful? She didn't know, she'd never witnessed another event like it. Not even the force-feeding came close. But at ten, when the body had hung for the stipulated hour, and she entered the pit to help remove it to the autopsy room, Emma realised there was worse, something far worse. The evidence lay in the drains beneath the body. It was hard to pull herself together and do the necessary. How would the rest of the prison react? She prayed it would be another twenty years before a hanging happened again and that she'd be long gone. Emma stared at the body. She didn't see her brother's bodies after they died. They'd met their end on a battlefield. She'd no idea what their injuries were, she'd never been told. Did they die with the same fear on their features that she looked at now? Had they even had faces left to look at? It brought it back, Ma's sadness and her own struggle to find a way to accept what happened.

When she finished she got given leave to take some free time. Preoccupied, she set off for the wardresses' recreation room, anxious to get there. Why so many gates to lock and unlock? At least each one she passed through put more distance between her and The Shed. After she locked one gate, she turned to see a woman watching her. She remembered seeing her before. The woman wore the uniform of the Discharged Prisoner's Aid Society.

"Are you all right, you look pale?" said the woman.

"Aye. I 'ad to perform an 'orrible duty today, one I ain't never 'ad to do afore and 'ope never to 'ave to do again."

"I understand. Were you present? It proved difficult to get through the demonstrators this morning. My name is Miriam. Would you like someone to talk to, I have a few moments spare."

"Aye, it would 'elp, if you've a little while. My name's Emma."

As she talked Emma looked straight at Miriam, and found herself staring into gentle, kind eyes. She couldn't remember ever seeing eyes like 'em before. Then she noticed Miriam's face, round-shaped, almost as wide as long, with small lips. Her dark hair had been tied back, but soft curls still escaped to frame her face. Miriam seemed about the same height as herself, but unlike herself, entertained a more feminine shape with bigger bubs and small waist. They only had a few minutes. Emma was conscious that she'd get into trouble if caught chatting too long. She'd be told to pull 'erself together, it being 'er duty and 'ow as she 'ad to get on with it. As they parted Emma experienced disappointment. She wanted to get to know Miriam better, but didn't know how to ask. It was now or never.

"Please…" she called out, frightened of being heard.

Miriam stopped, turned and smiled. "What is it? Is there something else?"

"When will you be 'ere again?" Emma asked.

☙ ☙ ☙

NANNY RUTH WAITED at the garden gate in front of The Old Forge. Emma was due. She'd taken a day off and arranged to come down from London to see her. They planned to go for tea.

"Uniform's canny. Our two 'eads together was good," said Emma.

"Enough of that," said Ruth. "You seem extra happy today. Happier than I've seen you for ages. I reckoned you might be gloomy, especially with that hanging. There's been so much in the papers. That's why I suggested you get away to see us."

"It were 'orrible. But good comes from bad, as Ma used to say. I made a friend through it. Name of

Miriam. See each other reg'lar now. Nice to have a body to talk to. Lots in common an' we 'ave fun together."

"I can see that. Any chance she might come to Northchapel?"

"Love to bring 'er and show 'er countryside. Lived 'er whole life in East End."

"Can't wait to meet her. If it's in summer we can go for a picnic in the forest."

"How's it going with baby? Still enjoying 'im?"

"I'll say. Mrs Elam stays out of our way. Keeps herself busy with her work. Mr Elam is quiet. Mostly goes along with what she says."

"Strange that, 'ow she don't seem motherly."

"I won't complain. Some people are like that. Suits me. I'm happy. I've a bonny child, who might as well be my own. Didn't want another husband after Walter, even if there were any around, so many died there ain't a lot of men to spare. So I got the best of it for now."

ଔ ଔ ଔ

EMMA MET MIRIAM as often as possible. One of their favourite places was a Lyons Corner House where they would enjoy afternoon tea. Emma looked forward to these outings. Meetings inside 'Olloway was impossible. Prying eyes and ears lurked everywhere, and the endless 'ard work gave little time to spare. Corridors was where they met most times. Miriam suggested they meet outside somewhere. Emma was nervous at first. Why was Miriam interested in her? Miriam was so pretty, spoke better than her, must've 'ad more book learning. Emma wanted to get book learning so she might get promoted. Perhaps Miriam would help her do that. It was nice having a friend who seemed to understand. Perhaps it were too good to be true, as Ma used to say. But somehow, it seemed right. They 'ad fun and never stopped talking about lots of different things.

"Do you feel better about the Mrs Thompson thing now?" asked Miriam.

"Aye. You 'elped me so much. Don't never want to see such like again. Lucky I saw you that day. Otherwise I mayn't ever 'ave gotten over it."

"Oy. We were both in luck. I watched you about the prison, and tried to talk to you for ages. So when I saw my chance I grabbed it."

"Right glad you did. Don't know 'ow as I never noticed you 'afore."

"Who'd have believed we'd find so much to talk about?"

"I always 'ad lots of questions. Thought it were me. Then with the war and losin' me bruvvers. Never 'ad no one to ask or tell about me worries."

"It's good you're as curious as me."

"Never met anyone 'afore who made me easy 'bout asking things. So, 'ow come you ended up a prison visitor?"

"It's a long story. In Jewish families the idea of community service is drilled into us from the day we're born. For girls that means marriage and children. We mother the whole community. I never wanted to marry. Always dreamt of escape by finding a career. Argued with my parents over it. They accepted this work as a compromise because it serves the people, although they still wish I'd accept a husband and marry. They're desperate for *aineklach*."

"What's that word? Can't hardly say it."

"Aineklach – grandchildren."

"Right."

"What about you? How did you end up a wardress?"

"My Da were army. Strict on doin' duty and obeyin' rules. Left army to be prison warder. It were 'im got me to work in 'Olloway. Havin' lost my bruvvers to the war, Ma and Da want me to marry. Same as your Ma and Da, they wants me to give 'em grandchildren. But I ain't interested in gettin' married neither."

"It seems our communities aren't so different. Lots of traditions to tell us how to live."

ᘓ ᘓ ᘓ

AFTER THE ANNOYING business with Nanny in the nursery, Norah hurried to her study, longing for quiet. Her stomach churned, she felt shaky and breathed so fast her pulse raced. How did she manage to get into this position, fall pregnant and saddle herself with a baby? How stupid. She went over it in her mind, the path to this disaster.

The first few weeks with the baby were hell. She couldn't get over her anger. The delivery had been long and painful and she'd no idea how to begin caring for the helpless creature that invaded her life. She'd no idea how to manage her finances. Her life's work destroyed, she didn't want to dwell on the responsibility involved. She hated to look at the child. Every time she tried, all she saw was the shame and stigma attached to a bastard child with her social ambitions lying in ruins around it. As for breastfeeding, if God existed he must be male. Only a man would inflict such discomfort on a woman under the guise of renewing life. It was the baby's fault. He was unnatural because he didn't do as expected and suckle. What sort of an idiot would he grow up to be? How would she cope? How would she manage? She needed to talk to Dudley.

"I've been considering how we might manage this situation," said Dudley.

"Has your consideration progressed far? Have you come up with anything?"

"Give me a chance. This hasn't been easy. I need to consider Ada and my children."

"Your children are almost grown up, they can cope, look after Ada. Tony and I need you more."

"It's going to break their hearts. Cause them shame and suffering. It's not something I can do lightly."

"You need to get on with it. Delay makes it worse."

"I'm aware of that. I've decided you and I will move out of London to a village in East Sussex, where nobody knows us. We can live quietly as man and wife until the scandal dies down."

"How far has this plan progressed?"

"I've rented a house, 'The Old Forge' in Northchapel. I've got a nanny who's preparing a nursery for Tony. As soon as everything is ready we'll move. It should be a week or so."

"When will you tell Ada and your children?"

"I'll do it the day before we move."

Norah's relief was evident. It meant that when things settled down she would be able to concentrate, uninterrupted, on what she wanted to do.

CS CS CS

THE FIRST FEW months of their lives together, Dudley spent time developing tactics to deal with Norah's demands and moods. His most important tactic saw him agree with whatever Norah insisted she knew his thoughts were, nod his head, walk away, but carry on thinking his own thoughts. Life until he met Norah had been steady, if unexciting, and he contemplated what part that played in his falling under Norah's spell. His marriage to a woman ten years older than him, had been uneventful. Their children grew up ordinary young people in a comfortable home. His personal resources had been sufficient to ensure that. War caused everyone hardship, but they got through it intact and had arrived at the brink of adulthood. The end of the war saw restlessness seize everyone's life, as if they'd been holding their breath and might now relax. The future held promise. He wondered if this might be the reason for abandoning the rules he ran his life by. He couldn't imagine another one. At least that is what he persuaded himself later, refusing to acknowledge that at the time, he ignored the strident pealing of the tocsin in his head.

Once the situation with Norah became known, he found it impossible to decide what to do. He envied Norah her certainties and solid convictions. He never made decisions. How could he desert his family? How would they bear the shame? His wife was devoted and dependant on him. The idea of her upset became unbearable, but he must do something. Visits to Norah left him in no doubt she wasn't coping, and took her anger out on the baby or anyone else who happened to get in the way.

For a long time he remained haunted by the scene that took place the night before he left his family.

"I need to talk to you," he began, "because I've decided I am going to live with Norah and support her and the baby."

Ada stared at him, stunned, as large tears streamed down her face.

"How could you?" shouted Carina. "How dare you do this to us? What has Mama done to deserve it?"

"Tell us what we've done to deserve it? Or are you too much of a coward to explain?" said Eustace.

"I'm trying to. You are both young adults and can care for your mother if I'm not here. Norah has a small baby and no support. If I have to choose between you, I must choose the most vulnerable."

"The most vulnerable?" said Eustace. "How did you decide who is most vulnerable? Don't you worry for Mama's reputation and the scandal and shame she will endure? Your reasoning is distorted. What did you do, draw up a vulnerability scale?"

"I care what happens to you, but I can't procrastinate any more. Norah's not coping and the baby is vulnerable. I need to protect the child and this is the only way I can do it. I'll make sure you are provided for."

"One thing is certain, you won't be giving me away at my wedding later this year," said Carina, "I won't let you anywhere near. You are a deluded moral coward and a disgrace."

"I agree," said Eustace. "If you choose to go and live with a dreadful woman who has persuaded you to desert your family, I want nothing more to do with you. I'm going to Australia to work as a farmer. It's arranged, and I won't take any money from you. I am disgusted with you and never want to see you again."

Dudley looked at Ada. She'd not opened her mouth the whole time except to take gasps of air in between sobs.

CB CB CB

EMMA AND MIRIAM spent all the time together they could. Emma lived for their outings. In moments away from prison duties, she'd daydream about Miriam, wonder where she might be, what she was doing, how long it would be until she saw her again. She was sure Miriam felt the same, but didn't know how to ask her about it. Emma had never been courted, and didn't know how to find out if Miriam had either. She had no idea how to go about it. What did you do?

Emma became frightened that if she asked Miriam questions she might lose a friendship that meant everything. What about Da and Ma, or Miriam's parents? None of them would understand the sort of friendship she wanted with Miriam. For now she'd to be patient. At times she'd get frustrated and angry. How could friendship with Miriam be perverted and unnatural? But that is what people would say if they found out. She slept badly, wondering how she might find a way to speak up, to tell Miriam how she felt. But what if she scared Miriam off?

Then one day, when they went out walking in a park, Miriam took her by surprise.

"Miriam, 'ave you 'eard about Mary Allen and 'er Women's Police Service?"

"Yes, Why?"

"What d'ya reckon? I know 'bout it 'cause Mary Allen were a suffrigitt in 'Olloway as I looked after. Saw something a few days ago what reminded me."

"I saw it too. Mary Allen got an OBE for her police work. They do a lot of child welfare work."

"But?" asked Emma. "You sound like you fink there's some'at fishy 'bout it."

"They say they want to rescue women from vice and

slavery. But I think it's rich women judging poor women's lives – lives they've little in common with."

"Aye. Nothing's ever simple, is it?"

"No. But on the subject of Mary Allen, can I ask you something?" said Miriam. "I hope it won't frighten you?"

"Why? Should I be affrighted?"

"I hope not."

"Aye, go on then."

"One of the reasons I'm interested in Mary Allen is because she's an invert, a lesbian. A lot of the women police are. Even if you don't accept that, it's hard to miss the way they like to dress in military uniforms. It's got them into lots of trouble."

Emma's right hand shot up to hide her mouth, which emitted an involuntary small gasp, while her left hand, fingers splayed, leapt to cover her heart. Her eyes widened as a blush spread upwards from her tummy, which began churning. "Oweeeee... Fiddlesticks. What you tryin' to say? Is it what I fink?"

Miriam moved to put an arm around Emma, whose hands now moved to smother her cheeks, which felt as if they were on fire. "I'm an invert," said Miriam, whispering in her ear, conscious of other people walking past. "I believe you are too. Thought so since I first saw you in Holloway. That's why when I saw you the day of the hanging I took my chance."

Emma made to sit on a nearby bench, her body shaking. *Mustn't cry. Mustn't cry. Don't let tears come.*

Don't cry. Don't cry. Why can't I find me 'ankerchief? Fiddlesticks to this 'ere bag. Why is there so much in it I can't find me 'ankie? Perhaps it's in me pocket? She kept rummaging as Miriam sat down beside her.

"Look at me... say something... please," Miriam begged. "There's nothing to be frightened of. I don't want to make you uncomfortable."

Trying to keep control of her runaway emotions, Emma looked up and stared into Miriam's face – those wonderful deep eyes, full of love, fear and hopefulness. Emma shook her head in disbelief, then burst out laughing.

"What does that mean?" Miriam sounded hurt. "Why are you laughing at me? Does it mean you don't understand what I'm saying? Please tell me, did I do the wrong thing?"

Emma, now holding her stomach with both hands, smiled into those loving, warm eyes.

"Does it mean as I can now say I love ya and miss ya when I ain't wiv ya?"

"Yes," cried Miriam, bursting into smiles and grabbing one of Emma's hands, while the other hand wiped a tear from her eye.

"I wish as I could 'ug you right now. D'ya reckon we could? D'ya think as anyone would guess?"

"I'm sure we can hug. Although I long to kiss you, but we can't do it here. We need to keep it secret. It's going to be difficult, but I love you so much I am sure we can work it out."

"Aye, it won't be easy."

Emma went back to Holloway and her duties that night unable to sort out her emotions. She was excited and fearful. Excited because she longed to have someone to belong to and who wanted to belong to her. A person she might turn to who would understand and share her secret hopes and desires. Someone she could do the same for. Fearful because this was something she never believed would happen to her. Worst of all, she'd to keep it a secret. Only a few trusted people could be told. On the positive side, it would keep others guessing as to why she frequently smiled to herself. She was sure she would be – smiling to herself that was – a lot from now on. Perhaps it was worth having a secret that gave you an advantage over others that they could never understand the reason for.

Emma confided in Ruth. Ruth would understand. She was so happy she'd to tell someone. Ruth expressed pleasure and made her promise to bring Miriam to meet her for their planned picnic.

So at the first chance they got, Emma and Miriam caught the train out of London to East Sussex. As they walked to meet Ruth and baby Tony near the Elam house, a car swept past and stopped at the gate of the house. Emma saw Ruth pushing the pram. They had almost reached the corner. To Emma's surprise she saw Mary Allen get out of the car, to be greeted by a woman that Emma guessed must be the baby's mother, Mrs Elam. As Mrs Elam stepped onto the street, Emma gasped. Miriam turned to look at her. Emma turned away with her back to everyone, and whispered to Miriam in a shocked voice–

"That Mrs Elam is Mrs Dacre Fox, the suffrigitt what I force fed in 'Olloway 1914."

Miriam turned back to look at the women, trying not to stare. "Well, who'd believe it?"

"Aye, and here's Ruth, my sister-in-law, with the baby, ready to picnic, coming from the 'ouse."

"You mean Tony is Mrs Elam's baby?"

"Aye."

"Oy," said Miriam, stunned.

CHAPTER 6

Childhood at The Old Forge

H AVING TAKEN THE job, although she didn't think of it as work, Nanny Ruth moved into the Old Forge appropriating two rooms at the top of the house for her nursery.

"These are the rooms I would like," she told Dudley as they stood discussing it when they met to plan for the nursery furniture and equipment.

"I suppose you've given it thorough consideration?"

"These rooms are the best because they are light, airy and spacious, and far enough away from the main rooms to ensure that Tony won't bother others at night when he cries."

"I bow to your wisdom, Nanny. Can see no reason to contradict you. I'm in your hands, as is Mrs Elam. She'll be pleased it is in hand and to be relieved of the worry."

"Thank you, Mr Elam. I can't wait for Tony to arrive. I haven't seen him, but babies are adorable. This little boy will be more perfect than the rest. He is special, I'm convinced of it."

Ruth set about buying everything she needed, including her uniform. When it arrived she rushed to try it on. She stood in front of the mirror, smoothing down the skirt, pleased with the result. Life may have robbed her of the chance of motherhood, but fate saw her longing; her dearest wish was about to be fulfilled. Luck intervened and gave her a chance to talk to Emma about uniforms on one of her visits from Holloway.

"I can choose my own. Do you have any suggestions, Emma?"

"Make it simple but comfy. You'll need to take care wiv the outdoor one. You'll 'ave to wear it when you go out wiv the pram. Maybe a blue cloak wiv a small 'at, same colour."

Emma gave good advice. The fitted calf-length dress in dark grey with white trimmings would allow for the lifting, carrying and general running after she had to do every day. She added a small white cap, like a nurse, to give the impression she was in charge. Nanny surveyed the five foot three slim woman with light brown hair reflected in the mirror; studied the face looking back at her. She hoped that baby Tony would see in that face the love that she wanted to fill his life with.

The day came for Tony and Mrs Elam to arrive. Ruth was beside herself with excitement. Like a duck paddling fast below the water but appearing calm on top, she controlled her feelings. The mask Mrs Elam saw shouldn't be allowed to betray her anxiety. Ruth longed to fill her arms with the warm bundle about to arrive.

"Welcome, Mrs Elam," said Ruth. "I trust the journey down from London was pleasant."

"Would have been if the child hadn't yelled the whole way."

Ruth smiled and held out her arms. "Adults find journeys difficult. Must be worse for baby. I offered to travel up to help, but Mr Elam said you would manage."

"That shows how silly he is. I wish you had."

"Anyway, you're here now. Shall I take him?"

"Help yourself. I'm looking forward to rest and proper sleep. You must be either a fool or a saint taking this on. Not sure which."

The first few days Ruth stood by Tony's cot, staring, unable to believe she had this miracle to lavish with care and attention. Tony's crying didn't distress her – meant she could cuddle him – enjoy the comfort of physical touch which healed so much of the hurt she faced in life. With Tony to herself, the grief at losing Walter and the horrors of the war begin to heal. Tony represented the promise of spring; newness and renewal.

Ruth established her routine. Nursery life settled to a satisfying rhythm. Except for the incident when she took the afternoon off, as a result of which she never left Tony alone with Mrs Elam again, everything went smoothly. Tony was an active, lively child and Ruth guarded his childhood milestones to herself. Sitting, crawling and walking were taken in their stride, although his teething upset her and she experienced sympathy pain in her gums. She did worry about Tony's health as Mrs Elam refused vaccination. Ruth spoke to

Mr Elam about it.

"Yes, Nanny, can I help, is there a problem?"

"I am concerned that Mrs Elam won't allow Tony to have his injections."

"Ah, well…"

"What has she got against it?"

"Mrs Elam has always opposed animal experimentation. As vaccines come out of that, she is against them."

"I see." said Ruth.

"Is it going to be a problem?"

"I can't go against her wishes. I'll take steps to protect Tony to make sure he keeps away from local sources of infection. That will mean limited contact with other children."

"I'll be guided by you, Nanny. You must do what you think is right."

At first, Ruth continued to worry over this, but later rationalised it to herself. What did it matter if he didn't socialise much with other children? They had each other. Mrs Elam never interfered or challenged her. It was strange, but Ruth was glad that his mother wanted little to do with him. Mr Elam visited the nursery, but never stayed long. The nursery was her domain and Ruth guarded it like a lioness.

Ruth recorded Tony's birthdays, marking them by physical and mental growth. He loved having stories read to him and was an inquisitive child. He would explore the garden with great excitement, hunting for insects and frogspawn in spring, wild blackberries in late summer and conkers in autumn. Long summer days allowed picnicking, walking and exploring in the nearby forests. Few people used the forests, so they had them to themselves. The forest seasons enveloped Ruth and Tony within their encompassing natural protectiveness. In them, they found contentment in each other's company, never tired of finding things to do. When Tony went to school at five, Ruth experienced the pains of first separation, spending her day in the nursery, ruminating on how he might be coping, and longing for the time to arrive when she would go to fetch him home. Ruth arrived at the school gate first, straining to catch a glimpse of Tony as he trudged out of class. This always became a run when he saw her wave to him.

When Tony went to school, Ruth became anxious in case he noticed things and asked about household arrangements. How would she explain why Mrs Elam got called 'Mrs Elam' by Tony and not 'Mama'? While he was tiny it didn't matter. Everyone in the household intimated she was his mother, but because they had little or no contact with other families he didn't realise that other children called their mothers Mama or something like it. Mrs Elam was content to keep her distance, sometimes enquiring of Ruth through Mr Elam about his progress. She never gave the child time. If she did, it happened by accident, making sure to keep a distance and observe. She never cuddled or held him after the day she handed him over to Ruth. Ruth realised her selfishness in going along with it, but was unable help herself. To ease her conscience she asked Mr Elam about it once, but he said that, as it was all Tony knew, Tony would think it normal. Nanny gave him the love and affection he needed and wouldn't question any further. She concluded he was right; told herself that as long as she remained, Tony would never be without love. She had more than enough to give. It didn't matter where Tony got it from, as long as he got it. But now the time approached when she would have to face the consequences. What would she say if he asked? Then one day, walking home from school, the question came.

"Nanny Ruth... Why do other children have mummies and daddies and I have you?"

"Your mother and father weren't able to look after you, so they asked me to do it for them."

"OK, Nanny," said Tony.

They passed round the edge of a pond where a small boy skimmed stones. Tony got distracted and, if he had further questions, seemed to have forgotten them for the moment. He begged to be allowed to watch. Ruth wasn't sure whether to be relieved or anxious. She expected more questions. As they watched, Ruth smiled to herself, temporarily relieved; she hoped that the issue would go away and sink like most of the little boy's pebbles. The ones he did get to skim lasted for two or three bounces and didn't cause too many ripples.

Ruth's devotion to Tony made her sensitive to tensions in the house, always arranging activities so as not to disturb Mrs Elam, but it wasn't possible to control for every difficulty. One day, thinking that Mrs Elam had gone out, Ruth planned a picnic in the garden.

"Tony. What are you doing? Come and eat your sandwich."

"OK, Nanny Ruth. After my sandwich, can we play catch with my new ball?"

"Of course, we'll do it over there on the lawn. I'll catch, you throw. We better make sure it doesn't go into the flowerbeds. We don't want to tread on the flowers and break them if it rolls in there, do we?"

They played for a while, then Tony dropped the ball and it rolled into the flowerbed. Nanny tried to retrieve it without damaging the flowers when an angry demand startled them. There was no mistaking the voice.

"What are you doing in there, Nanny?"

"Tony's ball rolled into the flowerbed. We're trying to retrieve it."

"Why aren't you controlling the child and making sure the ball doesn't cause damage?"

"We had an accident. We tried not to cause damage."

"Make sure you don't. Then get the child back to the nursery. I don't like to see or hear him down here. He disturbs me when I'm working in my study. He needs to be kept under control – out of my way."

☙ ☙ ☙

NORAH RETREATED TO her study. How could she be expected to think with a racket going on outside? At first she thought children were playing in the fields behind the house. When it started, she ignored it, hoping they might go away. She tried to concentrate on the task she was engaged in, but the noise wouldn't go away; it moved closer to the house near the edge of the field. Drat, she had to go and look and make them go away. What a nuisance! It turned out to be Nanny and the boy. *What on earth does she think she's doing? She knows I need peace when working in my study. She knows how important this work is, told her often enough. Why can't she remember, why does she have to be told so often to keep the child under control?* Words – words were all she had to stop animals being tortured. The child was taken care of. She needed quiet to assemble her weapons in the unequal battle to protect innocent living, breathing animals. Nanny got paid to do what she was good at, so that Norah could do what she was good at, stopping those inhumane torturers inventing more and more ways to inflict pain on creatures unable to fight back. She lifted her hand to her face and stroked her cheek. There might be no visible scar, but after all these years she still heard the dogs howling and the sting of the whip as it lashed her face.

Peace at last. Now Nanny and Tony had been dealt with, she must get on with understanding this wretched research into vitamins. Why make animals suffer so they could understand the effects of different vitamins on the body? The same experiments repeated over and over with different substances and mixtures. *Why call them 'vitamins'? Why call them anything? If we understand that eating fresh fruit and vegetables are needed to maintain good health, and not having them can make you ill, why don't we make sure everyone gets enough fruit and vegetables to eat? It's logical and simple. But when did men ever apply logic? Animals don't need to suffer to prove untenable claims by men. That is common sense.* But then, doctors and scientists never worked on instinct, as far as she understood. What they did was find more and more ways to ignore it. Look at those other disgusting products of animal experimentation – vaccinations.

The more she read, the more incensed she became. Since they added vitamins to that disgusting axle grease called margarine, the doctors and scientists on the board of the anti-vivisection society decided to put energy into investigating the issue. They came to meetings with papers to be poured over, and as editor of the journal she would write articles to accompany their submissions. She needed to get her arguments straight and make sure they hit home. They organised a visit to one of those dens of iniquity, a margarine factory. Now there was a place to kill your appetite for anything for a long time! She couldn't get the smell of fat and grease out of her nostrils. Slopping around in the gumboots they obliged her to wear, for hygiene reasons – what a joke – she struggled to keep upright, almost falling over at one point as she slipped on something on the floor. It reminded her of the time she toured the mines in Wales with Emmeline Pankhurst and got overcome by gas while underground. She remembered fainting and being brought round above ground. For some reason, the smells and production line in the margarine factory brought it back.

Her nostrils became so sensitised to margarine that she could smell it – from any distance. If she visited any of the local tea shops, they always made sure to serve her butter. She got them to understand that she wouldn't tolerate axle grease being served to her. Made sure they understood it was bad for business. She spoke to the tea shop owners personally and made sure they appreciated her argument.

❂ ❂ ❂

ONE VISITOR RUTH and Tony always loved to see was Aunt Dorothy. Her visits proved to be great fun and full of excitement. She never warned them when she might come. She'd arrive in a motor car after phoning in the morning to check they were there. Sometimes she'd take Tony and Nanny out for tea in her care, which always made Tony so excited he would babble on about it for days afterwards. Aunt Dorothy didn't have children of her own. Neither did Uncle Augustus's sisters. When Tony asked why, Ruth told him it was because they hadn't married. Aunt Dorothy told Tony that, because she didn't have her own little boy, Tony was special to her and that was why she liked coming to see him so much.

Aunt Dorothy's passion was monkeys. She told

them it was because she lived in South Africa, where she learned about them. She told Tony stories about a place she called 'The Bush', where monkeys lived. Tony asked her how big 'the bush' was and how many bushes there were, and what they were called. There were bushes in his garden; was it like them? Dorothy laughed and explained to Tony how bush didn't mean the same as in England. The Bush was large areas of countryside covered in different sorts of trees and plants, miles and miles of it, where different varieties of animal lived, not just monkeys. She brought him books about the animals and things she'd seen, and would spend happy times reading them with him.

Aunt Dorothy arrived in a whirlwind, dropping presents everywhere. She spent hours telling them stories about her work at London Zoo in the monkey house. One day, she arrived and caused such a hubbub that the whole household came to see what was going on. The servants rushed to the front door, the cook with her hands covered in flour, while the gardener stopped digging and sidled along the hedge to watch from a safe distance.

"Nanny, Nanny Ruth. Come quick. Aunt Dorothy is here. Looks like a monkey sitting in her car."

"No. It can't be. She can't have. Where would she get a monkey? Who let her bring a monkey out here?"

"It is a monkey. Look! She's getting it out of the car. Can I go and see?"

"Be careful. Let your aunt introduce you and tell

you what to do."

Dorothy caught Tony up as he ran towards her, giving him a hug.

"Let me introduce you to George."

"Is that his name? Can I play with him? When did you get him? Where did you get him? How long will he be with you? Does he have to wear that nappy the whole time?"

"Calm down, Tony. Let's go into the garden. I'll tell you and Nanny about George."

Tony held his hand out to George, who accepted it. In his other hand Tony took George's lead. George followed him into the garden. Ruth tried to ask questions but Tony interrupted.

"How long are you staying, Aunt Dorothy?"

"If Nanny agrees – I wondered if George and I might stay for lunch in the nursery."

Ruth nodded, at a loss to express her amazement. She was further astounded when she realised that George needed a place laid at the nursery table to eat lunch with them. That was nothing to the head-shaking and tutting by cook and the maid assigned to carry the food up to the nursery. Ruth was glad Mr and Mrs Elam were out and not expected back until late afternoon.

After lunch, Ruth asked if Dorothy might take George to use the toilet, as she was toilet training him! Ruth was nervous about this, but the nappy-changing had them in uncontrollable laughter, especially when

Ruth had to press some of Tony's old nappies into service. The visit was so successful that Dorothy suggested she bring George for another visit. Tony got excited and begged her to make it soon; a promise Dorothy was happy to keep.

Ruth learned the full story about George on a later visit. One day at the zoo, a pregnant monkey died giving birth. Dorothy pleaded to be allowed to nurse the baby, and was pleased when, seeing her devotion, the head of the monkey house gave George to her to nurse full-time. Dorothy drowned the monkey with affection and they allowed her to take it to live at home. Her mothering instincts came pouring out. Ruth understood what Dorothy meant; she recognised the feelings Dorothy described. The empathy she shared allowed Ruth to overcome her anxiety about George's visits to The Old Forge.

CB CB CB

RUTH DID NOT hear the conversation between Norah and Dorothy, and would have registered alarm if she had. During one of her visits with George Dorothy asked Norah about her relationship with Tony and its effect on her anti-vivisection work. Norah's zeal was unquestionable and her commitment to stopping animal cruelty complete. Dorothy wondered why Norah never once saw the irony in trying to stop physical violence to animals, but could be cruel to her own family. Dorothy couldn't understand why Norah had so little to do with her son.

"Do you think it wise to let Nanny do so much for Tony, while you show little interest?" asked Dorothy tentatively.

"Not that it is any of your business, Dorothy, but since you ask it seems to have happened that way. As Tony is content, I've no wish to interfere."

"Don't you think it will be more difficult to build a relationship with him yourself the longer it goes on?"

"I'll tackle it when the time is right for me, and not before. I don't want distractions. Nanny is capable and reliable, and relieves me of worry about Tony."

"As you say, it's not my business, but I wonder you don't think it cruel. You get angry when animals are treated badly. Some would say you are treating Tony in a similar fashion."

"Dumb animals deserve our respect and care. We have a greater responsibility to them because they are just that – dumb animals – they've done nothing to deserve the cruelty we show them."

"Quite so, but Tony is a child, and to that extent is as vulnerable as any animal."

"Tony will grow up to be a man. Men set out to harm others. Women and dumb animals are victims of male intransigence and cruelty. As such, they deserve everything they get."

Dorothy left it at that.

ಐ ಐ ಐ

TONY HAD BEEN at school four years. Ruth delighted in his progress. Mr Elam, whom Tony addressed as 'Sir', took a keen interest in his education and the boy developed a shared love of books with his father. Ruth and Tony still occupied the nursery quarters, sharing every aspect of their lives, content with their own company, with the occasional excitement of a visit from George.

In the midst of this routine, Nanny received a summons to see Mr Elam.

"I've asked to see you because I need to tell you about our problem," said Mr Elam.

"I've sensed an angry, gloomy atmosphere in the house for a while," said Ruth. "I'd like to understand what the problem is."

"As you are aware, Mrs Elam changed her name to 'Elam' from 'Dacre Fox' by deed poll in 1928. This wouldn't be a problem, except that Mrs Elam has been declared bankrupt."

"Ah. I can imagine that's made her angry."

"Maybe a little. The problem is that, with our married status, she is worried about what will come out and the social and financial consequences."

"I understand. You must both be worried. I need to understand if this will affect my position in view of Tony's attachment to me."

"Definitely not," said Dudley.

Days later, Ruth received a summons to Mrs Elam's study.

"I've decided that Tony is to be told to stop calling me 'Mrs Elam' and call me 'Mama', and that he will take meals with us in the dining-room every evening. From now on, when I'm here, I'll be involved in and direct his activities," said Norah.

"When?" Nanny was shocked and began to tremble, close to tears.

"Immediately. No point in delay. He's been reliant on you for too long."

"This is sudden."

"For goodness' sake. Stop dithering and biting your bottom lip. I've decided. I won't tolerate an argument. My decision is final," Norah shouted.

Ruth pressed on, concern overcoming her upset. "Surely you can see that you can't drop this on him. He's still a little boy. He's bound to feel overwhelmed."

"What's your problem? Children are like dogs, ripe for discipline and training. Tony will be too, whether he likes it or not. I won't be put off. He will be told and he will accept it. From now on, I expect to see Tony dining with his parents every evening."

"I am sorry, Mrs Elam. Can we not do it gradually? It will be hard for him."

"Poppycock. He's my son. I know what's best for him. You'll do as I say. Now get out and get on with it."

Ruth appealed to Mr Elam, who shrugged his shoulders and refused to get involved other than to help Ruth break the news to Tony. Ruth was angry. She could not understand the need for the sudden change.

She wondered if Mrs Elam planned it. Was she angry and lashing out after the bankruptcy? Thinking about how Mrs Elam reacted in the past, Ruth believed that Mrs Elam was venting her anger over the bankruptcy on Tony. Ruth would never find out. How was she going to tell Tony?

ᏅᏋ ᏅᏋ ᏅᏋ

NORAH'S ANGER OVER the bankruptcy was intense.

"It's not my fault, Dudley. It was those nincompoops and idiots who worked for me."

"That may be so. Unfortunately, you are the owner. You have to face the court."

"Another lot of lackeys and sycophants in the pay of the financial institutions ruining the world."

"That may be the case, but the only way to make this go away is to cooperate. You must go through their procedures. Then you can be discharged."

"What a bore. I wanted to use the printing business for political purposes, and now it's gone."

"If you want to resume public life, you need to cooperate. The sooner it's dealt with, the sooner it will be forgotten."

Cooperating with the bankruptcy procedures proved hard. They seemed interminable. Officious little men picking over her account books; how dare they? How to control her anger? She had to appear calm in court, but whenever she'd to look at the papers or prepare documents, she would sit staring at them, grinding her teeth. She couldn't concentrate for long, and wished the court officials could face some unpleasant torture invented by herself. Sometimes she would punch the arm of her chair or slam the drawers shut. If the inkwell on her desk dried out, the maid would get an angry rebuke. Every appearance before the court humiliated her, and despite the help Dudley gave, she vented the worst of her anger on him. She picked fights with him over insignificant things. At least she had her anti-vivisection monologues to work on, and the country-wide tour she had planned. That was going well. But these distractions couldn't stop her thinking about what she, and her colleagues, had achieved since their suffragette days. She concluded every time that the root of her difficulties lay in her frustration with how little women had achieved since getting the vote. She felt powerless.

☙ ☙ ☙

DUDLEY SAT IN his library, deep in miserable thoughts. He'd been responsible for letting the situation drift, but found it easier to put off than confront the problem. Norah never took an interest in the boy; they'd not built up any relationship despite living under the same roof. Dudley appreciated Tony would find it difficult to be told by Norah what to do and how to behave. He didn't like the way Norah ordered him around, and he'd put up with it for years. Nanny was more like his mother than Norah. Tony had Nanny to help and guide him, and her nature was different from Norah's. Nanny's pleading for him to intervene was the first he heard of Norah's intentions. But Nanny's pleading was nothing compared to the lecture Norah would give him if he tried to interfere.

He looked around his library, his solace, his place of refuge. Norah had always been so full of passion and impetuous anger. He wondered if the overriding dictum of her life was the misanthropic trait she displayed when involved in animal work. She hated to be interrupted or deflected when planning or executing something in connection with that work. At times she seemed to hate men with a vengeance, particularly when provoked by some external event she couldn't control, like the bankruptcy. When the notices arrived she attacked him first; then her anger spread like a tsunami, accusing men in general of being her enemy. Although he realised it was wrong, that was the reason he allowed the Tony situation to persist. Norah's restricted role in his care as a baby and small child protected Tony, as, when angry, Norah often threatened violence. Thank goodness she never carried out her threats, but confined herself to verbal abuse. Norah's bark was more painful than her bite. It used to frighten him when, hearing Tony laugh in the garden when playing with Nanny, Norah would glare into the distance and mutter, "That child will never control my life like Papa did. Let him try."

CS CS CS

RUTH NEVER FORGOT the look on Tony's face when she told him. Tony was frightened of Mrs Elam. He often asked why she lived with them; she was always so cross and unhappy. Otherwise, he seldom enquired about household arrangements. Why would he? It was all he knew. To him it was normal. After his initial cry of, "No, no," he dissolved into tears, ran to his bed, lay down, and turned to face the wall, refusing to talk to her. Ruth could not bear to witness his anguish. Tony refused to be comforted, increasing her unhappiness.

Mr Elam came to talk to Tony. He tried persuading Tony to attend an interview that Norah demanded to set out the new arrangements. Tony went, but Ruth got upset when he returned to the nursery – pale and cowed like a beaten animal – thinking he would never trust her again. Ruth wanted to cuddle him; to protect him from the upset she understood he felt. With every rejection she wept, searching for ways to show him how much she loved him. Eventually, her years of devotion won him over and he forgave her; at least as far as a young child was able to. Ruth was aware their relationship would never be the same, but found satisfaction in his acceptance of her ongoing support. Tony agreed to his mother's insistence that he call her Mama – to her face at least. Outside her hearing, he stubbornly referred to her as 'she'. Ruth recognised future menace in this little token of defiance.

CB CB CB

As Tony was expected to dine with his parents every evening, mealtimes became a battle of wills.

"Stop slouching, sit up and act like the well-mannered young man you were brought up to be," said Norah.

Dudley, looking at Tony, noticed his jaw clench. "How was your English lesson today at school? What book are you studying at the moment?"

Tony, who sneaked a brooding angry glance at Norah, responded, "Shakespeare."

"Any particular play?" said Dudley.

"Hamlet."

"For goodness sake, Tony, can't you be more civil. Why do we have to prise every bit of information out of you?" demanded Norah.

Tony glared at her. Dudley sensed his defiance.

"Come on. Answer me before I lose patience."

"Give the boy a chance."

"A chance. Every time he joins us at table he acts like a spoiled brat. His behaviour is recalcitrant, mutinous and intransigent."

"Norah, calm down. Language like that won't encourage him."

"He shouldn't need encouragement; he should do as he is told. Animals can be trained, so can children. Perhaps I should take a whip and give him a good hiding."

"Leave it, Norah. We'll discuss it later."

Dudley didn't know if Tony understood the meaning of the words Norah spat at him like bullets, but he did believe that Norah was guilty of the hypocrisy she so often accused others of. Tony's schoolmasters reported that he was an unpopular boy, who found it difficult to socialise, and who made a lot of enemies. Dudley became concerned for Tony. It reminded him of his older children's reactions when he told them he was leaving them to live with Norah. He'd never seen either of them since. There were occasions when he regretted that had happened. He hoped that he wouldn't live to have the same regrets for Tony, especially having given up so much for him.

C３ C３ C３

TONY HAD TURNED eleven and now attended boarding school in a nearby town. Ruth decided it was time to make changes in her life. She left The Old Forge and the nursery about nine months after Tony had been cruelly introduced to his mother's expectations.

"You're to leave us to get married, Nanny," said Dudley.

"Yes. I've been seeing Robert from the village for a while now. He has asked me to marry him."

"I'm pleased. Will you remain in the village?" asked Dudley.

"Yes. Robert has his work and his aviaries, and it means I can be here for Tony, if he needs me. My home will always be open to him."

"I'm grateful to hear that. Tony is reliant on you.

You've been the constant in his life, bringing continuity and stability."

"Tony brought me hope when I was hopeless and helpless. I'm glad I can be here for him. He isn't going to find life easy."

"I know… but without you he wouldn't stand any chance."

They were both aware of what lay beneath those words, their instinctive understanding that Norah's interest in the child fluctuated, dependant on chance reminders that would strike a discordant desire in her to do something about her neglect. Ruth dealt with the fallout every time.

Once Ruth settled into her new life, Dudley arranged with the school to allow her to visit Tony at weekends. During holiday times, Tony lived at her home, enjoying helping Robert in his aviary. These were happy times, but there were the dark times as well. Norah, during guilt-driven forays into his life, made it hell; on many occasions Ruth got called on to comfort Tony. So often Ruth felt inadequate, hoped she was providing a secure refuge to mitigate the bullying Norah inflicted on him. Norah insisted it was discipline, but Ruth and Dudley knew it was bullying.

One day Tony arrived on Ruth's doorstep, sobbing violently. It took every ounce of ingenuity to calm him down. When he stopped crying, she probed him to find out what happened.

"Come on, Tony. Sit here next to me, and tell me

what brought that on," said Ruth.

"She shouted at me, called me a bastard child, who should never have been born, who ruined her life," Tony sobbed.

"Did you do something to provoke your Mama? What did you do?"

"Don't know. I was playing in the garden with my ball. It hit a pot on the wall that fell down by her study and broke. She got angry and shouted at me that I'm a bastard. Then she wouldn't stop, she kept shouting and getting angrier and angrier, until Sir came and spoke to her, and I ran all the way here."

Ruth was taken aback. The use of the word 'bastard' had become a regular part of Mrs Elam's temper tantrums with Tony. Ruth had approached Mr Elam to ask her to stop.

"The boys at school use that word, Nanny. I know it's bad. But why does she call me that? What does it mean?"

Ruth long dreaded this moment. How to explain the shame and disgrace attached to the word, without making Tony unhappy? She tried to plan for this, but had no idea how to deal with it. How do you explain to a nine-year-old that his parents' sins were being laid at his door? She hoped she might put off the explanation until he was able to understand. But now she had to try to explain to him the implications if the family secret was to be kept and he was not to be exposed at school. Damage limitation was going to be difficult.

"I need you to understand it is a terrible word, used to describe a child whose parents are not married. Your parents aren't married. A lot of people disapprove of children whose parents aren't married. What you need to understand is that you aren't to blame for what your parents did before you your birth."

"But, Nanny, are the boys at school bastards too? They call each other that name, and then fight. The masters get cross with them and tell them not to use it."

"No, Tony, I don't think any of the boys at school are bastards. They are using the word to be nasty to each other."

"But if I am a real bastard?" Tony asked anxiously.

"Tony, you have to promise me, even if you don't understand why, you must never tell anybody your parents aren't married. You must never use that word yourself. Promise me, Tony, it is important that you promise me. We must keep this secret."

℘ ℘ ℘

DUDLEY RETREATED TO his library to prepare for Ruth's visit. Tony was about to have his twelfth birthday, and he guessed the reason for her visit. What would he say to her? He stared at his memento mori. He wondered if his mother realised how apposite her gift had been years ago when he first went up to Oxford. She took a lot of trouble to source it. The beauty and quality of the carving showed how carefully she selected it, inspired by the divinity studies he was to undertake. He remembered an expert telling him that the exquisite carved ivory skull with snakes weaving in and out of its various orifices was precise in every detail. These days, he thought the snakes represented Norah slithering into his mind, with him powerless to resist. He wondered what more he would face in life before the inevitability of death the symbol represented.

"Come in, Nanny. Sit down," said Dudley.

"You're aware of why I'm here?" said Ruth.

"Is it about Tony being sent away to school in Germany?"

"Is the decision definite?"

"Yes. Mrs Elam is insistent."

"I've mixed feelings. On the one hand, I'm pleased she won't be able to embarrass him by storming into his school when the fancy takes her, lecturing his teachers and masters, as she does now. When she does that, I'm never sure if she is punishing them or him. On the other hand, it's so far away, I'm scared for him."

"I feel the same."

"What preparations are being made? Is there anything you want me to do?"

"Would you prepare everything as Mrs Elam doesn't want to be involved. Here are the lists and information."

"I'll miss him. How long is he going for?"

"No idea at this stage. Hasn't been decided. Mrs Elam wants to see how it goes year by year."

"I hope he can cope. He must be frightened."

Nanny left while Dudley returned to his reflections.

He had to give way. Norah was never going to agree not to send him. Tony needed to make the best of it. It was just as well. Norah's growing involvement with the West Sussex branch of the British Union of Fascists meant she was going to be busy launching her new political career. He guessed that was the reason she wanted Tony out of the way. It would be convenient for him too, if he cared to admit it. He would need his energy to support Norah, although he did feel sorry for the boy.

CB CB CB

CHAPTER 7

Watering the Desert

ALMOST TWO YEARS to the day after Tony's birth, Norah stood beside her Mama's bed and watched her die, wracked with pain. She wanted Mama to be at rest from her suffering, but didn't want to let go. Why couldn't she take the pain and suffer it for Mama? But pain is peculiar to the individual. There was no chance to take it from Mama no matter how much Norah wished it. Watching Mama brought back memories of the different types of pain she'd experienced – force-feeding, childbirth, the pain of anger and frustration. Indignity caused the worst pain. She suffered large doses of that alongside the physical pain many times. Mama must be enduring all of them now. How would she cope without Mama? The idea of never seeing Mama again was unbearable. How to cope after they laid Mama, inaccessible, in a frigid coffin beneath hard ground? How to stop the suffocating dreams she was having? She tried to stay awake because they came every night now. If she managed to sleep, it was a relief to wake, even though when she did she would be cold and shivering, awash with the sensation of struggling up through dense, dark, damp earth, unable to breathe. Papa always stood there in the nightmares, observing her.

"Dorothy, what shall we do without Mama?" Norah sobbed. "Why has fate been cruel, taking her before Papa?"

"We both loved Mama to distraction, Norah, but she's been unwell for a long time. We should be thankful she's not suffering anymore," said Dorothy.

"Maybe, but Papa allowed idiot doctors to treat her who didn't do their job. He's to blame. It's his fault. He's responsible. You won't make me believe otherwise. Anyway, are we sure she's dead?"

"You've seen her; we stood by her bedside together and watched her breathe her last."

"But medical men are so stupid. Perhaps they got it wrong."

"I'm aware you advertise The Society for Prevention of Premature Burial in your Anti-Vivisection Journal, but Papa did what you wanted and made sure they did not seal the coffin for several days."

"But he wouldn't let me get one of those Bateson's Belfrys attached to the casket before we buried her."

"You're distraught, but must be sensible. No one can live forever. Her time had come."

"You're wrong. Papa is to blame. I'll never forgive him. He treated her with disrespect her whole life – like a chattel. He never dignified her with the equal status she deserved, and abused her loving nature endlessly." Norah was angry.

"Calm down. You're not going to get anywhere blaming Papa. We need to concentrate on organising her funeral. I'll put your anger with Papa down to your grief. I'm sure you don't believe he killed her. It's a preposterous idea."

Norah heard the sharpness in Dorothy's voice. "You're right, I'm sorry. I'm so full of anguish I can't concentrate."

But Norah was thinking hard. She hoped Dorothy didn't realise she'd beaten a strategic retreat. She might not be able to say it out loud, but Dorothy couldn't censor her thoughts. Papa was going to pay. She'd ideas to make him. She called them her 'No compromise – Bully back' plans.

CB CB CB

JOHN DOHERTY REMEMBERED each moment of Charlotte's funeral despite the pain and anguish clouding his mind. The turnout was extensive, including colleagues from the Spelthorne Bench, members of the National Liberal Club and other dignitaries. Immediate family attended, or if unable to come, sent bouquets. The local press reported the occasion, with comments that made him cry. ".......held in the highest esteem and affection by a large circle of friends…" "…Always interested in her husband's public work and political activities, she ably supported him in all his undertakings and like her husband, was ever ready to assist those in need of help…" He kept a rumpled, worn copy of the newspaper reports, reading them several times a day in response to some unconscious trigger like hearing 'Lead Kindly Light' or 'Abide with Me', her favourite hymns sung during the funeral service. Spring flowers proved to be another potent reminder on the anniversary of her death each May. Primroses, one of Charlotte's favourites, reminded him of how Norah laid a bunch on the coffin when everyone walked away from the graveside. Norah told him later she wanted to make a last loving private tribute to her mother. The gesture touched him, and it pleased him that Norah hadn't shown herself up by bringing that fellow she lived with and that bastard son they spawned.

Although unwell in the years before her death, Charlotte never faltered in her determination to support him, as John well knew. During the funeral he kept wondering how he would to cope. But five years later, here he was getting ready for his eightieth birthday celebration at the National Liberal Club. He wasn't sure how and why Norah and Dorothy became his support over the years. It surprised him when he bothered to consider it, but they had, and he accepted it as his right. Charlotte had imparted her sense of duty, albeit he reflected on how Norah often embarrassed or let him down, but was always there to help when he needed her. She seemed to have got that rebellious nature of hers under control, enough to be of use to him.

"Which of my daughters is coming today?" John asked the maid carrying bed linen up the stairs.

"Last week was Miss Dorothy, this time it's Miss Norah's turn," she responded.

"It must be her meeting week. Good to have the house bustling. Too quiet when there is no one here."

"They keep us busy for sure. Are you off to your weekly Justice of the Peace meeting?"

"Yes. The tram should be along soon. I better get going. Make sure you leave Miss Norah a tea tray."

"When is your next National Liberal Club meeting, sir?"

"Next week. Miss Dorothy will be here. I must drop her a note. She wants to bring her motorcar and drive me. I won't get into one of those confounded contraptions – ever. I don't understand why she uses one. They are the work of the devil. Anyone who drives one is a fool in his service."

"I won't tell Miss Dorothy you said that, sir. I am sure you'll make an exception where she is concerned."

"No. Miss Dorothy knows my feelings. She keeps trying to persuade me to change my mind, but she won't succeed."

He was pleased Dorothy enjoyed spending time with him. She would ask him about his Liberal Club meetings. She listened to everything he said and he loved the chance to reminisce.

"Good meeting at the Liberal Club last night, Papa?"

"Yes, my girl. Lively discussions. Usual political quagmires we seem to get into. Never find solutions, but have great debates trying. Like the bogs that littered the Irish landscape from my childhood. Lots of them, damp but springy, and devilish hard to crawl out of."

"You've always enjoyed the challenges of politics, haven't you, Papa?" said Dorothy.

"Yes, my girl. You meet many interesting people. But you also have to judge when to retreat, give up, and try another way. A lot of politicians are stubborn and inflexible, which is why it makes for compelling characters, I suppose.

"Is that why we left Ireland, Papa?"

"Yes. After we formed the Dublin branch of the Irish Protestant Home Rule Association, despite the number of prominent supporters like Yeats and Maude Gonne, I realised that being a Protestant in the south of Ireland represented a lost cause. Better to try and influence from the sidelines."

For three months he'd been laid up in bed. He struggled against his frailty, but was unequal to the challenge. Last year they diagnosed throat cancer and now an idiot commercial traveller had run him over in his car after he stepped off the tram outside his house one evening. Norah and Dorothy had been attentive and done everything they were able to. He hated having nurses around, and between them Norah and Dorothy managed to keep the need for them to a minimum. It came as a surprise how much time Norah found to spend with him. He knew she found it difficult, but admired her devotion. She'd come good. She'd fulfilled her obligations to him as Charlotte had taught her.

Two things kept him going: his determination to attend his eightieth birthday celebrations at the Liberal Club, and the idea of testifying against that hooligan driver. Summonses were issued against him, one for negligent driving and the other for failing to give audible warning of his approach. John was going to enjoy his appearance in court. Norah and Dorothy intended being there to support him.

"Mr Doherty, can you please describe what happened on the day in question."

"It was five forty-five p.m. on the twenty-third of June 1928. I was travelling in a tram car from Twickenham to my home at Longford Lodge, High Street, Hampton."

"Do you regularly make such tram journeys?"

"Yes, it has been my custom for many years, particularly as there is a tram stop a few yards from my house."

"What happened then?"

"I alighted at said tram stop, making sure the road was clear. I crossed the road to reach the pavement and was almost at the kerb when I was knocked down by the defendant's car, which came up from the rear. I was rendered temporarily unconscious."

"Did the defendant give any warning? Did he sound his horn?"

"No, I did not hear a horn."

"Are you quite sure?"

"The defendant did not sound his horn, I would

have heard it if he had."

"How can you be certain?"

"I have seen many narrow escapes from accidents among people alighting from tram cars. As a result, I am always particularly careful when alighting. One of my precautions is never to alight from the tram until it is stationary so that my hearing is not impaired by the noises of the tram stopping."

"Do many passengers adopt the same caution?"

"I don't know. I do it even though it might mean a considerable space of time elapses between the car stopping and my alighting. I am concerned for my safety, not the tram driver's wish to hurry up his journey."

"Are you quite sure the defendant didn't sound his horn?"

"Yes, quite sure."

"Can you confirm again that you are a regular traveller on the trams between Twickenham and Hampton?"

"I was until your client tried to finish me off."

His riposte caused laughter, and he experienced a glow of satisfaction when the defendant got found guilty and fined. His licence was endorsed.

Shortly after that, his eightieth birthday celebration took place. He so looked forward to it, determined to enjoy the luncheon. He saw the guest list and menu and had learned the Right Hon. Earl Beauchamp would preside. They went to a lot of trouble with the meal and he found the attention flattering. Home Rule soup, Limerick sole meunière, Donegal mutton cutlet and Doherty pudding reflected the value they placed on his service during the forty years of his membership. The appointment as a Vice-President some years before was an honour, but this was special. He'd remember the speeches for a long time, and wished Charlotte had been alive so he might tell her about it.

ඖ ඖ ඖ

NORAH SAT BESIDE Dorothy at John's funeral service. John and Neal, their brothers, sat opposite. None of the other brothers came; they'd fled and now lived abroad. She didn't need convincing; they'd gone as far from Papa as possible, away from the arguments and bullying and strict discipline. Even as adults they found Papa difficult to reason with. How much harder was it for her and Dorothy? Norah looked across the pews at John Junior sitting next to his wife. The man was ill. She observed him coughing, witnessed the pain on his face. Mama went the same way, and he'd been the only brother who worked with Papa in the printing business. *Look at him, worn out and exhausted. He'll not live long enough to inherit the birthright he endured so much to win. He'll be following Papa to the grave soon.*

Norah looked around at the dignitaries who came to pay respects. Norah regarded them with as much contempt as the man in the coffin, despite them being Sirs or MPs or magistrates or whatever. They experienced Papa's public face and allowed themselves to be fooled by it. She was glad he was dead, and she no longer needed to 'do her duty'. She anticipated his estate would be settled fast; that she and Dorothy would get control, so she might put Papa and everything he represented behind her. If he weren't being buried in the same grave as Mama she'd have wanted an old Irish curse on his gravestone – 'May the only tears at your graveside be the onion-pullers' '. Watching the casket disappear into the ground, she hoped he wouldn't find rest, but be tormented forever for the way he treated Mama.

After the funeral, Norah wasted no time arranging with Dorothy to go through Papa's papers.

"We're looking for his will, Dorothy. We need to find out if he appointed an executor or administrator, and who he left his estate to." Norah rummaged through Papa's desk.

"I'm not sure why I'm here. You could have done this yourself." Dorothy's annoyance showed.

"If we can't find a will, as Papa's oldest surviving child, you'll be the one with authority to have us declared administrators of his affairs. My solicitor colleague at the anti-vivisection society deals with this stuff on a regular basis. He'll draw up the papers for us."

"Do you really believe Papa didn't leave a will?" Dorothy sounded incredulous.

"I've no idea, but the quicker we find out, the sooner we can start sorting out the legal bits. Let's get on searching."

"But shouldn't John Junior and Neal should be involved?"

"Dorothy, if there is a will we will handle it. John Junior is close to death and Neal is a bankrupt. Everyone else lives abroad. It's up to us. If there's no will, they'll appoint us administrators of the estate anyway. Now let's look for any papers there might be."

Norah smiled as she discovered Papa's pile of press cuttings. It betrayed how much Papa valued his public career and sought validation from colleagues. It was a shame they didn't know him as well as she did. How soon he forgot Mama after she died. Except when he remembered something he wanted doing and she wasn't there. Norah looked for subtle ways to remind him of Mama. Like the In Memoriam notice she got him to insert in *The Times* the May before his death. He never commemorated the anniversary of Mama's death, but that year she put the idea to him. Her reaction when he agreed was one of amazement. They produced the wording together: *'In unfading memory of Charlotte Isabel Doherty, for 50 years the dear wife and wise help of John Doherty of Longford Lodge, Hampton, whose long, useful, unselfish life ended on 2 May 1924.'* That last phrase gave her particular satisfaction when he accepted her suggested draft. Perhaps he realised what Mama did for him. But then again, he'd been easy to persuade about many things owing to his mental confusion at the time.

She looked at the press cuttings of his eightieth birthday celebrations. Fancy that Lord Beauchamp referring to him as a 'little man with a great heart'. Mind you, that lot deserved each other, she reflected. Pusillanimous liberals to a man. She never forgave Papa's wishy-washy excuses when she challenged him during her suffragette years as to why Liberal governments took so long to give women the vote. Norah picked up the much fondled and worn cutting from her mother's funeral, which made her cry, but also got her to concentrate. She must stop her mind drifting off into the bogs Papa was so fond of alluding to in his jokes. Not allow emotion to distract her from what she must concentrate on.

Norah had worked hard since Mama's death to earn Papa's trust. She forced herself to ignore her impulse to reject him, except when she needed his help. She knew he'd help if their interests coincided, but he extracted a heavy price. This added to the festering sores in their relationship that would flare up and rankle like a noxious weed whenever they clashed. He haunted her sleep, where he always figured in some guise or other punishing or mocking her.

"I've been having more of those dreams about Papa," said Norah.

"What provoked them?" asked Dorothy.

"I suppose the funeral and everything."

"What are they this time?"

"Variations on the forest and altar nightmares."

"The one with the clearing, the shrine, the crowd, the sacrifice and the loaded cart carrying it away?"

"That's right."

"But how is it different on this occasion?" asked Dorothy.

"I'm pregnant, and Papa is standing there with disgust and disdain radiating from his eyes. In the dream I'm happy because I got revenge by conceiving through an illicit relationship."

"That sounds intense."

"Yes, but the euphoria soon evaporates because Papa starts shouting at me, 'You think you can plead for your independence when you have flouted convention and got yourself with a bastard child'. Then I wake up yelling at the cart carrying away my sacrifice."

"I suppose the most straightforward meaning is that the dream shows how difficult your relationship with Papa was."

"That rather states the obvious," said Norah.

Despite a diligent search, no will appeared to exist. Their solicitor advised them to proceed on the basis of intestacy and published notices inviting interested parties to come forward. No one did. Probate was granted and Dorothy and Norah declared the legitimate heirs, sharing the proceeds of five thousand pounds. More important to Norah was that Dorothy let her have sole ownership of the printing business, a valuable asset in view of the ambitions she nursed of a return to public life. She got her way because it was of no interest to

Dorothy, who wanted nothing to stand in the way of her main interest – animal welfare.

"Are you sure you want the printing business, Norah? I always believed John Junior would take it, but now he's died, I wondered if the other brothers might be interested."

"I need the business and will deal with our brothers if they contest the issue. Although I don't think they will," said Norah.

"I'll leave it to you then. I know you reckon you deserve it after your hard work. It can't have been easy for you, given Papa's reaction to Tony and Dudley."

"It was difficult, but we made his life comfortable for Mama's sake."

"For Mama's sake? If that's true I understand how you managed to overcome your antipathy towards Papa. You spent so much time with him I did wonder how you found the patience. He was tiresome the last year, what with his illness and accident."

"Are you suggesting ulterior motives?"

"Certainly not! Just curious. Found it hard to understand why he didn't leave a will, but put it down to his general decline. Did he never discuss a will with you? I did ask him about it once, but he insisted he had it in hand."

"Never discussed it with me, and I never asked. If you have something you want to say, say it."

"Norah, don't be so tetchy. You always did have a way of getting what you wanted. We always gave way in face of your impetuous, headlong, impulsive pursuit of whatever, whenever. You can't blame me for being curious."

"I've always been able to rely on you, Dorothy, so don't let me down now."

Dorothy dropped it, much to Norah's relief. If more was said, it would give the game away, supposing Dorothy thought there was anything to be given away. She hoped not. She relied on the fact that she knew Dorothy wasn't that interested anyway. With no children and no responsibilities to distract her, Dorothy and Augustus were happy to concentrate on their animal welfare work.

CB CB CB

EMMA, MIRIAM AND Ruth stood by the graveside. It was a warm, hazy, late summer day in early September. The sky was cloudless. Heavy rain fell earlier in the week, but the earth had dried out. Despite her sadness, the calm, warm weather reflected another side of Emma's mood. She was glad that the earth round the grave proved warm to the touch like last year, when they buried Ma. Da said then how he were glad Ma died in summer, and went into warm earth with warm mem'ries. She understood his reasons; two of her bruvvers got buried in winter, and she never forgot how the cold hard earth swallowed them. The war and everything connected with it fetched nuffink but misery. Now Pa was to join Ma in warm earth. Emma was pleased for him, although heartbroken for herself.

"Poor Pa," said Emma, "he never was gonna last long after Ma, but now he's peaceful."

"Inevitable, I suppose," said Ruth. "After losing three boys in the war, they only had each other to cling to. You saw more of them than I did, Emma, but they did get to Northchapel to visit me sometimes. They always enjoyed a day out in the countryside."

"They loved you," said Emma. "They was so grateful what you did for Walter. You made 'is last few years comfy."

"Walter was a wonderful man. So brave. The pain of his injuries never went away. I'm sorry I didn't get longer with him, but then Tony came into my life, so it wasn't all bad."

"I'll miss 'em, but happy they's togever now."

"By the way, how is Tony?" Miriam asked Ruth as they left the churchyard.

"Had a lot to deal with. Until recently, Mrs Elam wasn't interested in him, except to shout at him when reminded of his presence, usually when some accident or other happened. He asked questions about his parents a while ago. I responded by telling him I love him, and that not spending time with Mama and Papa the same way as other boys at school didn't matter."

"Must be difficult," said Emma. "Meself, I never bin able to fathom it. Mind you, she were awful difficult when she were in 'Olloway 1914. Real stubborn. Don't seem to 'ave changed much."

"Oy. Must've been a lonely boy," said Miriam.

"We'd trouble when Mrs Elam told Tony to start answering to her instead of me and to call her Mama and not Mrs Elam. Strange because she goes away campaigning and I do most of his looking-after."

"What made her decide that?" asked Miriam.

"Being declared bankrupt? Reckon she wanted to hit out at anyone around. Tony was the most vulnerable."

"Seems cruel," said Emma.

"I agree. It was too coincidental. I wondered how I might've managed the situation better. I feel guilty because I should've done something about it sooner, prepared him."

"But could you have done anything?" asked Miriam.

"Not sure. Mrs Elam has a powerful personality. If I resisted too far, she might have dismissed me. When Tony got told, I made it clear that I'll always be here for him."

"Astonishing," said Miriam.

"I worry what Mrs Elam will do next to upset him. Anyway, enough of that. I want to learn about how Miriam has been helping you, Emma. You've been working hard, I hear. About to be promoted? Is that right?"

"Aye. Miriam don't take much credit for it, but she 'as been 'elping me. Me reading an' writin' 'as got better and I been learnin' to talk posher. Fiddlesticks. It's hard not to drop me haitches, but when I 'ad, I mean 'had' my interview, I remembered an' never dropped one of 'em, I mean 'them', she's been helping me with me tee-haitches as well."

"She'll 'ave you talking right posh in no time," Ruth laughed, as she winked at Emma and smiled at Miriam.

Despite being sad at the loss of her parents, Emma found that their deaths ushered in a period of happiness. She'd worried and felt guilty in case her parents found out about her and Miriam. Miriam's father died some years ago, while her mother followed not long after Emma's Da, lifting the last restraint on their relationship. They saw each other about Holloway and surreptitiously worked together to help prisoners, but were careful not to let other wardresses or the governors realise. Their best times were when they met outside the prison, talking and enjoying each other's company. Ruth's support made this easier. Emma came to realise that the manipulating invert relationships she witnessed in Holloway weren't the only model for women's friendships.

Miriam suggested to Emma they look at getting together, but Emma was uneasy and fearful.

"Why won't you consider us setting up a home, Emma? A refuge where we can be together." Miriam asked.

"I have to live at the prison; it's me job."

"But you could bring personal things to my flat, and spend free time with me. It'll be much easier now my mother has gone. Bless her. No one will find out."

"But what if someone does? I'd get sacked. You

would too."

"Oy vey. Why are you so frightened? We love each other, that's all that matters."

"Aye. But folks'll say we ain't normal. They hate us for what we are. You was the one who told me about that writer woman Radclyffe Hall, and how they put her on trial for writing about folks like us."

"But we'll be careful. We'll make sure we don't get found out."

"It ain't that easy. It ain't so long since the funerals. I'm happy now, but can't quite get used to everything that 'as 'appened – I mean has happened – I need more time to get accustomed."

Emma sensed Miriam's disappointment. She'd come a long way in understanding herself and finding happiness with Miriam but she found it hard to shake off the hold of her parents' beliefs.

CƷ CƷ CƷ

RUTH UPDATED EMMA and Miriam on Tony's progress whenever they came down to visit.

"Tony's to go to school in Petworth," Ruth announced.

"How far away is that?" asked Emma.

"It's a small town down the road. He's a weekly boarder. Comes home weekends. Makes it easier, but I miss him."

"So you still see him?"

"Yes, thank goodness. Mrs Elam has taken to embarrassing him. She goes down to the school unannounced, then tells them how to do their jobs. He arrives home hurt and confused. I spend visits trying to help him. It's a mercy Robert understands. He's so tolerant with Tony. They spend hours in Robert's aviary together."

"You're both patient. Don't know how you manage it."

"I wonder myself sometimes."

Emma and Miriam were thrilled when, some nine months after Tony went away to school, they found themselves standing in the congregation in the church in Northchapel, while Ruth exchanged wedding vows with Robert. Robert was a local man who'd been a supportive friend for some years. When he realised that Ruth was no longer committed full-time to Tony, he asked her to marry him. Ruth had been reluctant, but Robert had been persuasive, and she gave way.

Mr and Mrs Elam joined the congregation. Ruth found herself amused after the ceremony, when the guests mingled outside the church, to see Mrs Elam approach Emma.

"Don't I know you from somewhere?" Norah said to Emma.

"Perhaps the village. I come down regular to visit Ruth. She was married to me brother who died."

"Right. War wounds, wasn't it? Then she came to be Tony's nanny. Have seen you in the village, but sure I recognise you. Who's your friend?" said Norah.

"This is Miriam."

"And what do you do with yourself when not attending weddings?" asked Norah.

"Social work at Holloway Prison."

"Now I remember your face," said Norah, turning back to Emma. "You were one of the wardresses when I was a suffragette."

Emma blushed. "Aye."

"Well, why didn't you own up? I was sure I could see you recognised me."

"I didn't want to remind you. Thought you'd rather forget."

"Wish I could. How long are you staying in the village?" asked Norah.

"We're visiting a few days with Ruth and Robert, 'til they go off for holiday."

"Well," said Norah, "you may remember Mary Allen, my suffragette colleague. The one involved in women's policing. She's giving a talk to a small invited group at my house tomorrow night. As you are both working in occupations dealing with female crime and criminals, perhaps you'd like to attend."

Emma hesitated, but Miriam spoke up, "Love to come, thank you."

Later she told Emma she couldn't resist the chance to meet Mary Allen. Despite her initial reluctance, Emma realised she also wanted to see the woman who appeared in public dressed in a police uniform. The images she saw showed her with cropped hair, always looking serious. Wearing police uniform got her into trouble with the authorities lots of times. From her pictures, Emma wondered if the woman ever laughed. Perhaps she had, and her face cracked so she never bothered again.

"That was interesting," said Miriam after the meeting.

"It seems women police ain't getting far," said Emma. "Men police don't believe they can do more than look after women prisoners, bit like my job. Wonder if we'll ever get to see female police doing the same things as male police."

"Men view women as prostitutes or drunks and never ask why," said Miriam.

"Not changed since I started at 'Olloway – sorry, Holloway."

"People like Mary Allen are comfortably off. They don't understand what poverty forces women to do. They've never been poor or desperate like the women in Holloway. That's why I spend ages trying to arrange for the children of female prisoners to be cared for by relatives. Families are ashamed, even though the mother stole bread because it was the only way to secure food for her little ones."

"Shame makes people do awful things. It's cruel when mothers in Holloway don't have any idea what's happened to their bairns while they're in there."

"Don't suppose it'll change much. Perhaps one day we'll get more female magistrates. Who knows?" said

Miriam.

CЗ CЗ CЗ

"SO WHAT DO you reckon to my proposition that democracy is undemocratic?" Norah asked Dudley one evening over dinner.

"That's quite a statement. On what basis do you make such a claim?"

"Well, for a start, what difference do you think women have made since they got given a vote?"

"Some, but it was always going to be a slow business."

"But what about the fact that the first woman MP elected was an Irish Nationalist traitor who never took her seat, and the second one, Lady Astor, was an American?"

"I realise the extent of your disappointment not to win a seat in 1918, but there has been some progress since then."

"Not enough. We need to find a way to expose the vested interests that hide behind our politicians, the power they abuse through Parliament, and the sham democracy it gives rise to."

"So what do you presume is the answer?"

"We need to get rid of the Parliamentary whip structure. It's corrupt, and patronising to MPs who want to challenge the system, especially women. It makes them impotent, while kidding them that they have the power of the vote behind them – that putting a cross on a ballot paper once every five years is worth the effort."

"You never start anywhere simple, do you? You always go for the most difficult thing you can achieve. The secret is to learn to eat the cake one slice at a time. You want to gobble the lot at once."

Norah changed the subject. She wondered if Dudley had any inkling of her plans to handle her frustrated political and social ambitions. Norah knew Nancy Astor quite well. They worked together to get Mrs Pankhurst to address meetings in Lord Astor's constituency at the outbreak of WW1. Through Nancy Norah met Oswald Mosley, who also campaigned on the Anti-Alien ticket at the 1918 Election. She'd followed his career since then, and taken a keen interest when he formed the British Union of Fascists in 1932. Her reading about his new party suggested it was based on an ideology she supported that would answer her frustrations with the current system.

"Dudley, I need you to do three things in connection with my plan to relaunch my political career."

"What is it? What would you like me to do?"

"I am cultivating contacts within the local British Union of Fascists."

"I'm aware that you've been to meetings and met William Joyce."

"That's right. There are plans for us to join the BUF. I'm to share a speaking platform with Joyce at a public meeting to announce it. My suffragette career is to be part of my credentials."

"You say 'us'. Am I to be consulted?" asked Dudley.

"I'm consulting you now. I hope you aren't going to argue. I've reasoned it out, and laid plans with Comrade Joyce that will make a big impact. I need your cooperation."

"It's as well I agree! What is my role to be?"

"You will write to the West Sussex Branch of the local Conservatives, resigning from the General Purposes and Finance Committee. Joyce and I have prepared a draft. Your letter will, at the same time, be published in the press, and we will join the BUF as a husband and wife team at the meeting I mentioned."

"Let me read your proposed letter. What else?"

"We need to make Northchapel a hub of fascist activity. We might turn a room downstairs next to the entrance lobby into a library with fascist literature. Then we can publicise it as open for anyone to drop in and take or borrow whatever interests them."

"I'll make arrangements. You said you had in mind three things?

"We need to establish our credentials. You must obtain portraits of your ancestors, the Clary sisters, Julie and Marie. Do it as soon as possible so we can display them where library visitors will notice them."

"I'll see what I can do."

A couple of weeks later Dudley sat at his desk reading his resignation letter. Norah stood behind waiting for him to finish. Her impatience was evident. He'd gone through it several times already, and she wanted him to get on with it. She worked with Joyce on the draft and enjoyed setting out BUF criticisms of Conservative Party policy. Dudley approved it, saying they crafted it well, but asked to put his personal stamp on it. So they agreed he would write the final passage. She was proud of Dudley; he understood what they were about to do. She re-read Dudley's last paragraph over his shoulder.

> '*I prefer to go out into the wilderness and start the fight all over again, in the hope that I may see a new spirit regenerated in the national interest, but this spirit can only lie in fighting for what is right, not by compromising with what is corrupt and evil.*'

She experienced a thrill as Dudley picked up his pen and signed above his name – *E Dudley Elam MA, Sussex – 26 March 1934.*

ᘓ ᘓ ᘓ

EMMA AND MIRIAM were on their way to Northchapel to stay with Ruth and Robert. It was summer. Their journey was uneventful and they were looking forward to days of forest walks and peaceful evenings spent chatting. The weather had been mild with little rain, and they were excited to be getting out of London. The prospect of the quiet and calm of the village and the forests was wonderful, and as they left London both felt the change and relaxed. But when they got to Northchapel, Ruth greeted them in a distressed state.

"What's the matter?" asked Emma.

"Tony is to be sent away to school in Germany."

"What! Why?"

"Mr Elam says it is Mrs Elam's wish. She won't be persuaded otherwise."

"How do you feel?"

"Anxious, but pleased that he will be away from her immediate influence. She causes him problems the way she flounces into his school demanding to interview his teachers."

"Hard to see why he needs to go so far though," said Miriam.

"I think it has to do with what occurred in March," said Ruth.

"What happened?"

"Mr Elam resigned from the Conservative Party and they joined the British Union of Fascists."

"You're joking," said Emma. "Has she told you owt about why?"

"I've avoided her, otherwise I'm sure she would have. Bet she can't wait to get a chance, though."

"I know a little about Fascists," said Miriam. "They have meetings in the East End. I don't like what I've heard."

"When it was announced, there was lots of publicity. You couldn't miss it: pamphlets, parades and handouts. She made a speech from the same platform as William Joyce. Nasty man, terrible scar down his face.

Gives me the shivers. The Elams' house has been busy ever since. Tony's been staying with Robert and me while we get him ready to go to Germany."

"What do folks in the village say?" asked Emma.

"Bit of a novelty still. They hold rallies at the local pub. The Elams have set up a library in their house full of BUF pamphlets. Anyone can borrow from it."

"Do you know much about them?" asked Miriam.

"Hadn't taken much notice till now."

"Well, I might have to visit that library. See what I can see. Will you come with me, Emma?"

CB CB CB

CHAPTER 8

There be Dragons

NORAH'S HAPPINESS WAS evident. Dudley's resignation from the Conservative Party appeared in the local press, and preparations for her to share a platform with William Joyce at a BUF rally at the Chichester Assembly Rooms were well in hand. She was ready to deliver her first public speech for the BUF. Having spent years preparing drafts of speeches to give on this occasion it took no time to adapt one of them. For what seemed like aeons, she had longed to find a way back to the political arena. Now the BUF had come along and provided the perfect vehicle. She read Mosley's ideas about the Corporate State and the role of women within it. Her chance had come. She saw how women might get recognition; play a proper part in directing their fate, controlling their destinies, and contribute ideas and talents to the life of the nation.

Her exhilaration got her firing on all syllables. No more observing from the wings, the political stage awaited. How annoying to be billed as Mrs Dudley Elam and not Norah Elam. But, to succeed, she had to play the game. It seemed that the way to fulfil her vision for women would be be through exploiting men. To follow their rules rankled, but would be worth it in the end. No point falling at the first hurdle by standing on principle over something minor that Comrade Joyce wanted. Mrs Elam it would have to be. Joyce is the BUF's rising star. She must grab this star's tail and hold on tight, bumpy though the ride might be. He was close to Mosley, and the place to begin achieving her ambitions.

"Our BUF partnership is already producing results," said Norah.

Dudley looked up from the local newspaper. He was engrossed in a report on the Chichester rally.

"It seems so. You made quite an impression according to this. It's also in *The Blackshirt*. I received the notices appointing me Sub-Branch Office for Worthing and you Sussex Women's Organiser. Mosley approved the appointments when Joyce briefed him about your suffragette past."

"I'm invited to meet The Leader's mother, Maud, Lady Mosley, in Worthing."

"You must be excited."

"I am. My speech is ready and I can't wait. It's good to be part of society again."

"What else is on the horizon? Anything we need to be ready for?" asked Dudley.

"The big event is Olympia in June. Joyce tells me The Leader wants to meet us before that, and looks forward to our taking part."

"What will we have to do?"

"March in the opening parade. Then sit behind The Leader on the main platform with other BUF officials while he delivers his speech."

"Will our Blackshirt uniforms be ready in time?"

"I made sure of it, don't worry."

When she met Mosley she wasn't infatuated; not in any physical sense – at fifty-five she was aware people would describe her as 'portly and mature'. Those butterflies in her stomach weren't a silly girlish thing, they fluttered from natural excitement. Intimate relationships were of no interest. Such things brought her a bastard son whom she found it necessary to keep out of the public eye. Nuisance, that. No, her intoxication arose from what The Leader represented. A member of the aristocracy with breeding, money, and power. His credentials gave him automatic access to institutions she wanted to join and individuals she needed to influence. Although sections of the establishment regarded The Leader as a rebel, he led a political party through which she would achieve her ambitions for women. He was a visionary, and she wanted him to realise that her vision was as big, and ready to serve him in whatever way required to make it reality.

Now here she stood, surveying a massive crowd, listening to the noise – that loud hum expectant crowds make. It penetrated her bones, all that excitement and buzz mixed with a little apprehension.

"Look, Dudley," she said as loud as possible to be

heard above the noise. "See the crowd in the hall! How many do you think there are?"

"Supposed to be ten thousand. Looks like it."

They stood at the back of Olympia, lined up with BUF officials, proud to wear their Blackshirt uniforms emblazoned with the flash-and-circle emblem. They were ready to march down the aisle behind their comrades. Front and rear standard-bearers bore Union Jacks, or black and yellow party flags. Other banners had been unfurled, which added to the general atmosphere, creating a blaze of colours as loud as the mass of people filling the stadium. She couldn't remember being this excited since childhood. Was this it at last? Everything she was certain she'd been born for. She was going to change the world for the better. Women were going to change the world for the better.

"Here we go," said Norah. "Look at the Blackshirts lining the aisle, standing to attention and saluting."

"That band at the front is doing us proud," said Dudley.

"We'll need to concentrate until we get to the platform. It's hard to hear above the noise."

Norah's senses attuned to the music as she marched under the arc lamps, glancing side to side at the massed crowd as they cheered and clapped. Elated and energised, she chanted the letters M O S L E Y followed by his full name, MOSLEY, in harmony with the crowd. She longed to listen to his speech. Previous speeches she had the privilege to attend left her with deep admiration for his powers of oratory. His voice overran with inspired intonation. It was possible to listen for hours. How could anyone fail to appreciate his message? She knew it emanated from his charisma and ability to create a mood of spiritual renewal. That was his destiny and now it would be hers too.

Norah and Dudley arrived at the platform. She was ecstatic. As they prepared to sit down, someone offered to introduce her to Baroness Ravensdale, The Leader's sister-in-law. Norah became almost breathless with elation.

"I'm delighted to meet you, Baroness," said Norah. "It's a good turnout. The Leader will be pleased."

"I'm sure he will. Are you the suffragette lady?"

"Yes, I am. But we can't rest on past triumphs. Dudley and I are anxious to get going on this campaign. It holds so much promise for the country's future."

"Let's hope so; we need it. The last years have been difficult."

"Didn't I read that you attended the Coronation of Emperor Haile Selassie in Ethiopia in 1930?" asked Norah.

"I have travelled widely, but this year I'm making myself useful in London. I'm to host the Blackshirt Cabaret Fund-Raising Ball."

"If you need help, I've a lot of experience. Don't hesitate to ask."

"Thank you, I'll bear that in mind."

The Leader entered the hall thirty minutes late.

Norah sensed his arrival when the band lowered its volume to play a German march and the arc lamps swung onto the Blackshirt-lined aisle she marched down not long since. Norah caught her breath as The Leader appeared behind six men carrying Union Jacks and the Blackshirt flag. She raised her arm in the fascist salute, and chanted his name along with the crowd.

Despite her thrill at seeing The Leader stride down the aisle and take the podium, the rest of the rally disappointed.

"Never imagined I'd be thankful for seats behind the leader last night and not in the crowd," said Dudley. "At sixty-two don't think I could get involved in fisticuffs and escape unharmed."

"It was terrible the way the hecklers shouted The Leader down during his speech. I found it annoying not to be able to listen uninterrupted. Don't know how he kept going for two hours. A lesser man would give up. What a clever tactic of the agitators to disperse themselves in the crowd so the stewards couldn't get at them. Learned that in my suffragette days. Very effective," said Norah.

"Still made it awful when the stewards needed to climb over our supporters and cause unintentional injury in the mêlée."

"A certain amount of violence is a natural part of political discourse. My father taught me that. But perhaps it did go a bit too far."

"Like when that idiot clambered sixty feet up among

the girders, where Blackshirts were forced to pursue him. When they fell to the ground together I thought my heart would stop."

"Wonder if we will ever find out if he got hurt or what happened to him. Mind you, if he got what he deserved who are we to question what went on?"

☙ ☙ ☙

EMMA AND MIRIAM set off for Olympia. Miriam had secured free tickets and persuaded a reluctant Emma to accompany her.

"I still ain't sure we should be goin'," said Emma.

"Don't worry, it'll be all right, you'll see," said Miriam.

"But if we gets arrested or injured, how will we explain to 'em at work?"

"We'll be OK. We won't heckle or do anything else to attract attention. I want us to find out what this lot are about."

"I'm frightened. Don't like the way they talk about your people, but some of the other stuff they say seems OK. What about work and jobs? Read as Churchill thinks Mussolini and Hitler have clever ideas about gettin' men working. How's folks such as us supposed to decide between 'em – I mean them?"

"Emma… because they have one or two policies that might be all right, doesn't make them good for the country. We need to learn what they're about. I think tonight you'll find as many for as against."

When they reached Olympia, a large crowd of communist demonstrators had assembled, but not many police. Emma overheard a police officer say that he'd no colleagues inside the building – inside being under the control of Blackshirt stewards. Emma shivered. Huge arc lights lit up the crowd and Emma became frightened by the pushing and shoving. Because of their tickets, she and Miriam went down a route guarded by a police cordon, but she felt scared as the police struggled to manage the crowd. She saw a squad of BUF stewards attack some protesters and beat them. It was the arc lights. They made it seem like daytime. They picked out people in the crowd. Mind you, thugs such as that didn't need no excuse, did they?

Once seated, Emma looked around and tried to listen. From muffled conversations, she gathered they had communists and anti-fascists sat near them. She whispered to Miriam, "I hope we'll be all right."

"Don't worry, we'll be fine," said Miriam.

Emma wasn't convinced. Then things got underway. A procession of BUF officials, accompanied by music and banners, marched into the hall and down a Blackshirted aisle to the platform.

"Miriam, look… there's Mr and Mrs Elam marching behind the band. Ruth told me she was going to be here. Who'd 'ave believed it?"

"I can see her. That Blackshirt uniform makes her appear more portly than ever. Those fascist emblems are hideous. The flash and circle is supposed to represent 'action within unity', but I've heard it called the 'flash in the pan'. Me, I think the lightning strike represents thunderstorms, grey skies and miserable weather to come."

"Maybe so," said Emma.

The crowd got restless waiting for Mosley. When he did appear, late, accompanied by Union Jacks and BUF banners, Emma watched as he marched to the podium in a great blaze of music while the crowd chanted his name. Miriam wasn't going to join in and neither was she. She wanted to hold Miriam's hand, but decided it was too dangerous. What if someone spotted them? When he got to the dais, after what seemed an age, he commenced his speech, but the atmosphere turned nasty as agitators around them kept shouting. Emma witnessed Blackshirt stewards climb over people to get to the hecklers, injuring their own supporters, and then beating up those they pulled from their seats. Now Emma knew why she felt sick when she overheard the police officer outside say there were to be none of them in the hall. The Blackshirt stewards had it their own way. Emma saw a woman protester carried along an aisle not far from her by five of 'em. Her clothes were half torn off and her head forced back by a hand over her mouth and nose. It made it difficult for the woman to breathe. The brute-force struggle made Emma shudder. She'd seen a lot of violence but this must be some of the worst. She didn't understand. Mrs Elam had been force-fed and had violence done to her, so why did she support this sort of thing?

Emma never knew how they got away to safety. The next day Miriam bought every newspaper report of the event she could find. It became clear that Blackshirt violence turned opinion against Mosley. Lord Rothermere and the *Daily Mail* said they'd stop supporting him. Without press support, Miriam said she hoped the BUF mightn't last long. After last night, Emma wanted Miriam to be right. It made her head hurt and she still felt sick from being so afraid. Miriam was so much cleverer than her. She tried to follow Miriam's arguments, but got lost, and would ask Miriam to explain it to her several times. Like men with no jobs. Miriam would talk about it lots. But it got so complicated and no one seemed to have an answer. The government sure didn't, from what Miriam said. What she did understand was that inside Holloway, not much had changed since the days when they called Mrs Pankhurst a dangerous criminal for wanting to talk to her daughter in the prison yard. Last week she dealt with a dangerous criminal, a mere slip of a girl, who got a month for being drunk and stealing. The girl told Emma she stole to feed her illegitimate baby. Someone had raped her, and the child was the result. What chance did girls like her have to work and support themselves? Men beat women and told them not to complain. Men paid to use prostitutes, but then got them arrested and locked up for doing what the men wanted. She saw such women every day in Holloway, saw the word 'vice' used to describe what they did in official reports she read. Perhaps she was wrong, but it seemed to her that it were women what got accused of 'vice'. Men never did. Miriam said that if you believed stealing because you was hungry was a vice, then wanting to eat must be a vice as well, given how many women was in prison for stealing food because their men had no jobs. That did make sense.

"What chance have women got?" asked Miriam. "They proved themselves able to do any sort of work during the war, when they did men's work because they were away fighting."

"Then men came 'ome – home – and women got sacked. Men wanted their jobs back."

"Seems we are always taking half a step forward to make things better, then ten backwards."

CB CB CB

DUDLEY FOUND OLYMPIA exhausting. The violence and rapid loss of control shocked him. They held an enquiry at BUF headquarters afterwards. The party line, pushed through *The Blackshirt* and *Action* magazines, claimed it was due to violence engineered by communists, anti-fascists and militant Jews, who managed to get hold of some of the two thousand free tickets. Norah insisted that The Leader's investigation arrived at the correct conclusion. Dudley let it drop. He experienced no jealousy of Norah's commitment to The Leader, but was resentful of her enthusiasm and inexhaustible energy.

She never did things by halves. To match that and appear her equal proved uncomfortable. He wasn't sure he had the physical or mental energy.

He sat in his library contemplating metaphors to help him cope. This had always been his coping mechanism. Found it helpful in the past. But this time, it didn't seem to be working. Every time he found an idea that helped, it would mutate. His mind seemed to be imitating a grindstone, crushing his thoughts down until they resembled fine flour running away through a sieve. Perhaps there was no point trying to understand. Maybe he couldn't do anything except placate her and do what she wanted. He felt like a fly imprisoned in amber. He hadn't escaped at the crucial moment. Norah exhibited so many good attributes, but for each good one, she displayed a corresponding awkward one. On the good side, Norah never accepted limits on her ambitions, allowed nothing to hold her back. Her brain percolated with political arguments refined by an intellect dominated by fierce logic that always demonstrated consistency and insight. On the obverse side, it made her impatient and sarcastic with anyone who couldn't see her point, or who produced counter-arguments as logical as her own. Dudley smiled as he conjured up a mental picture of her physical response to verbal challenges. She would draw in a deep breath, stand erect, and demand an explanation as to how anyone dare suggest the possibility of an alternative argument as valid as hers. She was right, always had been, and they were fools to think otherwise.

He reflected on her fierce loyalty to friends or causes she adopted. The trouble being, her loyalty was bestowed impulsively, while other people faced rejection for what appeared to be trifles. The fierce tongue-lashings she handed out resembled broadsides, seldom missing their target. She never stopped to consider the damage caused, collateral or otherwise. He admired the way she hated hypocrisy and unfairness, but confined that to issues to do with women and the role she wanted for them in society. It proved infuriating that she never made the same link when she behaved hypocritically or unfairly herself.

Then there was Tony. Dudley met Norah through their interest in anti-vivisection, anti-vaccination and animal rights, but he failed to reconcile this with her behaviour towards Tony. Why treat animals with respect, but not her son? Why did she see bullying and threatened violence towards Tony, and men in general, as acceptable? He wished he understood. Was it because of the violence she suffered as a child? Had it been the force-feeding in Holloway and the unrelenting battle she fought with the Church and political establishment? Now she despised them. Who knows? Perhaps with Tony it came because of her bitterness that her WSPU colleagues excised her from their collective memory after his birth. Mary Allen was the one suffragette colleague that stood by her over the years, probably because they were members of the London & Provincial Anti-

Vivisection Society. But then Mary Allen was an invert. Norah never discussed that with him, so he was unsure how much it bothered her. It must be that Norah ignored it because she needed Mary. They did work well together. Mary's commitment to her causes was as strong as Norah's, and those met in the animal welfare work. Together they made a formidable team.

It was impossible to escape. He had evidence enough. Norah was, at her core, a political animal that treated everything as relative to the situation in which she found herself. That added up to why Norah was a puzzle he'd never solve. He better stop trying to analyse Norah and get on with preparing the paper Joyce required from him on the India question.

CB CB CB

"IS EVERYTHING READY?" demanded Norah. "I'm determined the 1934 Blackshirt summer camp in West Wittering will go down in history for our part in it."

Dudley and Norah stood in the hall, which they had hired for the day. Norah surveyed the room again. It looked in order, but you never knew; something may have been overlooked. She contemplated the tables set out with glasses, cups, and saucers down one side, and plates the other. It may be a simple luncheon, but nothing must go wrong. There were people to impress and her reputation to consolidate. She expressed herself satisfied with the BUF banners and decorations that festooned the hall. She chose each one. No one in

Petworth was going to say they hadn't noticed what was going on. The tea urns bubbled away as she reached over, opened, and smelled a couple of the milk bottles to check the milk was fresh.

"No need to worry," sighed Dudley. "I spoke with the caterers and double-checked everything to make sure it's ready. Have some confidence."

"You're sure they've used butter on the sandwiches and not that disgusting axle grease they call margarine?"

"I made sure of it. Left the caterers in no doubt as to your instructions on that."

"I won't have my guests subjected to that foul muck. Everything has to be right. What time is the first contingent due?"

"Shortly. After luncheon we shall join the party and when we get to West Wittering, we will lead the parade into the camp and be met by Major Matthews, the Camp Controller this year."

"Good, it must all go smoothly. We need to make a good impression. Are the press lined up?"

"Yes, the report for *The Blackshirt* is ready. The local press will also receive a copy."

"Let's hope they print it. It's an exciting programme this summer and I am sure the young men and women will find it inspiring."

"Have you got your speech prepared for the final session?" asked Dudley.

"Yes, I've based it on the article going in *The Black-shirt*: 'The Tragedy of Passchendaele'."

"Good idea. I like how you linked today's effete politicians with WW1 Generals and their obsolete ideas. Accurate and to the point, as always. You never lost your touch with words."

"Hope my audience appreciates it as much as you."

They did. The applause and congratulations proved it on the day. Afterwards she received proof of her triumphant week. Joyce and Mosley wrote to thank her personally, as well as the Camp Controller. The letters went into her file marked 'Successful Outcomes' to await the time when she might compose a scrapbook for her family to show them her achievements and how proud she felt.

The next summer, Norah sat down to audit her BUF journey. Her propaganda skills and hard work had produced results. *The Fascist Quarterly* published her article 'Fascism, Women and Democracy'. In that article, she demonstrated how the women's movement had failed since partial female suffrage in 1917, and argued that the answer lay in the Fascist Corporate State. That was how women would get the freedom they hadn't achieved through the ballot box.

Other articles appeared on similar themes. She was pleased that people read her message but she wanted to impress more than the general readership. The people she wanted to get to were The Leader and those around him. Couldn't afford to waste any opportunity to attract his attention. Wanted to force acknowledgment of women's roles for when the old political guard disappeared and Mosley's Corporate State came into being. So she confined herself to issues where her arguments were compelling. No point wasting time on matters others were better qualified to deal with. Sticking to women's issues with powerful arguments gave her the best chance to get her points over.

CR CR CR

MIRIAM COLLECTED AS much BUF propaganda as possible for her and Emma to study. Articles by Mrs Elam came in for particular scrutiny. They attempted to study the latest one, 'Fascism, Women and Democracy'.

"This article is interesting. It raises a lot of questions I'd love to ask her," said Miriam.

"Like what?" said Emma.

"Well for one, having been a suffragette, how can she support an organisation run by men?" said Miriam.

"Good point."

"Then I'd like to enquire if she thinks of herself as a fascist first and a woman second."

"Blimey! You don't want to ask much."

"She seems to suggest women will get power through something called the Corporate State."

"How will that help?"

"Seems it means women will be able to take charge of women's affairs separate to men's."

"Fiddlesticks. It makes my head hurt," said Emma.

"Mine too."

"Will it change anything though?"

"Only for the worse, as far as I can see. Imagine if they do get elected what it will mean. Oy vey, I hope I never live to see it."

C3 C3 C3

NORAH LUNCHED WITH Mary Allen, now a secret BUF member. Norah knew this because she introduced Mary to The Leader. She was also aware that Mary didn't want the authorities to learn of her membership in case it jeopardised her police work.

"How did your visit to Germany go?" asked Norah.

"Productive and satisfying."

"Whom did you meet? Can you tell me anything about it?"

"I can't give details, but I can say that I met the Fuehrer. Granted me a long audience. He expressed interest in my role in the women's police force and how this has developed in England."

"What was he like? Was he what you expected? How knowledgeable was he?"

"I found him extremely knowledgeable, although he didn't give me any clues as to his intentions in Germany. He was as I imagined: easy to talk to, a great communicator, and his grasp of the issues amazing."

"I understand Diana Mosley and Unity Mitford have met him. They have good contacts with him and others in the Nazi hierarchy. I wonder if it I might get an audience with him."

"Don't know," said Mary. "I suspect you'd need to

have a specific purpose in such a meeting, unless you meet him as part of some delegation from the BUF or something."

"I'll keep talking to my contacts, hatch a plan and see if any of them can help me. Wouldn't it be exciting if I did?"

Norah stood in her hallway at The Old Forge looking up at the portraits of the Clary sisters. *You are about to start earning your keep,* thought Norah, *and I am sure you will give excellent service. You will help make the November 1935 General Election a memorable one.*

"I found it surprising when The Leader said he'd no intention of putting up candidates for the November Election," said Norah.

"So was I. But his reasons made sense. We aren't ready to fight an election," said Dudley.

"What do you make of his idea to run a campaign under the slogan 'Fascism Next Time'?"

"It is a good one, although how it will work isn't clear."

"I have ideas. You can start by finding a couple of workmen with tall ladders for one day next week."

"What for?"

"I've ordered a banner with the campaign slogan writ large, wide enough and deep enough to cover the entire front of the house, in large black lettering. No one will miss it."

"Done with your usual restraint then, Norah." said Dudley.

Norah ignored him.

"That's not all. I am arranging an event at the Swann Inn on the corner up the road from the house. John Beckett has agreed to speak and I'm sending out a hundred invitations. With John being editor of *The Blackshirt* and *Action*, it means we'll get a good write up. Nothing like getting the Director of Publications out to speak at your rally. After refreshments and speeches, we'll round off the evening with a march back here to The Old Forge under BUF banners and standards. We'll then open the library downstairs, and invite everyone to help themselves to the BUF literature you will stock up on for the occasion."

"Anything else, Your Majesty?" asked Dudley.

"I've speeches to prepare and pamphlets and hand-outs to get ready."

"What will your line be?"

"I'll tell women they should take a principled stand and not vote."

"Don't you reckon that's a bit contradictory? You were a suffragette, remember."

"Precisely. That's what gives me the moral authority to withhold my vote."

"On what grounds?"

"On the grounds that it's the only way women can register their disgust at the mandates the old parties are fighting the election on."

"But what if women reject that idea and still want to vote? What advice will you give?"

"I will suggest they question their candidate with care to find out what they will be voting for."

"You should be careful, Norah," said Dudley. "Your arguments are convoluted and questionable, and if I find that, voters are bound to."

The evening at the Swann Inn went well. Visitors to the library noticed the two portraits in the hall, and Norah got several chances to tell her story. No one got away, including Beckett, on whom she pounced the minute he stopped in front of them.

"You've noticed the portraits," said Norah.

"Such beautiful women. Who are they?"

"The Clary sisters, Julie and Désirée. Do you have knowledge of them?"

"No."

"Well, Julie married Joseph Bonaparte, becoming Queen Consort of Naples and Sicily. Désirée got engaged to Napoleon, but he broke it off to marry Josephine. However, Napoleon's General Bernadotte then proposed to Désirée, who accepted him."

"Interesting, are you an admirer of the sisters?"

"Yes, although, there is another reason we have them hanging here."

"Can I ask why?"

"Bernadotte was adopted by the King of Sweden to set up a new line of succession. The old king had no male heirs. When Bernadotte was crowned, Désirée became his queen. Their son, Oscar, inherited the throne when Bernadotte died."

"You know a lot about French and Swedish history."

"That is because King Oscar is Dudley's great grand-father."

"Ah! But that raises a question. Why Dudley is not part of the Swedish royal family."

"Dudley's grandmother was one of Oscar's illegitimate children."

Norah enjoyed the look on visitors' faces when this story climaxed. It fitted well. Royal connections remote enough to give her an air of respectability, an oblique suggestion that she had a claim to belong to the aristocracy, but an excuse for why she did not.

※ ※ ※

EMMA AND MIRIAM journeyed to Northchapel to visit Ruth. After settling in and enjoying a meal together, talk turned to the General Election and Mrs Elam. Ruth reported that Mrs Elam campaigned vigorously, although the BUF did not intend putting up candidates.

"How does that work?"

"The BUF slogan is 'Fascism Next Time'. They want to put up candidates at the election after this one. Everyone is asked to consider abstaining in this election as a protest."

"What does that mean?"

"Mrs Elam told me she isn't voting. Said if I intended to, I should question my candidate. If I don't like what he says, I shouldn't vote."

"It has a curious logic."

"You should see the house. There's a huge banner slung across the front emblazoned with the slogan. Quite something."

"Not ashamed and wants everyone to notice."

The next day, the three of them walked through the forest. The day turned out cold and crisp. Emma appreciated the quietness of the place and the nearness of Miriam. When they arrived, she felt drained of energy; denuded like the leafless trees. In the forest she relaxed and, in the same way that spring renews the trees, Emma took strength from Miriam.

It had been a hectic year at Holloway. Outside, women's lives improved, but inside, change came slow. The appointment of Mary Size as deputy governor in 1927 brought some improvement. Mary fought for women to have posters and mirrors in their cells and established training and education. The old guard resisted. Dr Morton, the Governor, died last June, and despite questions in Parliament about considering a woman for the job, the appointment went to Dr Matheson DSO. Miriam said the DSO stood for Delayed Switch Over.

"Mrs Elam is having one of her soirees," Ruth said. "Do you want to attend?"

"What's it about?"

"After the invasion of Abyssinia by Italy, and the League of Nations Peace Ballot in June, she's written a paper for *The Fascist Quarterly* called 'The Affirmative Guaranty'. It's about that."

"I'm interested," said Emma, "what wiv me bruvvers all dying in the war."

"A lot of people agree."

"I'd like to go," said Miriam. "I wonder what she'd say if she realised I'm Jewish?"

"Don't worry about it. I'll get us invited."

Miriam was nervous. Emma and Ruth tried to help her relax, but it proved impossible. Miriam shuddered as she stepped into the hallway. She felt uncomfortable, although curious to hear what Mrs Elam wanted to say. Miriam looked at the library of fascist literature to the left of the entrance hall, the two portraits hung in the hallway. Miriam remembered her amusement when Ruth told her about them. Mrs Elam was a social climber. But what about the trouble in the East End and the way Blackshirts rioted against her people? That was why Miriam hoped Mosley's fascists would never come to power.

As they left the meeting, Miriam remarked, "Mrs Elam sounds fierce when she speaks."

"Always has been. When I lived as the nanny in the house, I used to hear her in her study when she practised speeches for the Anti-Vivisection meetings," said Ruth.

The lecture itself presented a challenge to Emma and Ruth. Miriam made notes and took hand outs. She summarised it for Emma and Ruth, trying to explain how Mrs Elam made proposals supposed to stop war and how governments and other organisations had it wrong.

"I'm glad I've got you to explain. It makes my head hurt, it's so complicated," said Emma "Now I understand a bit, maybe she's got a point."

"Not sure. If politicians argue about how to get peace, how are we supposed to understand who's right or wrong?"

"Anyway, Ruth, enough of that. You never said if you got your birthday greetings telegram," said Emma.

"I forgot. I meant to say. It caused a stir in the village. It must have been one of the first Greetings Telegrams delivered here. How did you find out about them?"

"Saw it advertised last time I visited the Post Office. Reckoned it would be fun."

CB CB CB

THAT PROVED TRICKY, but worth it, Dudley thought as he examined his copy of *The Fascist Quarterly. It took some persuading, but Norah saw my point. This League of Nations article is good. Norah is impatient and intolerant, always thinks she is logical and incontrovertibly right, and argues endlessly. Silly thing is, after she slept on it, she saw my point, but then pretended she saw it and made the improvements.* What could he do with her? The prospect was for a busy year, what with The Leader about to announce the candidates for the next General Election. He hoped she would be pleased with the seat Mosley offered her. He went through the prepared press release.

'Mrs Norah Elam – Was one of the leaders of the Woman's Suffrage Movement in pre-war days, served three terms of imprisonment and endured several hunger strikes. On the outbreak of hostilities she placed her services at the disposal of the Government. Mrs Elam had a distinguished war record – recruiting in 'Red' South Wales working in a munitions factory and was a member of several important government committees. In 1918 she contested Richmond, Surrey, as an Independent candidate, was then for a short time in the Conservative Party, but joined the British Union almost at its conception. She is a popular and well known Fascist propagandist.'

That seems OK. He understood how much Norah enjoyed the political game of half-truths and outright dissembling, and this was up to her usual standard. She excelled at the ambiguities, telling him how the statements were true – relatively speaking. More work would have to wait until the seat announcement. In the meantime, he needed to tackle her on the article 'Women and the Vote'.

Dudley read the article. He realised how much she enjoyed writing this one. She hadn't held back, given full rhetorical flow to her obsession with how women, ex-colleagues in particular, sold out to Financial Democracy and allowed themselves to be exploited by Party wire-pullers. It proved a real tour de force, as he got her to work through her argument that women had fallen for it and let themselves be duped. He was unsure about her reference to women wearing '...the primrose in memory of the Jew Disraeli, the rosette in honor of

Sir Herbert Samuel, (and) the red emblem in commemoration of Karl Marx'. She hadn't liked it when he suggested that a similar charge might be leveled against her for wearing the Blackshirt uniform in honor of The Leader. In the end, she gave some consideration as to why her actions might be justified and her ex-colleagues were not. He was sure her idea that those women are exploited and she is not was inadequate. But he'd leave her to ponder that one.

CB CB CB

"DID YOU SEEN this, Emma?"

"What?"

"These press reports about Cable Street."

"Are they accurate?"

"It says a hundred and fifty demonstrators were arrested and a hundred and seventy-five injured, including police, women, and children."

"Is that all? I'm surprised the numbers are so low. We got few into Holloway, so it may be accurate."

"The anti-fascist demonstrators gave Mosley a bloody nose."

"Glad we avoided being in the middle of it," said Emma. "Would 'ave – have – been embarrassing gettin' arrested."

"I did enjoy throwing manure and rotten vegetables out of the window over the bobbies in Cable Street, though. A woman next to me emptied a chamber pot over them."

"Made me a bit sick, that did."

"I liked the shouting of '*No pasarán* – they shall not pass' and that chanting 'One, two, three, four, five – we want Mosley, dead or alive'."

"That was because the Blackshirts shouted, 'The Yids, the Yids, we are going to get rid of the Yids'. It terrified me," said Emma. "Then there was them fireworks and marbles thrown under the horses' hooves."

"I heard the Blackshirt column was three thousand strong and that two hundred women wearing black blouses marched with them."

"Might be right. Best part is, police and Mosley had to give up marchin' along Cable Street."

"Don't suppose Mrs Elam joined the march?" asked Miriam. "She must be about fifty-seven by now and considered a bit frail for all that."

"Bet she'd have been there if possible, though."

"Maybe, but at her age I bet she wanted a place of honour beside Mosley himself to get her to do it."

"Wonder what she thinks about throwing marbles under the horses' hooves?" mused Emma. "She's always said she hates animal cruelty. I don't like it and the horses don't deserve it."

 timezones timezones timezones

IN NOVEMBER, SEAT allocations were announced. Norah got offered Northampton.

"I hope you aren't disappointed," said Dudley.

"Of course I am. I hoped for a seat in the south where I've worked hard. But this is politics; I have to accept it."

"It's better to stand somewhere your background isn't well known due to the bankruptcy. Then there's little chance of awkward questions."

"It's helpful that Charles Bradlaugh stood for Northampton in the past, I am sure I can use that to my advantage."

"How?" asked Dudley.

"I'll play on his radical reputation for refusing to take a religious oath of allegiance when elected in 1880. He went to prison and lost his seat, although got re-elected at subsequent by-elections. What better example to assert my suitability?"

The day that would live in Norah's memory, though, was that November day when The Leader accompanied her to the Town Hall in Northampton. It represented everything she worked for. The Leader's presence confirmed his trust and respect for her. His words carried much significance. Norah stood beside him in her Blackshirt uniform – proud to be acknowledged, but knowing that she wouldn't be able to wear it much longer. It was to be banned under the Public Order Act. The Leader introduced her saying that '... he was glad indeed to have the opportunity of introducing the first woman candidate and it killed for all time the suggestion that National Socialism proposed putting British women back into the home. Mrs Elam had fought in the past for women's suffrage and was a great example of the emancipation of women in Britain'.

Norah set about her campaign with energy and enthusiasm, giving speeches on issues she might exploit with carefully crafted ideas. She attacked unemployment and the failure of party politics, championed the cause of shoe-making – the area's staple industry – and wanted to see an economic system built on national rather than international lines. She spoke to the Northampton League of Nations Youth Group, referring to her article on the Covenant of the League of Nations arguing against collective security. Her message was clear: 'collective security' meant 'collective war', and stressed the benefits of isolationism. She was ready for anyone who tried to attack her as xenophobic, solid in her belief that her arguments on employment would trump every other.

CB CB CB

"JOYCE IS GONE and Beckett with him. The Leader has sacked them," said Norah.

"When did you hear?" asked Dudley.

"Today."

"You must be pleased. Since we joined the BUF I admire the way you overcame your dislike of Joyce."

"Joyce's ambitions were no secret. Some BUF members saw him as The Leader's natural successor, but Francis Hawkins decided in October to marginalise him, taking over control of headquarters, internal affairs, and political machinery."

"We suspected something might be going on. The infighting was obvious."

"Rumour is the BUF is in financial trouble. The Leader needs to reorganise and restructure, close outlying offices, reorganise the women's section, and make London the administrative centre. Staff are being slashed and volunteers brought in."

"What are your plans?"

"I'll make sure The Leader knows he has my unstinting support. You joining the Executive Committee of the London and Provincial Anti-Vivisection Society will pay off. It means that as we are both in London, you can offer services as a part time volunteer receptionist at headquarters. We'll inform The Leader he can use the LPAVS offices for confidential meetings. Our colleagues have agreed. We should consider moving to London."

Norah's loyalty earned a reward that summer. A letter landed on the hall carpet one morning. Dudley was in his library indulging his usual reveries. Norah burst in on him – without knocking.

"It's paid off. Writing to Unity Mitford and pestering The Leader's office."

"Are you talking about the study trips to Germany?"

"I'm being included in one as part of a private delegation organised by Ribbentrop's bureau."

"I'm pleased. You worked hard. Will you meet Hitler?"

"As part of the delegation. I won't get a personal meeting like Mary had."

For the next few months, the household endured frenzied activity. Norah's excitement became hard to contain. *What a relief,* thought Dudley, when she left for her trip, happy that peace and quiet descended like a burst balloon.

But then came the aftermath.

"Can you credit it, Dudley?" Norah had arrived home.

"What?"

"I didn't get to meet him in the end."

"That must be disappointing. I assume you mean Hitler."

"Those stupid men are to blame. The ones who planned it on a day when they should have known it would rain."

"That's taking it a bit far."

"They said we'd time to go and change after standing in the rain so long. We were soaking wet and wouldn't have gone otherwise. Why didn't they appreciate Hitler was due to arrive? They organised it."

"You took a chance, and it didn't work."

"I so much wanted to meet him. I wanted to compare him with The Leader, but now my chance has gone and I won't get another."

"Never mind, you've more important things to concentrate on."

CB CB CB

THE LEADER HAD announced a change of name from BUF to the British Union or BU for short, accompanied by a change of party emblems. That settled it for Norah: she and Dudley had to move to London.

"I've made myself as indispensable to The Leader as I did to Emmeline," said Norah.

"I agree," said Dudley. "Our At Homes have gone well. The Leader says he always enjoys them."

"The Leader instinctively knows how to keep the BU at the forefront of British politics, and the people he meets at them help him do that. That's why he comes."

"You enjoy meeting them as well," insisted Dudley.

"I feel at home among them – that's why."

"I saw you talking to The Leader at the last one. Has he asked you to do something specific?

"There are municipal elections due. He wants to use them as a platform to launch a peace campaign. He thinks it will recapture popular support."

"And your role?" asked Dudley.

"My old comrade Flora Drummond and her Guild of Empire are protesting against BU candidates. He asked me how best to handle them."

"What did you suggest?"

"I told him to get groups of Blackshirt women to disrupt Guild meetings, the same as Flora and I did as suffragettes. Always worked well."

"Good idea."

"I got hold of a Guild pamphlet and will publish a response to their crackpot arguments for voting."

Norah locked herself in her study and spent hours composing a response to go in *The Blackshirt* entitled 'Suffragette in Anti-Fascist Circus'. Norah's pen spun away and Dudley listened to daily progress reports. Every caustic comment Norah could summon up went in. The result was a sarcastic vilification of her one-time colleague.

"Dudley, listen to this – *'WHAT', asks Mr. H.G. Wells, in his new book, 'has the tide of feminine emancipation left behind it?' and answers with the deadly retort, 'Liberties galore and no achievements at all.'* Don't you think that is the right quote to start my article exposing the stupidity of the Guild's position?"

"It does grab the attention and sets out your intentions," said Dudley. "What else are you going to say?"

"I've got some wonderful phrases to describe Flora and her Guild members."

"Such as?"

"'Extinct volcanoes' for one 'maiden aunts' for another, 'funny little back numbers', 'earnest ladies', 'mediaeval guild'. Shall I go on? Do you reckon I'm getting my contempt across?"

"No one will miss that," said Dudley.

"I'm saving my best phrases for Flora."

"Is it necessary to make it so personal? Won't your message be lost?"

"I need to show how well I understand her tactics and expose her for what she is," said Norah.

"How?"

"By exposing her outright hypocrisy in criticising the 'ism' of fascism, by saying it is little better than the 'ism' of communism and complaining about the violence that accompanies 'isms'. I propose the following –

This from the pen of a Suffragette, who from 1906 to 1914 defied all law and order, smashed not only windows, but all the meetings of Cabinet Ministers on which she could lay hands and was for long the daily terror of the Public Prosecutor and the despair of Bow Street! She seems to have forgotten that when she was trying to give voice to her policies in those hectic days, not only unrest and disturbances occurred, but that her meetings were smashed, as are Fascist meetings to-day, by hooligans of the street and that free speech was at a premium. But I do not remember ever hearing her say that there was little to choose between her and the rowdies who manhandled her and pelted her with rotten eggs and other missiles whenever she got up on the soapbox.

"What's your opinion?" asked Norah.

"It works."

"She states she knows how to get rid of 'isms' and tells us how. I'm going to quote her statement back at her, mocking it –

"But what's to be done about these beastly 'isms'? Why, simple as falling off the Eiffel Tower. The Guild is to persuade the women voters – hold your breath – to use the power of the vote!"

"You have it well in hand. I'm sure it will be duly appreciated by BU readers, if not by Flora's Guild," said Dudley.

In October Norah and Dudley were gratified when The Leader awarded Dudley a bronze medal for distinguished services to the Chichester area on the fifth anniversary of the founding of the BU.

CB CB CB

EMMA AND MIRIAM were enjoying a quiet weekend. Emma glanced at Miriam sitting reading in the comfortable old chair opposite, admiring her lover's soft flowing hair and still beautiful but gentle face. Emma marvelled at how Miriam retained her inner peace, which never seemed to dim, despite the horrors she saw every day. Miriam gave her strength to cope with her own work, and Emma felt guilty. They discussed how they might change their work and find a way to live together, but Emma was afraid to make that last final commitment. She made excuse after excuse, but Miriam had been patient and said she understood Emma's concerns. Emma thought that showed how strong Miriam's love was, and wished she was able to overcome her fears. But that would be difficult, especially if they were to endure scenes like that one on their last visit to Northchapel, when Mrs Elam had accosted Miriam in the village. Every word burned itself on to Emma's memory. She'd never seen Miriam so angry – never suspected Miriam could get that angry.

"I've seen you several times at my lectures," said Norah.

"That's right. I heard Commander Allen speak on women's policing, and you on peace."

"Does your name mean you're Jewish?"

"That's a direct question."

"I'd like a direct answer. I also want to know if you are an invert? Your behaviour suggests you are."

"If I am either or both, that's my business."

"You may be right. But you make it my business when you come to lectures at my home. I can't be seen to be encouraging people like you."

"How preposterous. How is anybody to guess who I am in a public gathering?"

"You may get away with it in the city, but in small villages like this people talk, and they have noticed you."

"Are you saying you don't want me to come to your lectures here?"

"That's right."

"I find that hypocritical, ambivalent and self-defeating. You are able to tell I am an invert because you and I both know that Commander Allen is an invert. Yet she is your long-time friend and colleague. I am forced to conclude that it is my Jewishness you abhor most."

Emma, though surprised, was even more flabbergasted to see that for once Mrs Elam was at a loss for words.

Dragging her mind back from that scene, Emma

realised that she had never believed such contentment possible, and never stopped reflecting on how lucky she had been to meet Miriam. She looked around the room, her eyes resting on mementos above the fireplace that she and Miriam had collected. Not one of them had any value, but they symbolised shared joy and love. Emma wondered how society saw love like theirs as perverted and wrong. Would attitudes to same-sex relationships ever change? The world outside may be swamped by talk of war, but Emma was glad that in this room, at this moment with Miriam, she was loved and safe.

"Look at this?" said Miriam.

"What?"

"You remember Mosley launched a peace campaign to coincide with council elections?"

"The BU did well. Now they can't wear those uniforms any more they look a bit respectable."

"Eugh," said Miriam, "changing clothes doesn't change policies. Some may be fooled, but the majority aren't."

"Thank goodness, but Mosley seems to be the only politician pushing for peace. Most politicians don't have any idea what to do. Most suspect we'll go to war. All I know is the armed services are recruiting and wardresses are leaving to join up. It means lots of short staffing."

"Does that mean less time together?" asked Miriam.

"I hope not, but it does mean I can't make plans to leave the service at the moment."

"Will we ever get a chance to live together?"

"One day, but what were you talking about?"

"This spat between Mrs Elam and Mrs Drummond of the Guild of Empire."

"I remember those two; they were close in the suffragette days, arrested for a stunt on Lord Carson and Lord Lansdowne's doorsteps. That was the first time Mrs Dacre Fox, or Mrs Elam as she now calls herself, came to Holloway and underwent force-feeding. Mrs Drummond had been there before," said Emma.

"They're exchanging public insults now. Mrs Elam's main complaint is that putting a cross on a ballot sheet once every five years is a waste of time."

"I would rather do that than have no vote," said Emma. "Who knows what will happen? If they do declare war, elections won't 'appen – I mean happen – fiddlesticks, still struggle to remember me haitches – so we mayn't get a vote anyway."

"Oy vey. What can we do? Perhaps she's right; our vote won't make much difference. What a dreary idea."

CB CB CB

CHAPTER 9
Mosley's Challenge

NORAH SAT IN her London drawing room and looked up at the Clary sisters. They provided great talking points for her in Sussex, and hadn't finished provoking stimulating conversations yet. Thank goodness she'd completed preparing the At Home guest lists. She could entertain more now they lived in London. She enjoyed seeing old friends, but with Mary's help, her guest inventories were full of people she couldn't wait to cultivate. Networking was one of her strengths, always had been. No one would turn down her invitations. She made sure of that. The Leader received an invitation to every one of them, then let it be known he intended to be at as many as he could – let everyone know that he valued the conducive atmosphere she created. Her talent was for creating situations where people relaxed. Knew how to ensure guests might chat with candour. How good was that? Mary's contribution had been invaluable, although she needed to be careful as Mary's BU connections had to be kept secret for the time being. Being on the council of the London and Provincial Anti-Vivisection Society together gave them legitimate reasons to meet, so Mary's confidentiality didn't need to be compromised. Between them they made a big impact.

"Dudley, come and sit down, I've something to say."

"Can't it wait? I'm reading the newspapers."

"No. I have an idea and don't want to waste time getting going."

"Well?"

"We need something extraordinary to raise our profile. That gets us noticed by the leadership for the right reasons. Demonstrates our commitment more than we're already doing. That sets us up as 'The' people at 'The' forefront, whom everyone wants to know."

"Should I be worried? What are you planning?"

"You know that gold signet ring of yours?"

"Yeeessss…," he said.

"You know the BU is struggling for funds?"

"Yeeesssssss…," He was uneasy now.

"Well, I prepared an article that we can ask Arthur Chesterton, who's taken over as editor of *The Blackshirt,* to put in one of the journals – I suggest *Action* – which talks about the indomitable spirit of Blackshirt comradeship etc, etc. I have a draft. It says that in this spirit, Blackshirt Elam is going to '…….give one of his dearest possessions that the Movement might survive in its struggle with the forces of materialism'. Then it refers to you giving your gold signet ring, suggesting that others might have valuables hidden away in drawers and cupboards that they could also give. We can make it more symbolic if we say it was a gift from your mother so is valuable to you and a great sacrifice."

"But my mother did give it to me when I turned twenty-one," said Dudley grimacing, but nodding his head at the same time.

"Your face tells me you aren't sure about the idea."

"I'm not," said Dudley, unaware that Norah observed him rub his earlobe between his thumb and finger.

"For goodness sake, Dudley, it's a signet ring. Our reputation and what we are trying to achieve is worth more than that. Why would you need a more convincing argument? It speaks for itself. And it's logical."

"But it's a tough decision, and you caught me off guard," said Dudley, closing his eyes while his hand moved to rub his forehead. Norah's impatience began to rise.

"Backbone is what is required, man. Backbone and sacrifice. Pull yourself together. Look at what we will gain, not what you will lose."

"But I need time to consider it," said Dudley, trying to clear his throat of a frog that had lodged there.

"You don't need to. I did that for you already. This is a good idea. You'll agree when you hear the other part of my plan."

"Which is?"

"The next week another article will appear saying that amongst the donations received, Mrs Elam has sent her wedding ring. That will make us seem a devoted couple committed to the Movement. What do you reckon?"

"I suppose it's a good idea. I never liked you wearing Charles's ring as a symbol of our relationship. Now you'll have a good excuse not to wear one."

"I'll arrange to see Arthur, then."

She left him sitting at his desk among his papers, staring at his memento mori. She may not have married him, but her wedding day incantation of 'Aisle, Altar, Hymn' worked whether you had a wedding certificate or not.

The pieces appeared in *Action* in April. Chesterton resigned from the BU immediately before, but the agreed articles got published, the second one appearing a week before her first At Home. Norah experienced relief – the invitations had gone out before the articles appeared. She didn't want anything to spoil her plans.

Norah stood in her main reception room the morning after, watching the housemaid clear up. Looking up at the Clary sisters, she offered a silent paean of praise and thanks. They presided over a triumph – at least their spirit had. Everyone commented on and admired them, and anyone who didn't know the story before knew it now. Her old friend from West Sussex, Muriel Whinfield, and her son Peter had been there, as well as Lord Cottenham, Viscountess Downe, Geoffrey Gush, Dr Margaret Vivien and the Domviles. The Leader dropped in and circulated with her at his side, talking to

Muriel and Peter about their recent travels in Austria after the Anschluss in March. Peter's friends Peter and Lisa Kruger also attended and The Leader spent time discussing Peter Kruger's book on the Jews.

Norah reviewed her triumph over breakfast.

"Yesterday evening went well, don't you think, Dudley?"

"The temperature seemed quite febrile at times, with the discussion about Hitler's victorious Anschluss. The Leader spent a lot of time talking to the Whinfields."

"I find it amazing that the Allies, despite making noises about upholding the Treaty of Versailles, puffed warm air and wind at Germany. They made themselves look impotent and helpless."

"Seems like it."

"It shows Hitler is in control in Europe, and the Allies can't do anything about it."

"You may be right."

"I'm convinced of it. Mary keeps me informed about plans to unite fascist organisations here. When that's done, The Leader's time will come."

"There'll be a lot of political manoeuvring before that."

"I'm doing everything I can so The Leader can grasp the initiative. I'm sure with our help and others like us, people will realise he's the only leader in Britain with the right solutions."

"If your determination is anything to go by, I don't doubt it."

"Changing the subject – Tony is sixteen this May, and will be home soon," said Norah.

"What do you want to do about it?"

"I don't want him in London under my feet. I've too many other important things going on. He'd be a nuisance if I had to explain him away."

"What do you suggest?"

"Go and see Nanny Ruth. Ask if he can live with her in Northchapel until we decide what's best. Tell her to find out what work he wants to do. He always responded to her."

"I'll visit her," said Dudley.

Cß Cß Cß

TONY MET HIS father and travelled with him to Northchapel. Tony hadn't seen him for so long, he wasn't sure how he felt about it. His father looked old and careworn. Tony wondered why and how hard he was working. Nanny Ruth wrote and told him about their move to London, but he hadn't read too much of her letter. He didn't care because he was certain they didn't care about him. His mother didn't. Else why would he be sent to stay with Nanny Ruth? He'd been away ages, grown up a lot, and wasn't sure whether to call her Nanny Ruth. Must ask her about it. Perhaps he should use her married name, Mrs whatever. He couldn't remember it. He didn't recollect having seen it written down. She'd always been Nanny Ruth. He heard his father say that he would stay to see him settled

at her house. Not bothered, he shrugged his shoulders –
"suit yourself, Sir" – but his voice sounded distant even
to himself. It was a relief not living with his parents. His
mother hadn't come; didn't seem to care he had arrived
home; although he couldn't say so to his father. He
wished he was someone else – someone whose parents
cared about him no matter who or what he was. Instead
he was a bastard and an embarrassment.

Tony listened as Nanny tried to talk about what he
might do. Nanny always wanted the best for him and he
still trusted her.

"Let's sort out the name thing – Nanny Ruth is silly.
You're grown up now. I'm happy for you to call me
Ruth if you want to."

"OK."

"Any ideas about what work you might pursue?"

"Not considered it much, but don't want to do
anything bookish. Fancy something to do with my
hands."

"Are you sure?"

"Yes."

"Why?"

"Mama would want me take a desk job. Despises
what she calls 'manual labourers'."

"If there's something you want to do, why not do it
despite what she thinks? Being happy with what you do
will annoy her as much as doing something she doesn't
approve of."

"Whatever I decide to do, there'll be problems."

"Let's talk about it then."

"If I try to do something serious, questions may be raised over my birth. I don't want it discovered."

"Is that the reason? Those issues may not come up."

"If it costs money, my mother will object. Say she can't afford it."

"You don't know 'til you ask. I'm sure your father would support you."

"I want to be independent. Be far enough away so she can't visit or interfere. Lucky she's busy saving the country at the moment. At least, that is what it seems like to me."

"Whatever you do, Tony, don't do it to annoy your mother. Do it because you want to. Don't show her she has control over what you do. That will be the best way to irritate her, not by taking a job she won't like."

When Dudley left, he gave Tony some BU newspapers. Told him to peruse them to help him understand what he and Mama were doing that was so important. Although Tony resented his mother – thinking about her made him angry – he did read them, out of boredom. He agreed with BU policies on Jews. They were the same as he read about while he was away. These were easier to understand because of being written in English. They explained in language he comprehended that Jews were responsible for manipulating and polluting the world. His mother used the same rhetoric to describe him when a child. He understood hate. He loathed himself the way his mother loathed him, having heard from her often how he should never have been born and had ruined her life. Reading the papers when tired, the ideas got muddled in his head. He found it difficult to separate out whether he was reading about despicable Jews or hearing his mother's words shouted at him.

CB CB CB

DUDLEY AND NORAH breakfasted. Norah was, as usual, preoccupied with how her At Home had gone the evening before. Dudley wanted to talk about Tony but Norah was full of excitement and political gossip with ideas for outmanoeuvring opponents she regarded as dangerous to The Leader. Dudley knew it was useless to try turning the conversation until she finished, wondering how he might gain advantage. If he tagged what he had to say onto the end of the discussion, she might not notice. He surveyed the room. He noticed the china and careful arrangement of family pictures on the sideboard, the fascist writings and the literature on the bookshelves, stopping to take in the maid's barely hidden amused smile. Everything displayed to impress visitors with her commitment.

"Did you hear what I said?" demanded Norah.

"You said that nobody matched The Leader's political stature, and anyone saying anything else should be put in the Tower."

"So you did listen. We must work hard to see no one gets a chance to suggest anything negative to or about him. He must hear that he is right in his plans for the country."

"That may not be good for him, Norah. Political leaders need to learn to absorb criticism. It isn't healthy otherwise."

"Don't be exasperating. You know what I mean."

"But sometimes, in your enthusiasm, you lose perspective."

"You know I'm right. War is looming and he's the one working tirelessly to achieve a negotiated peace. Why can't his detractors see it? Britain's interests aren't threatened by Hitler's expansion plans. Germany is pursuing them because of the Versailles Treaty. Germany is not our enemy."

"I agree, but shouldn't you eat your toast before it gets cold?"

"Why can't people see The Leader is not a pacifist? If Britain were menaced or attacked, he would fight, but that's the only reason. He wants to save the country and the Empire, and lift us out of poverty."

Dudley reckoned Norah had forgotten she was at home, and imagined herself on a platform addressing a crowd. She stopped, drew breath and ate some toast. Dudley decided to try his luck.

"While you eat, Norah, I need to tell you about Tony."

"Must you? Go on then, what grand plans are there?"

"He's settled on an apprenticeship as a pipe-fitter on

the Isle of Wight."

Dudley paused, expecting the volcano to erupt, and that international peace negotiations might be easier.

"Silly boy, he has more potential than that. Suppose if that's what he wants, he better do it. If he wants to lower himself to be a manual labourer, how can I stop him? I suppose it also means it won't cost us anything much to support him. Good."

ↃↃↃ

MIRIAM AND EMMA strolled along an estuary path leading out of a small village on the Essex coast. They wanted to stay with Ruth, but she wrote to say that Tony had come back from Germany, and because of difficulties between him and his mother, was staying with her. Ruth suggested they might be more comfortable elsewhere. Tony was struggling and needed her. The sky was clear with bright sunshine and Miriam noticed the sun's reflection as it danced on the water. She drew Emma's attention to its gentle lapping as it caught shafts of sunlight on its peaks. The inlet was shallow and the silt below the surface so dark that even in full daylight it didn't reflect the blue expanse above. Swans and ducks bobbed, floating through the beams of sunlight breaking the water's rhythm.

Emma pointed out the gulls swooping above the estuary that drew her eyes past the harbour lights near the flood gates protecting the village, to the tall ghostly mooring poles standing in the silt alongside a jetty.

Beyond the warning lanterns they saw evidence of boat building, but this side was where private boats moored, their lanyards clinking in the wind. The empty sound invaded Emma's thoughts, reminding her of Holloway, hollow lives and hollow relationships.

"Is something the matter?" asked Miriam in response to an involuntary sigh from Emma.

"Not really. It's wonderful here with you, relaxing, but that hollow sound reminds me how lucky I am."

"Lucky? How?"

"Having you in my life. Work is difficult at the moment because of war fever. It's tiring. I couldn't manage without you, now more than ever."

"That makes me happy. Your sigh suggested more?"

"I was reflecting on why we're here. About Tony, Ruth, his mother. About his time in Germany. How life deals out problems. How we handle them. We have each other and our relationship has survived despite it. Tony seems sad and angry."

"That's a lot of reflecting. What provoked it?"

"I wondered about us. We talked about changing jobs and living together, but I've always been nervous about finding different work, wondering what I might do. Maybe we left it too late. Holloway is all I've ever known. If war does come, the chance will evaporate. We'll need to wait till it's over."

"I was thinking that. I'm frightened to make changes at the moment. Don't regret what we've done, but we must carry on the way we are for now."

"I hoped you felt like that. It might be easier if we weren't who we are, but it will be ages before anything gets better for us."

"Times like this make people more suspicious, not less. We need to be careful."

"I suppose we should be thankful we live in England and not Germany, from what I hear."

CƷ CƷ CƷ

"DUDLEY, IT LOOKS as if The Leader's 'Britons Fight for Britain only' campaign is vindicated. He was right about the Sudetenland, and his claim that British soldiers shouldn't be sacrificed."

"Chamberlain agreed that the Czechs refusing to recognise Hitler's moral claims has threatened the peace."

"That's why he had to sign the Munich agreement."

"It's working out as The Leader predicted. September 1938 will go down in history as the month he achieved his breakthrough. I'm glad I finished that article 'J'Accuse – Failure of the Women's Movement'. It's being published in *Action* as part of the publicity. It criticizes those warmongering women I am always complaining about. Here – read the first two paragraphs."

"NOW that the 'Pride, Pomp and Circumstance of Glorious War' has passed into the shadows and breathing space returns, the reputation of organized political women stands before the bar of public opinion awaiting judgment.

At a moment of supreme crisis, when the whole world trembled on the brink of disaster; what were the women of Britain doing to denounce the madness of a war, which Democracy up to a few days ago was working overtime to bring about?"

"It's good – as always, Norah, you get straight to the point."

Cʒ Cʒ Cʒ

EMMA AND MIRIAM went to the cinema to see a romantic comedy *The Divorce of Lady X* staring Merle Oberon and Laurence Olivier. They enjoyed films like this, light-hearted escapes from everyday life. But discussion on the way home was not about the film, but the Pathé newsreel before it, showing Chamberlain returning from Munich with the agreement signed by Hitler guaranteeing 'Peace in Our Time'. The newspapers were full of praise for Chamberlain with phrases like 'One man saved us from the greatest war of all'.

"Do you reckon it means peace?" asked Emma.

"Who knows? Chamberlain and his cronies seem convinced, along with the press and lots of others. Mosley must be pleased. Mrs Elam as well."

"People say Chamberlain should get the Nobel Peace Prize."

"They'll wait for a bit to see what happens."

"Everyone believes Hitler is lying when he says he has no more ambitions in Europe. If that's true, it means war will come whatever occurs."

"Most suspect it will – that what's going on now is delaying it."

"Many say the Munich Agreement is buying time to re-arm. I read somewhere that's what Churchill thinks."

"It makes my head spin. Perhaps it's me, or is everyone confused?"

"I'm not worried if YOUR head spins. I hope the politician's heads aren't spinning."

"What do you suppose the politicians should do?"

"Nor sure. At the moment they seem to be ignoring it and hoping it will go away."

"I suppose we better make the most of peace while it lasts."

γ γ γ

NORAH'S EUPHORIA EVAPORATED. Within six months Hitler's army invaded the rest of Czechoslovakia and he tore up the Munich agreement. The British government, together with France, vowed to support Poland. The situation collapsed so fast Norah found herself unable to grasp the immediate implications.

"This is terrible, Dudley. It's impossible that Hitler reneged on Munich. They must have provoked him. War seems inevitable. The Leader's efforts failed. I agree with him when he said '…any Englishman who won't fight for Britain is a coward, but that any Englishman who wants to fight for Poland is a fool'."

As 1938 shuffled into 1939, Norah became busier

than ever. Although war seemed imminent, she carried on supporting The Leader's attempts to secure peace. *If we rally people to the cause*, she thought, *he will emerge as the natural leader. Thank goodness he can use the offices at the London and Provincial Anti-Vivisection Society, where Barry Domvile and Archibald Ramsey feel safe meeting.* She was in conference with Dudley and Mary, comparing notes.

"The latest meeting went well."

"The momentum to get the various patriotic societies working together seems to be succeeding."

"The problem is The Leader's hesitancy. He's concerned it might be counterproductive if he becomes the centre of such a group."

"He's worried about government spies – is being careful who he speaks to and when."

"It's good our offices are secure."

"Have they found a hall for the peace rally in July?"

"Earls Court. I can't wait. It's going to be thrilling. Twenty to thirty thousand are expected."

Everyone came on the day. Norah took her seat amongst the Domviles, the Fullers, Lady Redesdale and the rest of The Leader's family. A trumpet fanfare announced the opening of the rally. Norah's heart went into overdrive. She hoped it didn't show on her face. Composure was vital. She watched the BU drum corps lead massed flags and honour standards down the aisle and join in shouting 'MOSLEY' as his name echoed around the hall. Quiet descended when The Leader appeared in a dark suit, black shirt and tie. After a dramatic pause, he commenced his lone march to the podium. The cheering was so loud Norah thought the roof would collapse. When he got to the plinth, he raised his hand and silence fell. Every nerve ending in Norah's body responded to the rise and fall of his voice. The speech resembled gold dust sprinkling wisdom and strength. The waves of applause that greeted parts of his delivery meant that he had to halt sometimes, but his words branded themselves onto Norah's memory.

"My friends, can we conceive of a policy of greater insanity, heading more straight for suicide, than this; to be prepared to fight a world war over a few acres which do not belong to us, but to make a present to the whole of mankind of the land which was won by the sweat, blood and heroism of our forefathers?"

When Randolph Churchill and others walked out, Norah believed this confirmed the ignorance of the old guard. She labelled them contemptible and dismissed them from her thoughts, concentrating on The Leader's words. Although Norah thought she'd been through every emotion it was possible to experience, his final comments inspired her to face anything.

"To the dead heroes of Britain in sacred union we say – like you we give ourselves to England: across the ages that divide us – across the glories of Britain that unite us – we gaze into your eyes and we give you this holy vow: We will be true – today, tomorrow and forever – England lives!"

It had been two hours of pure emotion. Norah felt elated and exhausted. The Leader delivered a consummate speech full of pathos, funny moments and sarcasm, timed to perfection. What a master of oratory. Her attempts, though praised many times, bowed in recognition to a man with far greater skill. She held the attention of large crowds, male and female, when younger, but this was different. She would remember the day as a high point for a long time.

෫ ෫ ෫

EMMA AND MIRIAM entertained Ruth in London. Ruth had acquired tickets to the Earls Court Peace Rally from Mrs Elam, and they were going. They made the most of Ruth's rare visit and spent time visiting the sights and enjoying themselves. The day of the rally, Miriam developed nerves. Attending a fascist rally was like Daniel entering the lions' den. Despite her anxiety, Miriam determined to support Emma who still said that every side of the argument should be rehearsed. Miriam was sensitive to Ruth and Emma's personal losses, knowing that the pain never goes away. It becomes less sharp.

The crowds were large, threatening and not well-controlled. This was the largest fascist rally in London for some time, and everyone wanted to be there. Following the Public Order Act, the BU found it hard to secure venues. Miriam suggested this had good and bad aspects. While she hated them having a public stage, the more the idiots spouted idiocy, the sooner the world would realise they were idiots. After anxious jostling and pushing they found their seats. They scanned the platform for Mr and Mrs Elam. They spotted her sitting in the front row near Mosley's family. "She's got herself in there," whispered Ruth to Emma.

Emma sensed Miriam shudder and attempted a discrete reach for her hand as the trumpet fanfares sounded and the BU drum corps led in the flags and banners. They endured an awful moment when the shouting of Mosley's name echoed around the hall. Not wanting to join in, they didn't know what to do. They relaxed as they noticed people around them hadn't joined in either. Mosley appeared dressed in the black outfit that replaced his uniform. As he marched to the platform, Miriam wondered if Emma was thinking the same as her, "Thank heaven that dreadful uniform is banned, although it doesn't make the procession or his arrival any less threatening."

Afterwards they discussed phrases that stuck in their minds.

"Thought that would never end," said Emma. "Must be the longest two hours of my life."

"Randolph Churchill made the best argument by walking out."

"Did you listen that rubbish Mosley spouted? What did he say? 'A million Britons shall never die in your Jews' quarrel'," said Miriam. "Then he threatened a revolution to sweep politicians from power."

"That terrifies me."

"I agree."

"He may be right about censorship though."

"You mean his rants about newspapers' vested interests and how they '….impose undemocratic censorship….' At least that's what I think he said. I got a bit muddled."

"It sounded confused. Perhaps that's because I hope he never comes to power."

"Let's hope so. Tonight has convinced me he doesn't have the answer, despite his support for peace."

"He wants peace because he doesn't want to fight Hitler, not because he believes in peace for its own sake."

Emma and Miriam were busier than ever at work. Irrespective of hopes for peace, staff training in civil defence and air raid precautions took place, while air raid shelters had to be got ready. Emma observed with a heavy heart. She and Miriam relied on each other more than ever. Evacuation procedures had to be put in place, and that involved both of them. If war was declared, prisoners within three months of the end of their sentence would be discharged. When that did happen in September, two hundred women and girls benefited. While Miriam was happy for them, she felt overwhelmed. Families had to be visited, arrangements made for prisoners to be welcomed home – or not in some cases – and alternative accommodation found for the homeless. Emma got embroiled in preparations for the seventy long-term inmates being sent, together with staff, to Aylesbury Prison, forty miles from London. Emma and Miriam watched them go, despatched with haste, while they remained at Holloway. New Defence Regulations, including 18B, came in from the beginning of September. Emma sat through the briefing explaining them. It seemed endless at the time, but their importance registered fully when she and Miriam discussed them afterwards. The Regulations allowed the government to suspend *Habeas Corpus* and intern suspected Nazi sympathisers, taking away the prisoner's right to see their case taken before a judge. This was serious. No sooner did the regular inmates depart, than enemy aliens arrived, many arrested for being foreigners. They soon became known among the prison officers as the 18Bs.

Emma and Miriam caught up with each other in the wardresses' room. Both were tired and exhausted and looking forward to free time.

"What chaos. These so called 'alien' women are a challenge. Many of them are hostile and angry. I don't blame them."

"Arrests seem to be indiscriminate. When you talk to them, you discover some escaped Nazi persecution, to end up in here."

"It must be hard. I remember my grandparents and parents would talk about fleeing Eastern Europe, and how disorientating and shattering they found it. To think the place you come to for refuge sees you as a threat."

"We are trying to persuade them to work with us and not resist prison routine. It's hard. Patient persuasion will take time. I wish the staff would exercise more understanding and tolerance, but they often make it worse."

"We've a lot to do. Let's hope we can make their lives easier. It would be helpful if the volume of arrests slowed down."

"Women get thrown together that shouldn't be. It's taking time to understand the sensitivities of the various groups. We're used to receiving prostitutes and drunks. These are different – like the suffragettes. We still haven't learned."

"It is a shame they didn't build it into the training. Some of our more insensitive colleagues failed to see the significance."

CB CB CB

"LOOK, DUDLEY, LOOK," said Norah holding out a picture frame that arrived by post.

"What is it?"

"A photograph of Diana Mosley, signed and dedicated to me."

"How thoughtful – you must be pleased."

"I am. Diana noticed my hard work at that dinner party The Leader held after the peace rally."

"You had a long chat with her."

"I enquired after Unity and the rest of the family. It doesn't take much, but pays rewards, as you can see from the note she has sent."

"You and Mary worked the guests. Did you get Lady Domvile and Annabel Jackson to offer to host At Homes?"

"I lined up a lot of people with offers of venues and help. We need to move the secret meetings around so the authorities can't follow who meets when and where."

"We are summoned to a meeting with The Leader. He's making contingency plans in case war is declared."

A few days later Norah and Dudley attended a gathering of the inner circle. The Leader laid out his plans. Norah got given a letter signed 'Oswald Mosley', stating 'Mrs Elam had his full confidence, and entitled to do what she thought fit in the interests of the Movement on her own responsibility'. The document spelled out her duties. She had permission to move funds and hide them in the Anti-Vivisection Society accounts for a period before or after war was declared. This would keep money out of the hands of the authorities, so the Movement might operate if The Leader were to be imprisoned or assassinated. Dudley's contained the same wording and indicated he was one of eight men The Leader trusted to take over running the BU if he could not. Dudley received a list of the other seven men handed a similar document. Norah was flattered that The Leader invested so much trust in her, and determined to live up to his expectations.

Shortly after on 1 September 1939 she received a

reminder of how timely The Leader's actions had been — Hitler marched his troops into Poland.

November and December became frantic with meetings of the Mosley-Ramsay-Domvile group and the proposed collaboration. In December, Norah attended a luncheon arranged by Mary for BU women at the Carlton Club. Diana Mosley and Annabel Jackson attended as well as Viscountess Downe and Lady Howard. Mary addressed the meeting, calling for a negotiated peace. At the end of the meeting, they drank a toast to The Leader, who they believed the only man capable of uniting and leading the right-wing patriotic societies.

Not long after Mary's luncheon, Norah and Dudley were at home when the police arrived to search their flat. Norah's indignation knew no bounds, but with Dudley in a separate room she had no one to rant at except the policemen guarding her. They kept telling her it would be better if she cooperated, but she resisted, glaring at them and shouting, "How dare you?" "Who do you think you are?" "By what right do you this to me? You are a load of filthy bully boys, sent to subdue an old woman, who you are frightened of. I am a veteran at this. Have experience of the worst men like you can do. Was force-fed and tortured for my convictions as a suffragette. Don't think you frighten me." The amused grins some officers tried to hide infuriated her more when she caught glimpses of them.

Norah and Dudley were taken under escort to her

offices at the LPAVS, where a forensic search also took place. Papers got taken away. Norah overheard them discussing the envelope found in her desk containing The Leader's authority to act as she believed necessary in the BU's interests. What excited them was that they found it in an envelope addressed 'Private and Personal, Mrs Dacre Fox'. They asked Norah to identify Mrs Dacre Fox. In her haughtiest tone Norah stated, "Mr Dacre Fox was my first husband." She hoped this would satisfy them and stifle further questions. She knew it to be a pseudonym for her and Dudley in connection with the secret meetings. Norah realised the police knew more than she suspected, and caught an upside-down glimpse of a note made on the file into which the envelope got bundled, 'Investigate name further'.

Dudley was concerned. Tony arrived for a Christmas visit while Norah seethed for days after her arrest and release, venting anger and frustration on everyone. Meal times became hell. Every day, Tony and Norah argued. Tony went out to avoid his parents as much as possible, but Norah insisted he attend meals. She never once relented, even though they always ended with angry scenes.

"Tony, what are you staring at?"

"Why – what do you care?"

"Show respect. I'm your mother."

"Why? You never showed any to me or my father."

"What did you say? Speak up. Why can't you be polite and hold an intelligent conversation instead of responding with grunts?"

"You don't care what I say. Why don't you go back to ignoring me like you have most of my life, except when you want a punch bag?"

"What do you mean? I only ever considered your best interests. Discipline is necessary in everyone's life, whether you approve or not?"

"I see – discipline is what you call it when it applies to me – but when the police come calling dishing it out because of your obsession with 'The Leader', it's intimidation and bully boy tactics."

"Dudley, tell Tony to treat me with more respect."

"Why drag him into it? He's another of your punch bags, accepting blame for everything to placate you. You insisted on following your 'destiny' with your political career. Now you're holding us to account for your stubborn selfishness."

The angry tones kept rising and often resulted in Norah grabbing a knife and chasing Tony round the table, with Dudley trying to intervene. Dudley suggested Tony leave if Ruth would take him in Northchapel and experienced relief when she agreed. He and Norah needed to concentrate on what was coming; this thing with Tony proved an unnecessary distraction.

Norah's rearrest came on 23rd January 1940. After her release she reported at length in angry outbursts to Dudley. Sudden reminders would jog her and she would shudder and shout fragments of statements from the questioning. Norah would then get angry with Dudley because he found it difficult to follow the gist of her frustrations, or what it related to in the context of the questioning.

"What did they ask you about?"

"They seemed to concentrate on three things."

"Which were?"

"The letters I posted to Peter Whinfield in Germany on Muriel's behalf."

"Interesting – perhaps they believe he is a spy. What else?"

"They asked about our marital status. That came out of the name 'Mrs Dacre Fox' that The Leader put on my envelope."

"What did you tell them?"

"I repeated that Dacre Fox had been my first husband's name."

"The third thing?"

"They were aware of my bankruptcy. Seemed suspicious about my financial competence, suggesting I was some kind of criminal mastermind. Asked about whether the Anti-Vivisection Society served as a conduit for funds coming from Europe. They want to prove The Leader got money from Mussolini, and whether that was the source of the cash I handled."

"What did you tell them?"

"I denied everything."

"You better arrange to see the Leader and report on

your questioning so he's prepared if they visit him."

MI5 did visit Mosley about information gathered during the raids and questioning of Norah and Dudley. Afterwards The Leader briefed Dudley and his deputies. Dudley reported to Norah.

"The Leader pronounced himself pleased to be prepared for MI5 by your briefing."

"What else did he say?"

"He said you had his full confidence. He authorised you to handle funds if war was declared and he became incapacitated, so that the organisation might continue."

"Did he think they left satisfied?"

"Who knows? Once these people get ideas they don't let them drop. He said he told them that nothing illegal or improper had occurred with regard to funds, only what was necessary in case of an air raid, or his headquarters being unable to function etc."

"What else did The Leader report?"

"He got the impression their main concern related to your connections with the Whinfields – in particular Peter Whinfield's relationship with the Krugers. I suppose that's because of those letters you posted to Peter from Muriel."

"Why?"

"The Leader thinks they suspect Kruger is a spy, and that Peter Whinfield worked with him. The Leader admitted he met the Krugers at our flat, but had no idea what MI5 could be talking about, insisting Kruger couldn't be a spy. He told them he considered Kruger a scholarly man, who wrote a scholarly tome about the Jews, that was all."

"We need to be careful. Things are reaching a crisis."

With the arrest and questioning, Norah could no longer make meeting facilities available. She contacted Annabel Jackson and arranged with her to host the collaborative meetings between The Leader, Domvile and Ramsay during February, March and April. Norah, Dudley and Mary attended every meeting. It was obvious to The Leader and those around him that their time was close, and they had to be prepared. Plans existed to pull the disparate groups together and ensure a large secret revolutionary organisation ready to march to power by armed force. Norah's concern, expressed to Dudley after her questioning, was that she wished they might get on with it. Events moved fast. Unless you stayed in the lead, you'd end up behind.

The BU annual lunch at the Criterion at the beginning of March buoyed Norah up. She enjoyed this luncheon every year, but this one was special. The Leader was to address five hundred guests, and Mary was to come out as a BU member with a seat of honour. Everyone who was anyone came, and Norah listened to The Leader's speech in rapture. It was full of the anti-Semitic, anti-war and pro-German rhetoric she needed to hear after her encounters with the authorities. She left on a high, believing that nothing would stand in the way of The Leader and his followers in the quest to return sensible government to Britain through fascism.

The hammer blow crushing those dreams fell on 23 May 1940.

 CB CB CB

CHAPTER 10

War and Habeas Corpus

EMMA GRABBED A break in the officer's duty room. She'd been briefed a short while ago on the arrival of the new prisoners and wanted to relax while she waited to be told that the Black Maria had arrived. It would be busy for hours once that happened and she craved a quick cup of tea to prepare herself. Yesterday's briefing covered the expanded Defence Regulations 18B. She'd been lectured on the basic regulations last year. The talk about Habeas Corpus made her head hurt. Real old Latin words – Miriam called them obscure – but their meaning and impact would have an enormous effect on everyone in Holloway. As far as she saw, whatever Miriam said they meant, in practical terms they involved a lot of work. Her memory would be tested to its limits. As well as guarding the prisoners, part of her duties with these prisoners involved listening to everything said, writing it down, and handing reports to the Governor to file with whoever. Miriam description for 'whoever' was that they were one of those invisible entities that spawn and grow limbs during times of crisis.

Holloway was ready to receive the first batch of BU fascist women. Since last September, a few hard core Nazis had been detained, German and Austrian, although naturalised British citizens. On receiving her orders, Emma realised Mrs Elam would be amongst this first group of British born traitors today. How strange? They'd crossed paths over the years due to Ruth's involvement with Tony, but she was sure Mrs Elam wouldn't realise how much Emma knew about her, or how closely she and Miriam had followed her career.

She was sixteen when she first got involved in force-feeding Mrs Elam. Emma wore a different uniform then and was called 'wardress' not 'officer'. Would Mrs Elam remember her? What would she do if she did? How would she react? Miriam insisted that Emma hadn't changed, apart from being older than when they first met. Others told her the same. But this was different, and Emma knew she had to control her nervous anticipation and remain professional.

As for Holloway itself, she was never sure how much relaxing the rules changed the place; to her it remained much the same. The walls had been painted white, but conditions continued unaltered or, in some cases, had become worse. It survived as a Victorian prison where Victorian ghosts stalked and echoed its cells and corridors.

How peculiar it seemed. She remembered her brothers and the price they paid in the last war. Now the country found itself faced with conflict again, carving new scars into everyone's lives. Would she have met Miriam if the fighting hadn't taken Walter and the others? Who knew? It changed so much, took so many men, nothing was the same after. It didn't change that Miriam had been the best thing that happened to her. Although their private life stayed secret, the quiet place of peace and refuge they made together brought her much happiness. She wished her parents had been able to understand, but it would have been too difficult for them. She felt guilty at being unable give them grandchildren, but she wasn't the marrying sort. Ma and Pa said she married her work. They never suspected about Miriam.

Her last chat with Miriam took place during one of those hurried evenings that now constituted their lives. Long hours of work because of staff shortages meant little personal time, and what free time they got together seemed to be wasted talking work.

"It's been a tiring week, Miriam. I wonder if we'll ever get control again. The chaos seems to go on forever."

"The secrecy requirements make it more difficult than usual. We're denied access to political prisoners. I understand it, but they still have families – some of them young children – who are suffering."

"It reminds me of when them suffragettes first came. No one was ready for how it turned out. I remember force-feeding them women. It was about then I took to wondering 'bout myself."

"The rules didn't help then either. Despite being relaxed, they've reinstated them because of the crisis." Miriam's deep sigh made Emma glance up at her lover, where she read the concern registered in the creases on her forehead.

"In suffragette days, we got told never to look in a prisoner's eyes, never to answer to anythin' they said. Stopped us feeling anythin' for them – took away their dignity. That's the one thing as has never changed."

"That's why you caught my eye," said Miriam. "I saw compassion in you and it was one of the things I liked."

"You taught me to be interested in how women got here, show 'em I cared and wanted to help, but keeping limits. It was hard."

"Everyone's being tested now. The press is full of the army retreat to Dunkirk. We're terrified the Germans will invade."

"We're expectin' lots more prisoners, but don't know when."

Emma's musings were abruptly ended by someone announcing that the prisoners had arrived. She better get on with it, then. There were four BU women: Mrs Elam, Mrs Whinfield, Mrs Brock-Griggs and Mrs Olive Hawks. As prominent BU leaders they were part of, or privy to the secrets of, the inner high command. As dangerous traitors she'd to start recording every word they uttered from the moment of arrival. This was going to be interesting. Mrs Elam deprived of civil liberties.

What a twist of fate! In 1914, Mrs Dacre Fox, as she called herself then, wanted to be a First Division political prisoner. Claimed it as her democratic right. Wanted the privileges that went with being First Division. It was denied then, but now here she was detained as a political prisoner, suspected of being an enemy of the democracy she battled for as a suffragette. She would get privileges now, but not the same as back then. Wonder what she'll reckon to 'em now?

Emma spent the following few hours overseeing arrival, initial processing, admission and assignment to a cell. The shortage of cells would be aggravatin' all round. Couldn't be helped; it would settle down – it always did.

"She recognised me straight off," said Emma, the next chance she got to talk to Miriam.

"Been surprised if she hadn't."

"She looked at me with a cross between a scowl and an amused grin. Didn't say anything to me. I gave her a strict look. Enough to put her off tryin'."

"I'm sure she found it hard to curb her tongue."

"Didn't bother. Talked out loud to anyone within earshot, about how she'd been in Holloway as a suffragette – that the torturers who force-fed her then was still here."

"You must've been tempted to say something."

"Not really, put it in me notes. Them's the orders, but in a funny way doing that helps me get over horrible things the prisoners shout."

The next weeks proved more onerous than Emma imagined. She toiled long shifts. Large numbers of detainees arrived and they had no time to sort out separate accommodation. Political prisoners got mixed with remand criminals. They set up such howls of protest they must've been heard outside Holloway's walls. Did war make it worse? Maybe it came from the general mood of fear and distrust that hung about everywhere. Big battles outside, bigger ones inside. The 18Bs never stopped going on about how they weren't convicted felons and shouldn't have to share cells with common scum who were. Emma took a lot of abuse. She ignored it. They was lettin' off steam. Although she polished up a hard shell over her years of service, some comments still stung. What she'd to remember was to stick to duty and not show feelings. During the worst moments, she'd think of Miriam, who taught her that they were mere words. She'd the upper hand and ways to exert discipline. She had to be strong. Some 18Bs ended up sharing cells with aliens. Emma thought this bad, for the aliens not the 18Bs, who were capable of showing their dislike with slurs new even to her – and she reckoned to have heard it all down the years – but there was nothing to be done, except carry out orders. She never lost that intuitive suspicion that nagged away since she started here that they were all prisoners of Holloway's pecking order.

Over the months, another sixty or so females arrived, including Lady Diana Mosley, Lady Domville and Lady Howard. No special arrangements existed for these women, despite 'em having grand titles. Treated same as other prisoners, they was. Wasn't a problem, but she felt sorry for Lady Mosley nursing her newborn. Ten weeks old, the baby was. The child went to stay with relatives, and Lady M to see the doctor with her painful swollen breasts. That would be uncomfortable for any woman. But then Emma reminded herself that other Holloway inmates didn't get any choice; there weren't no exceptions. It was something that seemed hard no matter who the prisoner was.

Cells were small and shared. Loss of privacy was part of the punishment. Some prisoners had to put up with a temporary straw mattress on the floor with dirty blankets from storage. The terrible smells from the lack of toilets clung to the nostrils. The slopping-out areas were often awash with faeces and urine because the drains became blocked. It was something Emma never got used to. It haunted her dreams. Food rations were meagre and because of the numbers, yard exercise was thirty minutes a day. So there were long periods of lock-up and lights-out.

"Wish other officers wouldn't provoke 18Bs," said Emma in another snatched conversation with Miriam.

"Is it a big problem?"

"Some are real nasty. No shame. Don't seem to realise it makes 'em as bad as them they're guarding."

"They have control, so why do it?"

"If what's said is true, the women is traitors, but

they haven't been up before the beak. Isn't he the only one can say who's guilty or innocent?"

"They're paying a heavy price for their beliefs, that's for sure."

"I agree with 'em that soldiers shouldn't die without good reason, but my good reason is different from theirs. Doesn't make me want to treat 'em bad, though."

☙ ☙ ☙

RUTH HEARD THE knock on the front door. Who might that be at this time of night? How did they find her in the blackout? She opened the door.

"Tony, what on earth are you doing here?"

"Can I stay for a bit?"

"Wondered if you would come. After your parents' arrest, I got the spare room ready."

"Didn't know where else to go. Been fired. Had a hell of a time getting here."

"Come in. Close the door in case the light attracts attention. Have you eaten? I'm sure we can find something despite rations. By the look of you, you need rest."

Ruth didn't know whether to be grateful that his exhaustion had robbed him of the ability to talk. She got some peremptory answers to questions about how he got to her, which involved a lot of walking. Otherwise he communicated little, grunts and shoulder shrugs being about all he managed. Ruth watched helpless as he sat in front of her cracking his knuckles and chewing the inside of his cheek. He fidgeted and kept rubbing his jaw or the back of his neck. Ruth wanted to hug him but his slumped shoulders and downcast eyes made her conscious that would be unwelcome. Ruth saw he wanted reassurance, but at the same time his moodiness pushed her away. He played with the food she gave him and every mouthful he took looked as if it tasted of sand. She had no idea how to comfort him. He was in a bad way and it would take time and patience to extract proper sense from him.

After he went to bed, Ruth sat down. Like everyone else, she read about the Elams' arrest in the newspapers, along with the news about Dunkirk and the Allied retreat. Everyone was anxious, angry and preparing for a German invasion. The febrile atmosphere invaded every part of life. War hit everyone hard, with food and petrol rationed, and suspicion rife. A few days ago there was an incident. Captain M, the BU District Leader for Chichester, who lived in the village with his wife, moved his caravan to a temporary parking space on the edge of a field near the village centre. With the publicity surrounding the arrests, some men got it into their heads that Captain M and his missus were spies and that the caravan was transmitting signals to German aircraft. They decided to set fire to it to stop the German bombs they believed would drop on them if they did nothing. No one got harmed, but it did highlight the rampant fear and paranoia.

The following morning, preparing breakfast with

the sparse household rations, Ruth prepared to listen to Tony. It was going to be difficult. He slept badly and his emotions fluctuated, much like the country, which seemed to be on a rollercoaster, frenzied one day, miserable the next. Ruth watched, unhappy, as one moment she saw a fiery, angry flash in his eyes, then abrupt deflation signalled by a slump of his head and shoulders. Then he would remember something – some humiliation he had suffered – his fists would clench, and the veins on the back of his hands would bulge bright blue. Ruth had never seen him so defeated and frustrated. It would take all her resources to help him.

"Come on, Tony, tell me what happened?"

"Don't know where to start. Everything is ruined. I won't be able to get another apprenticeship. I enjoyed this one and did well, apart from a few fisticuffs with some of the other men."

"Start at the beginning?"

"It was the newspaper headlines. At first I reckoned that if I kept quiet, no one would realise it was my parents who they arrested."

"So what do you think alerted them?"

"No idea. Got called to the main site office. The manager knew who I was, handed me my papers and said I wasn't needed."

"Did you ask why?"

"I tried to, but then he got nasty."

"What did he say?"

"That the authorities were aware of me and if I left

without a fuss, nothing more would be said."

"Nothing else?"

"Said I had fascist sympathies, that he wouldn't be surprised if I was a traitor as well and he wanted rid of me. If the police or military did come, he wanted to say I'd gone, so they had no excuse to search his premises."

"That seems pretty definite."

"Why can't I get out from under her shadow? Her whole life has been one long selfish thing after another – sod everyone else. Why was I born? She hated me from the beginning. When she ranted about politicians and dirty Jews in front of me, I used to think she thought I was one of them and wanted to treat me the way she did them."

"I'm sorry, Tony. I understand your upset, but we need to decide what to do now."

"What can I do? I've nowhere to go, and no job."

Ruth had a plan, but wanted to investigate before saying anything. Last year, Mr Elam visited and told her he'd been preparing in case war came. He gave her a letter granting authority to act on his behalf together with a key to the London flat. He'd paid advance rent for several years. Although difficulties intervened, Ruth managed to contact the authorities and found out that if Tony presented himself with the proper papers, he would be allowed to take up residence.

"Tony, I have solved part of your problem. You're going to live in your parents' flat. The servant has agreed to return so you'll be looked after."

"How did you manage that?"

"Your father had the foresight to make plans. I've managed to put them into action."

"I've been so worried about my father," said Tony. "She deserves everything she gets, but my father's been ill. Not sure how to find out how he is. Might be easier in London."

"You'll also benefit from being anonymous. In Northchapel, even though you've not lived here for a while, you are known about, and people talk."

ভ ভ ভ

DUDLEY ARRIVED AT Brixton in the Black Maria shocked and numb. This was something alien – he never expected to experience anything like it. He had no idea how to control his emotions. His usual props were unavailable, added to which his health was indifferent. The doctor diagnosed mild heart disease. At his age it might be anticipated, but despite advice to rest and take things easier, Norah's pace of life did not allow that.

From bits and pieces of information he distilled, he realised that he faced internment, without charge, as a potential traitor, with his civil liberties suspended. The full horror worked its way through his consciousness when he learned that The Leader had also been arrested, together with most of the BU hierarchy. Dudley's first thoughts, as always, turned on his duty to others. What if the other seven men who, like him, had received letters from The Leader, were rounded up? Who would run things? Not knowing made it difficult and he ruminated on headquarters routines, what he should be doing and who would be doing it in his absence.

After immediate processing and assignment to a small cell, in conditions that he never imagined human beings having to endure, it dawned on him what it meant. As he lay on his straw mattress the first night, with his cell companion making the most amazing noises during his sleep, Dudley experienced physical and mental pain. He visualised his memento mori and beloved library and the things that gave him comfort, worried about whether they would be confiscated or destroyed. He comforted himself with the idea that perhaps those in charge of carrying out the orders to arrest him would not be so barbaric. Memories of Hitler ordering the burning of books before the war flooded his mind. Surely the English authorities wouldn't do anything like that? England was a civilised place, where literature and free speech were valued. Weren't they?

Dudley realised how little he had worked through the consequences of what Norah proposed. He had no strength to withstand the long arguments that always ensued, something which had been truer of late. He allowed himself to be carried along on the tide. Although angry at those he believed undermined the country's greatness, his was not a nature bent on revenge the same way as Norah. Even then, despite threatening much, sometimes physically, most of her destructive power lay in words and the way she turned them into missiles.

After a few days, he asked permission to write to The Leader. The authorities agreed. He was pleased to be able to express to The Leader his sorrow at what happened and to say how he hoped their plight would not last long. After this, Dudley got transferred to Stafford Prison.

CR CR CR

NORAH ARRIVED IN the Black Maria overflowing with her usual indignation and anger at the idiot authorities, who didn't understand who they had arrested. They'd be sorry when they realised what fools they made of themselves. That must be why they left her in the holding cage for ages waiting to be processed. Too ashamed to come and sort her out. Some lackey brought her a mug of cocoa and a couple of slices of bread and margarine. How dare they put that disgusting axle grease on her bread? She couldn't bring herself to eat it. Not having an implement to scrape the vile filth off, she went hungry. It had been hours and she got cold. Didn't they care? Would she have to spend the night in this dreadful enclosure with its wire mesh roof?

At last they commenced their admission routine. How degrading, being fingerprinted, weighed and having to answer questions by that idiot doctor. She recalled Dr Forward, the torturer from her suffragette days. Still at it, subjecting women to disgraceful indignities. Did she look like she might be pregnant, have VD, head lice or scabies? Couldn't the fool see she was a woman of some standing? The whole time, that Baxter woman oversaw the process. She remembered her the moment she saw her. How could you forget someone who held you down and forced a filthy tube down your throat? Then she'd popped up in the village, with that Miriam woman, related to Nanny by all accounts. *Wonder if that Miriam person works here now?* Whatever this Baxter woman has been up to, prison life hasn't done much for her. Might be in charge, but she is still thin and mean-looking. *Prison life must have killed her ambition, that's why she's here resembling a dried up old prune.* The one good thing about Officer Baxter was that she was an adversary Norah understood well. She wouldn't be frightened by her; would do anything necessary to let Officer Baxter realise that no one was in charge of Norah unless Norah allowed them to be. *'No compromise, bully back'* was my slogan then and shall be now.

Determined to display defiance, she took every opportunity to inform prison officials, and anyone within earshot, of her opinion on the suspension of her civil liberties. If she was a criminal, why didn't they put her on trial? No, they'd no evidence, so the cowards decided to punish her anyway and incarcerate her for loving her country, wanting peace, and the best for its women. This was little different from the torture they inflicted during her suffragette days. They wanted her to recant and deny what she believed in. She posed no danger to the system, they did. She soon realised that the officers in charge had instructions to ignore her. If that was the case, she had to pick her battles; otherwise she'd exhaust herself and become ill. But whatever they did, she would never give up complaining about her loss of privacy and the dreadful damp, unhygienic conditions.

Lock up at night was the worst part. Nothing altered except that they had painted the walls white. When that metal door, with no handle on the inside, slammed shut, she cringed as visions from the past flooded her thoughts. She longed for knowledge of Dudley and wondered about his living circumstances. How could he bear it? He'd not been well, how would he cope? He'd not been to prison before like her. At least she was ready, understood what to expect. Having to lie down on the narrow plank bed was hateful. The coarse, grey-stained sheet and blankets got changed once a month and were disgusting. It proved impossible to get comfortable or to sleep. If unconsciousness did come, she found herself troubled by dreams of Papa. Some of those turned into nightmares, where she experienced the crack of a whip across her face and tubes being forced down her throat. She would wake pained and exhausted. These visions became muddled in her mind and sometimes Papa would look like the prison doctor and she would come to dazed and cold, angry with herself for letting them make her feel this way. Other dreams, while not nightmares, nevertheless featured Papa. One of the most annoying concerned Papa as he stood in an Irish bog. She stood beside him while he laughed, comparing her hopes, political ideals and principles to a quagmire and taunted her, "Well, my girl where are they now, these things you say you have been fighting for? Got trampled underfoot, it looks like, and will only be good for making peat fires."

Then came that night. The horror of bombing raids came accompanied by the freedom after lights-out to join friends in their cells. One blessing at least. But then came the constant nagging worry, wanting to learn whether Brixton had been hit, if Dudley and The Leader were safe. The women huddled down and talked to each other about their families, wondering if they lived, and if they did, had they been made homeless by the bombs? Some of them were able to see the skyline through the filthy windows in their cells. They scraped the dirt off the panes, and reported flames leaping high in the sky every night. If you were not able see the flames, the sound of the fire engines would be enough to alert you. They got the chance to ask prison visitors about their loved ones once a week. During one of those she recognised Miriam. So that woman was still around.

Then a bomb hit the wing that contained her cell. She huddled under the plank bed in the cell she was visiting and they covered themselves in the dirty blankets, coughing from the dust and debris thrown up. Her cheek throbbing, the sound of the falling bombs reminding her of the whistling and rush of air she remembered from that whip at the end of her father's arm. She tried to expunge that vision but then found herself overwhelmed by the smells. The gas escaping from the damaged mains mixed with the reek of sewage. Broken water pipes sent water cascading down walls, accentuating the denseness of the damp smell that hung over the whole place. Then came the stench of un-washed bodies, fear making them perspire into filthy clothes already ripe from being worn day and night. It was the only way to keep warm – wear everything the whole time.

When the all clear sounded, they emerged from under their blankets and inadequate shelters to survey the damage. While huddling beneath their makeshift shelter, Norah tried to check her imagination, reasoning that if she didn't imagine the worst, the worst might not happen. The hope proved vain. Her wildest flights of fancy never did justice to what now confronted her. It took a while to find out if anyone had been killed. Searching in the rubble was as bad as any nightmare. In the end, no one died. She stopped believing in God long ago, but this happening she found herself forced to chalk up to a miracle. They spent the rest of the night trying to put out the fires, and by morning were enervated. But greater indignities awaited. Lack of space led to her ending up in a cell with cracks that let the wind whistle through and whenever rain fell, it would seep through fractures in the roof and run down the walls. For weeks they had no gas or fresh water so that drinks got rationed. She'd been right to want peace, if this was the price of war. How could anything be worth this? Nobody listened to The Leader, the only man in the country who understood what war meant. It would be agony waiting for news of Dudley. She worked her whole life to get animals and women treated with dignity and respect, and now that work was blown to pieces by this wretched war. No one had any vision any more except for destruction.

ᘓ ᘓ ᘓ

EMMA AND MIRIAM enjoyed a few days' respite. The nights drew in and the prospect of the long winter evenings seemed gloomier than ever this year. They were exhausted. German bombs fell on the city in September and every night was filled with sirens, explosions and fires. Just a couple of days ago, Emma spent the night in terror for her life at Holloway because it took a direct hit. Miriam tried to comfort her. They'd come out for a walk along the Thames. Emma stared at the water, thinking of tides and flooding, and how life could be washed away in an instant.

"Talk to me, Emma. Tell me about it so that I can help you."

"You've heard it before, but this was the worst."

"It doesn't matter, tell me. Don't worry if you repeat yourself."

"It was awful, I thought as I was on me way to heaven for sure. There's no Anderson Shelters and seeing as how we can't do proper black-out, the electric mains is switched off at five every day. We don't lock the cells and the inmates wander around trying to share and comfort each other. It don't help with having King's Cross Station along the road a bit. What with the sirens and the anti-aircraft battery down the road as well, the nights are like bedlam. Having to listen to the prisoners crying with fear and shouting out as how they're goin' to be dead if Holloway takes a direct hit ain't pleasant. Everyone's nerves is on edge. You've heard the plane engines every night, buzzing like angry wasps, then the bombs falling with that loud whistling sound, then silence for a second then the crump followed by the explosion. Then there's the fire engines and the flames what light up the sky. But this was dreadful. We took a direct hit and it was like nothing' I ever knew, nor want to know again. It tore through B wing roof, smashed landings to pieces, blew out doors and left walls crumbling. I wished it had taken E wing, that terrible place where I helped with that last hanging. I hate going there to deal with the prisoners they put there now. They reopened it because of lack of space. I realise them women are supposed to be traitors an' all, but it don't mean they ain't as terrified as everyone else when bombs start dropping on them and they can't get no news of their families in the East End."

"Oy vey. All we can thank God for is that you are alive," said Miriam.

"And that we have things to laugh about."

"Are you sure? I can't remember much to laugh about."

"I can, but you had to be there."

"What on earth are you talking about?"

"You remember. I told you about when I had to keep my face stern – couldn't laugh. You know. Mosley's forty-fourth birthday. You must remember. The Governor agreed M'Lady M might have a small party in her cell, so they organised a tea dance. You should've seen it."

"Wish I had. I bet Mrs E was there in full swing."

"Of course. Is good friends with Lady M. During their parties, makes herself heard loud and clear. Goes on about how things was when she was a suffragette, how she never gave in to their torture, and how they was afraid of her."

"How did you stop yourself laughing?"

"Thought about what to write for my Guvnor's report. For sure, the women are instructed to be careful what they say. They tell themselves that with Mosley leadin' them they won't be beat. Mrs E behaves like she was on an actin' stage."

"Why did Mrs E refuse an appeal to an Advisory Committee?" asked Miriam.

"Stubborn. Bet she got Lady M to believe she did it on principle, though. Lady M is worried about Mr Elam, what with him being sent to Stafford an' all. Maybe that is why Lady M appealed to her own Advisory Committee hearing on behalf of the Elams –

saying how Mr Elam is ill and it would be difficult if Mrs Elam got exiled to the Isle of Man."

Christmas was over. Miriam was nervous. Emma tried to calm her as she escorted her through Holloway. They were on their way to attend a prisoner with news of her family. What Miriam called the 'Holloway Discord' – clinking keys and rattling door locks – made her jittery. Through the years, Miriam learned not to let the sounds bother her, although like Emma she could never ignore them completely. But today, they sounded louder and clinkier than ever. They arrived at the meeting room to find Mrs Elam waiting. Miriam struggled with her feelings. She tried hard to block out memories of her last encounter with Mrs Elam. It was long ago, before the war, but the minute they asked her to see Mrs Elam to tell her about what happened, anger and anxiety rose to the surface in equal measure. Why? She'd nothing to be frightened of. Mrs Elam had no power now. She was a prisoner. Nevertheless, a lot of Mrs Elam's power lay in her ability to say things in a way that left you in no doubt as to how she regarded you.

"Well, well. Like old times," Norah bristled. "Except you aren't here at my invitation, although I am sure I can deliver a lecture if you'd like."

"Enjoyable as that would be," Miriam smiled, "I have come to inform you about your family."

"Why, has something happened?"

"Nothing awful. Mr Elam is released from Stafford,

and at home with Tony at your London flat."

"How is Dudley – Mr Elam –He's been ill, but I received no official news."

"He is unwell, but being cared for. Ruth, Tony's old nanny, has been there offering support."

"Well, that is some comfort. But why is Tony there?"

"Got dismissed from his apprenticeship after your arrest, and been living in the flat on his own since then."

"Nobody told me. But then it's typical. They'd no right to sack him because of my political activity. I presume that was the reason."

Emma and Miriam, ever attuned to each other, sensed that Mrs Elam was about to start delivering the lecture she threatened at the beginning. They decided to end the meeting before she got into her stride.

ᘓ ᘓ ᘓ

TONY EXPERIENCED IMMENSE relief when his father came home after release from Stafford prison, but found himself horrified in equal measure at how ill he was. He'd no idea how to begin looking after him. He was suspicious of medical men. She taught him that. You didn't go to the doctor if it was possible to avoid it; you got on with it. Doctors made you worse with their quack medicine based on filthy animal experiments. Tony was grateful that Ruth came to stay for a few weeks to help him. Thank goodness they still had a housemaid as otherwise he would be out of his depth.

Tony wandered around the flat. The uncertainties of war inflicted on civilians seemed magnified. He didn't know whether to be ashamed of his parents' activities and their notorious reputation, or whether to be proud. They taught him so much of what he believed, but now it was chaos and confusion. Everything that seemed certain was now uncertain. His misery made him unable to decided what to do about it. He tried going out for walks, but the streets seemed endless and he had no idea where to go or what he might do when he got there. Bomb and fire damage were evident everywhere. That increased his misery. He had no purpose, and no idea of how to guess what the future might hold. He decided to get drunk as often as possible.

"What you doin' here, mate?" Tony looked across the bar and stared the questioner in the face.

"Having a drink."

"Is that all?"

"It's a pub, what else can I do?"

"You ain't wearin' uniform."

"It's not a crime, is it? At least, not last time I looked."

"Men like you should be fightin' for your country. If you ain't in uniform, it's suspicious."

"What if I changed before I came out?"

"Anyone proud to be fightin' for the country wears his uniform."

"Look, mate, it's none of yours, so get your nose out."

"You must be a conchie coward or a misfit, otherwise you'd be wearin' your uniform."

"Like I say, it's none of yours, mind your own."

Tony left, but round the corner found three men, who gave him a good kicking. After several days of discomfort, he decided not to go out again. He existed trapped between the unrelieved gloom of the flat and his fear of the streets.

Around June they received news that his mother would not be sent to the Isle of Man. While his father expressed relief at knowing she would be nearby, his own reaction was indifference. She was to blame for his situation, and feelings of resentment against her were never far from his mind.

They were breakfasting when the maid put the post tray down on the table. Tony looked around the room. It was the first morning his father had been well enough to get up and join him. He had plenty of time to rifle through everything while there on his own. The authorities confiscated most of the fascist literature and books connected with the arrest, together with personal papers. But the portraits of two women hanging in the drawing room were left or overlooked. Tony had no way of determining which. He spent ages glaring at them, with no idea who they might be, or why his parents would want such pictures in their flat. He wanted to ask his father about them, but must wait until sure he was well enough. When the maid told him his father would be getting up for breakfast, he determined that today would be the day. He observed his father pick up the letters and rifle through them, waiting for an opportune moment. But then his father examined one envelope, turned it over and over, and from the look on his face, Tony sensed his father's unease.

"What's this? The markings on the envelope are official. It's from the army," said Dudley.

"It'll be connected with my enlistment and training in the Royal Armoured Corps. I intended to tell you. I must report on the seventeenth of July and pick up papers and travel details for Catterick Garrison in Yorkshire. Maybe that's the confirmation of my orders."

"Why did you want to enlist? This is the first indication to me of your plan. Why didn't you speak to me? I hope you aren't doing it to spite your mother?"

"As she doesn't care about me, why should she be bothered?"

"You're wrong."

"If she showed any interest, it would be to give her an excuse to accuse me of 'consorting with the enemy'. Then she'd have a go because I'm going to be a trooper and not an officer. She'd moan on about how I'm a fool for accepting a position and rank beneath her social standing."

"You know how to make her angry."

Tony concentrated on opening his letter.

"What's the problem? What's the matter?"

"The bastards are saying 'my services are no longer required'. That I shouldn't report for duty."

"Any reason?"

"They don't say."

"Why do you suspect they did that? What did you put on your enlistment forms?"

"The usual – this address, details of parents. I declined vaccination, but apart from that didn't put anything unusual."

"That must be the answer. The minute they read our names and your refusal to be vaccinated, they decided you were unsuitable."

"I couldn't lie on the forms, could I?"

"I suppose not," said Dudley. "Are you sure you didn't do it so you did get turned down? You could have put information on the forms that didn't arouse suspicion. Could have agreed to a vaccination, put Nanny's address or something."

Tony didn't know. What he did understand was that he believed himself unwanted, unfit and useless. The thing he did wrong was to be born in the first place. He'd never been able to live up to her expectations. Never got anything right. He failed at everything he tried to do. All those years of exile, he felt alone, and although he joined in and learned how to be like one of the boys, he did it so he wouldn't stand out. He wanted to please everyone and be part of the gang. But it was never good enough, never had been. His mother did not love or respect him. And he forgot to ask about the portraits.

CB CB CB

EMMA FOUND SOME of the routine of dealing with the 18Bs rewarding in a funny sort of way. That realisation came one day while reporting on prisoners' conversations to the Governor. A lot of things she noted were serious and necessary to record in detail, but other things amused, especially when she overheard Mrs Elam giving accounts of life in Holloway in her suffragette days. Mrs Elam knew how to keep the younger 18Bs entertained with her past victories. Emma was aware how exaggerated some of the claims were, and often wondered why Mrs Elam didn't take her presence into account, tone down some of what she said. Time must be playing tricks on Mrs Elam's memory, although she loved telling her stories. A lot of the time Emma found it ridiculous and felt sorry for the women forced to listen to Mrs Elam.

Whenever officers had to deal with Mrs Elam, her response was predictable. Like the day a note came from her sister Dorothy about the death of their brother Redmond in Australia. Emma delivered the letter.

"I suppose you are aware of what this says. Relished reading my private business before me," said Norah, sarcasm dripping with every word.

"I know what it's about," Emma responded, refusing to rise to the taunt.

"I wonder why Dorothy was keen to tell me Redmond donated his body to Sydney University Hospital for use as a cadaver." Norah turned away from Emma and talked to herself, distressed.

"I can't comment," said Emma.

Norah, reminded that Emma was still there, took an opportunity for a lecture.

"Well, see here, this is what happens when you allow doctors to get their grubby paws on you. Not content with experimenting on animals, they cut up human beings and degrade them. No respect even in death."

"I can't comment, but will say I am sorry about your news," and with that she extricated herself and left Mrs Elam alone with her letter.

Emma's duties became more onerous with the arrival of Sir Oswald Mosley at Holloway in December 1941, when he and Lady Diana got assigned a flat together in the prison grounds. Emma had to be present at every meeting between Sir Oswald and his solicitors, as well as family visits by Lady Redesdale and other family members. Emma sometimes wondered if, apart from the actual surroundings, Lady Mosley, whose soirees for the BU women created great anticipation amongst the internees, realised that prison was intended to be a punishment.

On 1 August 1942 a Suspension Order was issued and Mrs Elam and her friend Muriel Whinfield were notified they were to be released. As Mrs Elam left, Emma suspected that she would miss her old sparring partner. But this was not the last time they were to meet.

Emma knew from her reports to the Governor that Lady D nursed a fondness for Mrs Elam. After Mrs

Elam's release Lady D encouraged her mother, Lady Redesdale, to visit Mrs Elam at her London flat. Lady Redesdale said she would. Later events made Emma believe she understood why.

"Why do you suppose Lady Redesdale visited Mrs Elam for tea?" asked Miriam

"Unity and Lady Redesdale make regular visits to Sir O and Lady D. Unity has to live in the country, so it's difficult travelling and visiting on one day."

"Because of Unity's health?"

"The bullet is still in her brain from when she shot herself in Munich. The reports describe her as 'fragile'."

"They reckon she got off lightly. No detention, despite being a traitor."

"Friends in high places. Anyway, Mrs E offered for Unity to stay at her flat before a Holloway visit."

"I can't imagine Mrs E enjoying looking after her."

"Mr and Mrs E went with Unity on the visit the next day so they got to see Mosley. They were the only BU members who did."

"The crafty woman. He refused to see anyone except his solicitor or business people. So that was what she was up to."

Emma remembered the visit well. At the beginning, Mrs Elam started excited and happy, but as it finished she became downcast. Emma overheard Sir Oswald tell the Elams that they must not make anyone aware they visited him. He made a rule that he would only receive relatives and business callers. He came along to this visit because he had the impression Unity would be accompanied by his mother-in-law, Lady Redesdale.

Emma never did discover whether it had been a mistake. She had her suspicions, but was unable prove it. Emma had her ideas about Mrs Elam, and her latest stay in Holloway gave Emma a long time to observe her. Apart from regular discussions with Miriam, Emma kept her opinions to herself, but did express surprise when she received indirect confirmation of her own idea of Mrs Elam's character during a visit by Mosley's solicitor, Mr Swan.

Emma recorded their conversation. Mosley indicated to Mr Swan that he wanted to talk about setting up a committee to work at informing MPs of the facts about the appalling conditions of the 18Bs. Mosley suggested Mrs Dacre Fox should be on the committee after her release. He suggested she understood first-hand what would be required. Emma, who wondered why Mosley referred to her as Mrs Dacre Fox and not Mrs Elam, struggled to suppress her surprise when Mr Swan's replied, '…. I do not think that Mrs Dacre Fox would fit in with the other people. She is domineering and not of the same class as the others'. Even more surprising was Sir Oswald's response when he agreed to cross her name off the list. Mrs Elam always gave the impression she belonged to the same social class as Mosley, revered and esteemed by him for her contribution to the BU. Her intimacy with Lady Diana and her family seemed to confirm this. But this revelation confirmed Emma's instinctive feelings about her.

❧ ❧ ❧

NORAH LOOKED UP at the Clary sisters, agitated. *Come on ladies, bring me luck*, she intoned, *you did it before, you can do it again.* She had already checked that the maid had the tea trays laid out and ready. She got the maid to make some sandwiches for their afternoon visitor. It used up most of the butter ration, but was bound to be worth it. Dudley had been briefed and Tony sent out to make sure he didn't get in the way. He'd been none too happy to be told that Mr Swan, The Leader's solicitor had requested a visit, and that she didn't want him around. Mr Swan was calling at The Leader's request to see her on an important matter, and she didn't want anything to go wrong. She'd have preferred it if Tony had gone down to Nanny like when Unity came to stay, but Mr Swan gave rather short notice and it hadn't been possible to arrange it.

Norah registered the bell ring, her ears aware of the maid answering the door. A few moments later, Mr Swan entered the drawing room, followed by Dudley. The maid was dispatched to bring the tea.

"I see you admiring the portraits, Mr Swan."

"I am informed about them, but have never seen them."

"Ah, then you know who they are?"

"I believe they are the Clary sisters."

"I always think they are so beautiful."

"If I remember correctly, Napoleon passed over Désirée for Josephine, while Julie married Joseph

Bonaparte."

"Napoleon's loss proved Bernadotte's gain."

"Quite so."

"Anyway, my guess is that The Leader has sent you. As he knows, I am at his disposal to help with the cause in any way I can. Has he a task for me to carry out?"

"Lady Redesdale has briefed Sir Oswald on your anxiety to see something done about the unjustness and indiscriminate nature of the 18B Regulations. He is anxious to form a charity to campaign and raise funds to secure legal defence for 18B prisoners during their appeals hearings. Margaret Vivien and Viscountess Downe have already agreed to work with George Dunlop, who is to be the head of the charity."

"It would be an honour to work with those individuals. I'm well qualified. I enjoy fund raising and making speeches, and my own recent experiences will give me authority when it comes to talking about being incarcerated with my civil liberties suspended."

"Then I take it we can begin work as soon as possible. I'll get details sent round about the meetings that are to take place."

☙ ☙ ☙

IT WAS A beautiful day. Whether there were clouds in the sky, rain beat down, snow, ice, sunshine, whatever the weather, it was a beautiful day. It was VE day. It was spring and it was VE day. Emma and Miriam woke together with plans. Truth be told, there had been partying everywhere for a few days now, but today was the public holiday, the day after everyone knew the surrender was signed at Rheims. Emma had the day off, and they were off to Trafalgar Square and Piccadilly Circus, and to see the King and Queen at Buckingham Palace. Too excited to eat breakfast, they dressed in a hurry, pulled on their coats, pinned their victory rosettes firmly to their lapels, picked up their Union Jacks and set off to find the crowds. They wanted to be part of it, wanted to join in and be free. After years of making do and mending, food rations, no bananas, restrictions on everything, somewhere people found the resources to stage big street parties. No one could guess how long it would take to get back to normal. Everyone had forgotten what normal was, if it ever existed. But for the first time in what seemed forever, Emma wanted to get up and face the day. That was despite the party that went on long into the night before. Everyone seemed to be drunk on happiness.

As they approached Trafalgar Square, avoiding ladders that appeared everywhere stringing up banners and bunting and Union Jacks, it proved impossible to ignore the singing. Emma wanted to get to the steps by the lions. The way to do that was to join a long conga line, while the music blared out of the loudspeakers. Everyone was befuddled with excitement and relief. Someone said Piccadilly Circus was the place to be, so holding each other's hands they tried to make their way there. Emma wondered where the loudspeakers came from. Like the bunting, most of them had remained hidden for years, only coming out to help the authorities when needed to deal with some emergency. Now what blared through them was joy and happiness.

Emma would never forget how the crowd hushed as over the loudspeakers came the voice of Winston Churchill. From the ecstatic deafening noises moments before, you could have heard a pencil land on the pavement, rubber end first. The crowd seemed to hold its breath while they listened. Emma sensed the tears streaming down her face. Miriam squeezed her hand and she squeezed back. Then they listened to those final words of his speech – "Advance Britannia – Long live the cause of freedom. God Save the King." A moment later the loudspeakers echoed to the call – "Three cheers for victory, hip hip – HOORAY!" came the deafening roar, "hip hip HOORAY!" – another roar. After the final hip hip, Emma was sure they heard the HOORAY in Scotland and France.

How they got to the Mall, Emma didn't know. At one point she lost Miriam in the crowd, but a little while later observed her standing on some steps a little above the crowd, shouting her name. How she reckoned to be noticed above the din, Emma had no idea. Having got hold of each other again, arms threaded together at the elbows, determined not to be parted again, they danced along with the crowd and got to the gates of the Palace as the King and Queen appeared with Princess Elizabeth and Princess Margaret. It was so hard to accept it was over. So hard to accept that the long years of endless struggle could soon be behind them. Despite common sense telling her that there was hardship still to come – six years of war wouldn't be fixed quickly – today the crowd were jubilant and it was good to let go and join in. The hangover would wait until tomorrow.

They parted that evening outside Holloway. Emma due on duty the next morning, needed to say something to Miriam before they parted. She'd been ruminating over it for some time now, and with the end of the war determined she must take the chance to change her life.

"Miriam, we aren't getting any younger – I'm fifty-four now."

"Oy vey. I've the same problem."

"I've decided that I'm going to leave the prison service and try to find different work for the years left with any strength in me."

"Does that mean for me what I've hoped for, for so many years?"

"It does. I want us to live together."

"It won't be easy. If the rumours circulating amongst my people are true, there are terrible days to come, and a lot of grieving to be done, but for now I will be content knowing that we will be together."

CB CB CB

"Dudley, Dudley, where are you?"

"About to go to my study. What is it you want?"

"Did you send that birthday telegram to The Leader

at Crux Easton?"

"I have a copy here, see. Just as you said. Read it for yourself."

Norah looked at the words – 'Heartiest greetings and best love. Dudley and Norah Elam.' She'd not heard from The Leader since he announced that he wouldn't be taking part in the election called for July after the war ended in May. She worked so hard for the 18B charity these last few years, it was hard to accept that The Leader giving up like that. She couldn't believe the way that the 18B charity ended, recriminations all round and nasty arguments. The Leader accused some of petty jealousy, saying that bad publicity killed any chance of a comeback for him. If she had a chance to talk to him or Lady Diana herself, they'd appreciate how much The Leader was still admired. There was no doubt that even if they put up candidates for the election, she would be too old to accept a nomination, but there must be something she could do. She craved to be involved and be active again. Dudley's health meant he had to be careful what he did, but they could both still wield a pen and organise things.

Surely their political hopes and dreams would not end like that. It must be the people around The Leader who persuaded him to give up. If he went, so would her political home. It was like losing a whole family in one terrible disaster. But as the days passed and no message came from The Leader, she realized that she would never again play any part in campaigning for the things she believed in. Others took over her animal welfare work during her internment, and it proved impossible to get back to that in the way she wanted. Why was it necessary to accept a seat on the sidelines? Her rights had been suspended while an 18B prisoner, but did that mean that she would never be able to participate in democracy again? That seemed perverse. Wasn't that what the politicians claimed to be fighting for and won a victory for?

The telegram on his birthday was her last hope. If he didn't respond to that, she would take it as a sign.

CB CB CB

THE LEADER DIDN'T respond. Dudley watched her agony, his own misery expanding in sympathy with those around her. *Every day that passes her frantic longing to be acknowledged by The Leader or Lady Diana erupts in anger at any poor soul in her immediate vicinity. She directs most of it at me, but that poor maidservant, how does she cope? Maybe she'll walk out soon. Wouldn't blame her if she did.* The barrage was endless. Norah's ears had developed a sixth sense. He watched as she went towards the telephone and stood waiting beside it before it rang. How did she realise it was going to do that? He watched as she picked up the receiver, her face settled into that calm 'I'm in charge' look. Then she realised it wasn't The Leader, Lady Diana or someone to do with them. He watched as her face changed to that defeated 'my lover has deserted me' look, amazed how the angry mask descended in a flash. It was the same with the post. The minute the maid arrived with the post-tray, she would snatch the letters off, then discard each one in turn, until the entire floor was scattered with them and her hands were empty. Then she would commence to shout, accusing the maid of not bringing every letter delivered and hiding post from her.

Other times he would find her sat at her desk, staring into space, grinding her teeth and clenching her jaw, holding a pen poised over a blank sheet of paper. Then, distracted, she would get up and start pacing, clenching her fists, unable to contain her misery. Her sleep became almost non-existent. Dudley kept her company at night when nightmares interrupted what little sleep she got. He would get up and sit, watching her pace up and down and attempt to utter comforting words. She met his efforts with angry rants about how others must be lying to The Leader and turning him against her.

Mary Allen kept her up to date, but the news wasn't good. Perhaps The Leader had deserted them for reasons he chose not to divulge? Who knew? She kept repeating how The Leader's silence was hard to comprehend. Dudley listened to her insistence that The Leader owed her a personal explanation. She'd been faithful; he'd do the right thing. Mary reported that he seemed to have some strange ideas, and if true, it was over.

Dudley felt ill and exhausted. Norah's grief had become intolerable. The latest visit with his doctor told him that the situation must be resolved. He needed to do something, couldn't go on with things the way they were. So he made plans for them to move out of London to a cottage in Twickenham. Once accomplished, he felt sure Norah would begin to come to terms with the end of her active political life. She had to; he didn't have the strength to go, otherwise.

CB CB CB

CHAPTER 11
Aftermath

DUDLEY LOOKED ACROSS the table at Norah. B*een here six months*, he thought, *but Norah is still restless, unable to overcome her disappointment at the abrupt ending of the 18B charity work and Mosley's retirement from political life.* He hadn't considered it at the time, but yesterday he realised that moving to 'Gothic Cottage' entailed a cruel irony. Gothic tales dealt with outcasts from society, who experience personal torment and uncertainty about the nature of man and his salvation or destruction. What an apposite metaphor for Norah's experiences the last year!

"Will Mary Allen or Arnold Leese be visiting to-day?" asked Dudley.

"Mary will be here. Arnold is coming to dinner later in the week."

"Is he still talking about writing his biography? What's the title?"

"*Out of Step: Events in the Two Lives of an Anti-Jewish Camel Doctor.*"

"How far has he got?"

"Says it won't be finished for a while. At the moment he is describing Kashrut and why he loathes Jews because of it."

"What's Kashrut?

"The laws governing ritual preparation of animals and food for slaughter. It disgusts him."

"I hadn't realised that. I was aware he and Mosley never agreed about anti-Semitism. Mosley said he was too radical, while Arnold insisted Mosley was never radical enough."

"They considered Arnold an extreme radical before the war, did some controversial things. Went to prison as a result. Another reason Mosley kept a distance."

"Same as William Joyce, I suppose. It was right for Mosley to sack him from the BU. Look how he fled to Germany immediately before our arrests. Does Mary make any suggestions about what people think of his Lord Haw Haw activities, and whether he deserved to be hanged as a traitor?"

"Opinion is divided," said Norah. "Couldn't stand the man, but to execute him as a British traitor was wrong. He wasn't English; was Irish – born in America."

"When they captured him, the passport he travelled on was British."

"Semantics serving politics."

Dudley had mixed feelings about Norah's visitors. He understood how much she missed political life and meeting people. Mary and Arnold helped her maintain the idea she still had involvement somehow. Mary's soothed Norah's anxieties. Her immersion in organisations connected with Mosley, meant Norah enjoyed being kept up to date. But the aftermath of Arnold's visits left him exhausted.

"I'm sorry I had to go to bed last night and leave you with Arnold," said Dudley.

"You do tire easily."

"Did you come to any conclusions then?"

"What are you referring to?"

"Arnold's proposition that if Hitler killed that many Jews, why do so many survive?"

"Arnold says the reports of five million dead are fantasies. Hitler never did away with the numbers claimed."

"What does he say to the pictures in the press?"

"Bogus. Falsified to win sympathy for Jews."

"What do you reckon?"

"Not sure. Can't accept so many died. Can't believe Hitler approved what they call 'The Final Solution'."

"Evidence keeps coming to light, though. I read the papers but find it difficult to tolerate the idea Hitler sanctioned genocide. Perhaps he didn't appreciate what might be happening, perhaps they kept it from him. Perhaps he did try to rid the world of Jews and failed."

"So many questions. We know how governments use propaganda. Maybe this is done to make Hitler appear bad now the war is over."

"Who knows? Perhaps more facts will emerge and we'll get a better picture."

"I'm convinced the publicity is to discredit fascism –

make sure it can't come back."

"It looks that way. Perhaps Arnold's question is the right one?"

CB CB CB

TONY STOOD IN the crematorium chapel next to his mother, watching his father's coffin slide away. As it disappeared and the black curtains closed behind it he stared around. *See those fuddy-duddies sitting on the hard pews over there,* he thought. *Stark and cold, like dead fish with their eyes popping. There's no more life in them than this building, or my father who's gone to get toasted. The only things with any colour are the flowers standing either side of the catafalque. Even the miserable bits of pale sunshine that get through those grubby windows up there can't make anything warm. It reflects back off the white walls emphasising the general gloom and misery. My father's been in hell these three years since the war ended. I am glad he's now at peace. My mother went mad when her political life came to an end, and he had a difficult time handling her moods. She peopled her twilight world with rejects and exiles from public life like her. That Arnold Leese was a right one. My father tried to give an opposite view, but never got far. It's good I've been able to set up the business in Southampton, and not live with them. Can't wait to go home, but first must go to this meeting she's demanded.*

"I'll get straight to the point," said Norah.

"Good. I need to get back. I've a lot of work. The

business is going well."

"Your father loaned you the capital to start the company. As his sole beneficiary, I require repayment in full within the next fourteen days."

"But if you take the capital out, it will collapse."

"Nothing to do with me. I didn't want him to loan you the money. Now I want it back, with interest. As it's mine, I shall also need you to pay over any profit made so far."

"If you insist on that, I'll be in debt. No one else will lend to me. If you let me carry on, I'll pay you back over time, including good interest. Job contracts are pouring in."

"I'm not interested. I need the cash now – for me."

"Why? My chances of getting work are non-existent. What jobs there are go to ex-servicemen and people without notorious parents. To set up my own business is the only way I can earn a living."

"If you are trying to be sarcastic, don't bother. Re-pay or I'll sue you."

Tony left angry. Why do it? What would she gain? Why couldn't she accept that patience on her part would secure her a regular income? Wouldn't that be better than him having no work? He convinced himself that spite drove her, and promised to find ways to pay her back.

ങ ങ ങ

THE WEDDING TOOK place at the Southampton Registry Office in August, less than nine months after his father's death. Olive was a merchant seaman's daughter, small, under five foot high, slim, with dark curly hair. Always neatly dressed, her fine features in classical proportions always reflected a smile. To Tony she was perfect in every sense except that she had one annoying habit – she would shake her head in a small tick whenever nervousness got the better of her. "The service was lovely," said Mrs Tanner. Mrs T owned the boarding house where Olive and Tony had temporary lodgings, and she'd invited them for drinks to toast the bride and groom after the ceremony.

"It was. I was ever so nervous, though," said Olive.

"Did you get the horror on the registrar's face when you signed the register?"

"You mean when he asked Tony's mother about his father's occupation?"

"Yeah."

"I noticed him wince, but he hid it well. Her best Trafalgar Square voice is rather frightening. Don't suppose I'll ever forget her glaring at him and announcing – 'He didn't have an occupation. He was a gentleman of independent means'."

"No wonder Tony finds her difficult."

"I'm glad we're living here for now. I wouldn't want to live with her. What a scary idea!"

ෆ ෆ ෆ

WHY DID MARRIED life need to be so hard, Olive wondered? Food rationing was bad enough, but finding somewhere to live proved a real pain. They searched and searched, but every time she enquired got told 'ex-servicemen and their families have priority'. It seemed they'd always be last on the list. Would there ever be enough money to build houses for every family that needed one? They located a small flat in an old mansion that had seen better days. It had once housed an aristocratic family and a horde of servants. *Must have been splendid once, but look at it now. Cramped living space for several families, its glory days long gone.* Shared bathrooms were the worst. She hated the squabbles over who was entitled to use them and when. Then came the day she brought her baby girl home. She stood in the bathroom cuddling the child and looked around. The birth had been a difficult one. They had to call the priest to baptise the tiny bundle in case she died and ended up in Purgatory. Despite the child crying for a feed, Olive's thoughts centred on how amusing it was that no one ever squabbled over who should clean the bathroom. *Need to get on and do it myself after feeding the child, then.*

Tony struggled to find a job after Norah collapsed his business. How they managed, she never quite understood, but they did, somehow. When daughter number two came two years later, Tony found himself forced to start searching further afield. Work came up in Surrey as a long-distance lorry driver. Olive faced an agonising decision. It would be steady, permanent employment. The first time he'd been offered such a thing. But there would be a price to pay for the security.

"Now I've got this work, my mother has said we should go and live with her at Gothic Cottage," said Tony.

"Are you sure that's a good idea?"

"It will solve our problems, won't cost much, and we'll be able to save a deposit to buy a house."

"House buying is the last thing on my mind. I'm worried whether your mother will cope with Carina and Mary."

"Why? They aren't babies. Carina's five and Mary's three. They're easy enough to control."

"They're children. I don't think she likes children."

"Because she wants them disciplined and well-behaved, doesn't mean she doesn't like them."

"Are you sure? You aren't rewriting the song sheet, are you?"

"Don't argue. There's no choice. Gothic Cottage is big enough for you to keep them out of her way. We're going to live with her, and there's an end to it."

His mind appeared settled on what should be done. He ignored her attempts to reason with him. She had to trust him for her daughters' sake. So why be so worried and nervous? She'd noticed how Tony never referred to his mother other than as 'she', spitting the word out in anger. Whenever he talked about her, which wasn't often, he would bite his top lip, while the bottom one quivered with fury. The few occasions they'd been to visit her, Olive observed nothing in the way of tenderness between them. He exhibited a determination to keep silent about her, and what little he did reveal came out under duress. Whenever they went to see Norah, she never failed to tell Olive, in her best commanding voice, about her days as a suffragette and her anti-vivisection work. Olive would listen politely while watching Tony's eyes. There was no doubt about it – if looks could kill his mother would be long gone. Afterwards she would try to get him to talk about why he nursed such anger towards Norah. He would brush her question aside with dismissive statements like, "She always did care more for animals than anyone or anything else." Olive came to the conclusion that Tony had been starved of love and affection, and that if Norah devoted as much time to Tony as she had to her causes, he might have been a happier person. In the meantime, she loved him, but faced a dilemma. Why had Tony decided to live with Norah? It may be fine for him; he went away a lot of the time, driving his lorry. Why throw her and the children to the lions? Hard up they might be, but that hard up? And was this was the solution? Her head hurt trying to fathom the answer. For now, she would trust that he loved his family, and wouldn't put them in danger. At least, that is what she kept telling herself. Trouble was, it didn't matter how frequently she repeated it, it never did quite silence her fears.

C03 C03 C03

THE BELL RANG downstairs and Olive tensed. The maid had the day off. She supposed Norah needed her to do something. She wondered what on earth it might be this time. She hated being the substitute maid. Hated leaving the children upstairs for too long, but despite trying to explain it to her, Norah didn't want to understand the trouble small children got themselves into. Or maybe she didn't care. Who could fathom? She roused herself to go and find out what was wanted. She hated the room Norah occupied as a study/bedroom. The smell resembled stale damp woollen socks put away in a cupboard soiled and wet. Then there was the tray of dog food and the litter tray that gave off a repulsive odour like a filthy toilet – because she wouldn't let the animal out. It didn't make sense why Maximilian – the name said it all – had to sleep in the room under the sheets at the bottom of the bed. It was disgusting. How did her visitors put up with the stench? More than a few moments in there and she began to feel ill. Enough to kill your appetite for anything, never mind food.

"You rang the bell. Did you want something?" asked Olive.

"Mary Allen is coming to tea this afternoon. Go and prepare a tray to put on the desk here for when she arrives."

"Hasn't the maid prepared everything? I can't leave the children too long, but if you tell me what time she's arriving, I can make sure they're having their afternoon nap."

"There are two jobs. Get the tray ready now then come back this afternoon to pour the boiled water into the teapot and carry it through here."

"If I must. Will three-thirty be in order?"

"You might be more gracious about it. Three-thirty will be fine. Mary should arrive about then."

Olive went to find the children. Lost in her reflections, she climbed the stairs. It was awkward living in this house. They'd no privacy, even though Norah was unable climb the stairs to their part of the house. Tony spent much of the time away on his long-distance trips, and never witnessed Norah's behaviour during his absences. Every time Olive complained, Norah told him she lied or imagined it, and Tony would defend Norah. Surely he wasn't that frightened of his mother? How much longer could she stand it? She was never sure if she'd be allowed to use the kitchen, and Norah's rules about the children playing in the garden were a nightmare. She tried not to listen when Norah said nasty things about what she called Olive's low-class common family, and her merchant seaman father, but it proved difficult. She hoped the children would settle later without a struggle to facilitate the tea ritual. She wouldn't be able to cope if they played up as well.

Later that afternoon, Olive carried the tea-tray into Norah's room. The desk was scattered with papers and she'd to stand holding it while Norah made room.

"Put it here. Carefully, if you please," said Norah.

"The tray is heavy. It would help if you cleared more

space."

"There's enough room, put it down and don't argue. Hurry up, there's the doorbell. Go and let Mary in. When you've shown her in here, fetch the teapots, then pour the tea."

"I don't have much time. The children are resting, but won't stay that way long."

"Nonsense. Do as I say."

Olive showed Mary in, then fetched the teapots. Shaking with anger and nervousness, she turned over the cups to pour out the tea. Disaster. As Olive picked up the two cups to carry to Norah and Mary, a saucer hit the edge of the tray, the cup toppled off and fell on the desk, and tea spread across and through the papers. Olive rushed to the kitchen to grab a cloth to starting dabbing and mopping up the liquid, but with every wasted moment it dispersed further.

"You stupid, clumsy woman," shouted Norah. "Look what you're doing. What's wrong with you?"

"It was an accident."

"Accident? I watched you, you did it on purpose. Your lack of breeding means you can't even pour tea without doing something stupid."

"Do you think I wanted to spill the tea and get told off?"

"Look what you did. Look, Mary, look what she did," said Norah, holding up her silver-framed signed photograph of Diana Mosley. "The tea has spread under the picture, got soaked up at the bottom and is spreading and making the ink of the signature run. Wait till Tony gets back from his trip. I'll make you pay for this."

Olive retreated from the room as fast as she her legs would carry her. She ran up the stairs sobbing, wondering how she and the children would pay.

෬ ෬ ෬

SHE WOULD MAKE Tony answer for bringing that woman and her brood into her house. He married Olive to spite her. Olive couldn't stand up to her; was timid, stupid and socially inept. Tony tried to make excuses for her. But to insist that because Olive's mother had died when she was five and she'd to live with a stepsister who treated her badly did not excuse the women's clumsiness. On top of that, Olive displayed pride above her station. She'd told her and Tony often enough that she'd pay for private education for those children, but Olive refused to allow it. The stupid woman used the argument that if the children had to go to ordinary schools later on they would suffer. "Rubbish, she talks rubbish." She needed to find a way to get Tony to realise that he shouldn't have crossed her and married beneath himself.

"Tony, there's something you should realise before you speak to your mother," said Olive.

"I just got back. She caught me at the door and told me I must go straight back down and see her once I've changed. Can't it wait?

"You ought to understand before you go down," said Olive.

"Hurry up, then. Tell me. What is it?"

"She's sold your father's books. Every one. The dealer came several days ago, paid her in cash and collected them this morning."

"But she can't. They were mine. My father told me he left them to me. There were beautiful first bound editions, a valuable collection."

"Your mother doesn't seem bothered by any of that."

"They were mine. She agreed."

"That's why she wants to speak you. I thought you should be ready."

Tony went down to his mother's room, bitter and ready for a fight.

CB CB CB

OLIVE SAT AT the top of the stairs listening to the angry voices below. The words swelled and rolled up the stairs in waves to where she sat in the darkness, hoping they wouldn't wake the children. The stairs were steep and easy to fall down because of the poor lighting. She looked at the frayed stair carpet held in place by bent or broken stair rods, like the tempers being aired down there. Inadequate lights did not hide the dust ingrained into the bare wood either side of the stair runners. Olive stared, thinking how it proved impossible get it out of the cracks and holes when she cleaned. It resembled the atmosphere in the house. Bad temper accumulated, proved highly sensitive to disturbance, was impossible to get rid of, and permeated everywhere.

"How dare you sell my books?" Tony shouted.

"They weren't yours," Norah shouted back.

"They were too. My father left them to me."

"Not according to his will. He left everything to me."

"Show me his will. Prove it to me."

"I'll get the papers out for you."

"But he's been dead for a long time. It was father's wish the books came to me. I always believed they were mine. Why didn't you tell me when you got probate?"

"You didn't need to be told," said Norah.

"That has always been your answer, 'I didn't need to know'."

"That's right. You didn't."

"Why? Fact is I did, but you never had the courage to tell me. You never told me I was a bastard, you shouted it at me though. You never told me about Father's other family, just lied. You never explained why you never married Father. You never told me why you never loved me like a normal mother."

"Tony, stop now or I'll lose my temper."

"You haven't already?"

"I tolerate you in this house, Tony. Don't forget that. This is my home, left to me by your father. You have tried to spite me by bringing that lower class, inept woman to live here. If you carry on, I will evict out."

"Lost the argument, have you? Resorting to the 'get out' line to end it?"

"You will pay, Tony. Mark my words."

The door slammed and Tony started up the stairs. Olive rose to go back to the bedroom so that he wouldn't realise she'd been listening. Norah would extract a price. Never said what she didn't mean. Except that Olive had a foreboding that Olive who would pay. Norah would make sure of that.

A few days later, Tony left for a long trip to the north, and Norah summoned Olive to her room.

"I've visitors arriving. Come with me to the kitchen to prepare the tea tray."

"But the children will be home soon. Where's the maid? Has she got the day off?"

"She's busy elsewhere. Are you defying me, refusing to help?"

"No. But it's late and I need to get food for the children."

"I don't care. This is my house. My priorities take precedence."

Olive sighed and followed Norah to the kitchen. She laid out one tray with the cups and saucers and cake plates, then a second with the cake. She carried them through to where tea was to be served. The bell rang, and Olive let in Mary Allen. Instead of going to the room for tea, Mary followed her to the kitchen, where Olive had gone to fetch the now full teapots, extra hot water and milk. The tray was heavy and Olive felt nervous with Norah and Mary watching her, as well as worried about the children. Passing a table covered in china objects the maid had collected up for cleaning, she tripped on the edge of a loose rug. The tray flew from her hands, and Olive fell to the ground, landing on her elbow. In great pain she sat up with Norah standing over her, the tea pot and milk jugs smashed to pieces with tea and milk running down the cracks in the floorboards. Looking past the liquid mess, it dawned on her that she had also knocked the figurines off the table and one or two lay broken on the floor.

"What have you done, you stupid, inept, clumsy idiot?"

"It was an accident. I tripped on the rug."

"You did it to embarrass me in front of Mary."

"Norah, I am sure Olive wouldn't do something like that," said Mary.

"She would."

"Do you think I wanted to hurt myself like this? Now I have a mess to clear up and the children need me."

"Damn the children, damn you, damn that son of mine for bringing you into the house."

"Norah, calm down. Let's go and make more tea. But we'll do it together and let Olive get on, shall we?

"She'd better go. She had better get out of my sight, and keep her brats out of my sight as well," shouted Norah.

Olive retreated upstairs shaken, crying and in pain.

Eventually, the visitors left. She put the children to bed and went down to the kitchen to tidy up and get some tea. The kitchen was locked with a note on the door in Norah's handwriting.

> *'Because of your total disregard for my home and the things in it, you are no longer allowed to use this kitchen. I don't care how you manage, but make sure you and the children stay upstairs out of my way'.*

What was she going to do? Tony was away for another five days. How would she manage? *The children must have hot food, we need hot water.* The next day Olive devised a plan. Outside her bedroom window, the roof led down to a raised bank of ground where the pantry window overlooked the garden. Lucky the roof was almost flat, the window never got locked, and Olive was small enough to get through it. It might be dangerous, but the only way get access to the kitchen. Once in the kitchen, she knew where the maid left a spare set of keys. At night she would creep out of the kitchen, carry things up to the children, and slink back down, lock the door, and return via the pantry window to her room.

CB CB CB

NORAH WAS AWARE of the staff bustling about around her bed. Idiots. *Pumped me full of drugs to stop me giving 'em what for. Must know I can hear — every inane word —*

how dare they talk about me – how dare they. If only I could…

"Her son's coming again today. Always makes her more agitated. Mind you, she looks pretty wound up now," said the nurse with the whiny voice.

"Pity the staff on duty this evening after visiting hours," the other nurse replied.

"Especially if her daughter-in-law comes as well."

"Her. Sits outside the ward cowering. Too terrified to come in. Small little woman. Has a nervous tick. Seems to get worse while waiting."

Idiots. Are they pretending they think I can't understand? I'm well aware what's going on. Haven't lost my marbles despite those disgusting drugs they pump into me several times a day. Always knew doctors weren't to be trusted. No proof needed of that now – if proof were needed. Think they can bully me because my body has let me down. 'No Compromise, Bully Back'. That was my slogan in the old days. They'll never get the better of me. Never.

"Heard tell as she was a suffragette way back," said whiny nurse.

"Apparently so. At least that was what the staff at the nursing home where she came from said. The one that came with her here in the ambulance told me they were glad to get rid of her. Said she shouted and cursed at them the whole time. Accused them of being torturers like when she was in Holloway being force-fed to get women a vote."

Idiots. Who do they think they are? Got no standards, no idea how to treat people and then moan when I tell them how to do their jobs. Isn't the Eichmann trial set to start in Jerusalem soon? Wonder how come they captured him? He'll put up a good defence. They won't best him. Don't know how they managed to capture him in the first place. Wish they'd turn me over; been lying in this position too long. Why can't they hear me? Aren't they listening? Aren't the words coming out of my mouth clearly enough?

"Time to turn her over, according to her chart," said whiny nurse. "Hope they come and give her the next dose of tranquiliser soon. Don't want to risk her flailing around and shouting if she gets fully conscious. Patients say horrible things when they are in pain, but this one takes the biscuit. Must have been real feisty in her day."

Idiots. I've only ever done what was good for animals and women. I've been loyal to my causes. Pity my stupid son came along and ruined it. If I'm gone, who's going to get those daughters of his in line? Certainly not that common, inept mother of theirs who behaves like an idiot most of the time.

"I heard tell as she was also an 18B prisoner, you know a fascist in Mosley's Blackshirts," said nurse two.

"Hadn't heard that. Do tell. How long did she spend in prison during the war?"

"Don't know. But I'd sure like to know how she justifies that – we read the terrible stories of what went on in Nazi Germany."

Idiots. Bet they never fought for a righteous cause in

their lives. I wanted peace. The Fuhrer never wanted war with England. Everyone blames him, but I'm sure he didn't know what was happening. Anyway, I'm sure Mary or Arnold told me that if he did, it was because he was a victim of the Zionists that needed him to do what he did to justify the creation of the state of Israel. It was our idiot politicians who couldn't see The Leader was right. These chits pretending to be nurses wouldn't understand an honourable cause if it hit them in the face. They're so ignorant and soft, they don't even vote at election time. Don't have any inkling what real sacrifice is, not like the sacrifices we made back then anyway. If they'd let me wake up properly, I could teach them a thing or two. Why won't my body respond?

"From all accounts, sounds like she's left a trail of broken lives behind her. I'd sure like to find out whether she thinks it was worth it in the end."

Idiots, especially that whiny voiced one. Why can't she see that militant action is the only way to make progress? I know how I would answer if I was in Eichmann's shoes. Always did my duty to the cause I believed in. Followed orders. Anyway, if those Jews did go to their deaths, they went quietly. Otherwise why didn't we read more about it? Silently acquiesced with their fate. No more justification needed for what went on than that. When I was put in Holloway and tortured to get women the vote, I didn't go quietly. I struggled. They may have got hold of my body, but they never got my mind. Not like that lot, they gave in, undressed and went and breathed in the gas without a fuss – at least that's what they say happened. One day the truth will out. Everyone will learn that a lot of the propaganda produced since the war is just that – propaganda by the victors to justify their pusillanimous stance.

"Her face is twisted and she looks so bitter," said whiny-voiced nurse.

"Looks like she'll go as she lived. Angry and with no peace."

"Wonder what her eulogy will say. A woman who died frustrated that she ran out of life before she ran out of ambition," said whiny voice.

"Better still," Norah heard the other one say, "a zealot who died full of zeal but lacking in wisdom."

CB CB CB

TONY STOOD IN the crematorium chapel next to Olive and his daughters, Carina and Mary. It was a few years after the kitchen incident at Gothic Cottage That was what had persuaded him he had to move his family away from Norah. Now his mother was dead and he didn't know whether to feel relief or anger. He felt bitterness flood through him at the hymn they were playing as the curtains closed behind her coffin. How ironic! He'd left the choice to the crematorium staff as he didn't have any idea what was appropriate. When they suggested the tune Crimond together with the words of 'The Lord is my Shepherd' being spoken above it, he laughed. As he listened, he hoped the mask of his face had not betrayed his true feelings as he forced himself to stop grinding his teeth and control the grin that involuntarily contorted his lips. He tried to distract himself by dabbling his foot in a single ray of sunshine that had managed to penetrate the gloom and was highlighting the dust around his feet – but that served to remind him of his father's funeral.

Outside, after everyone had filed out, he overheard a woman he didn't recognise talking to Mary Allen. She was bragging about how she had inherited what was left of Norah's home and property, and that she was in the process of clearing everything out. Tony took Olive and the children and went to Gothic Cottage to see if what he had learned was true. When they got to the house, he rushed around the empty rooms in a rage. It was – at the end she had denied him even the smallest memento.

He saw Olive and Carina standing at the bottom of the stairs looking up at him. He was as angry with Olive as he was with his mother. Why, today of all days, was Olive's nervous tick worse than usual? He could tell because she couldn't stop her eyes rolling back in every time her head jerked. It was a sure sign she wasn't coping. He struggled to control his fury and muttered with sarcasm, "Bet the old biddy died with a smile on her face knowing what would happen when she was gone." Then he noticed Carina try to surreptitiously push her hand into her mother's. He watched Olive force Carina behind her, then saw the child pull her mother's skirt about her as if it would magically transform into some sort of protective shield. Why was the brat crying? What was that about? Why couldn't Olive control herself and the child? Why couldn't she make the brat follow his instructions? Why had he been disobeyed?

"What's she doing here?" he bellowed. "I said she'd to stay in the car outside."

"Your mother's death affects us all and it may surprise you to learn that you are not the only one who has mixed feelings about it."

"My mother may have been wrong about many things, but one thing she was right about was what a useless waste of space that girl is. She should never have been born!"

"Typical!" said Olive. "You can no longer get at your mother, so you round on those who are closest, most vulnerable and can't fight back. It saddens me to say it, but the pair of you deserved each other!"

By the Same Author

The Alice Band

Carole and Alice have been friends for years, bouncing happily off each other in ways that mystify onlookers. No one could explain how or why the friendship worked, least of all Carole and Alice. Carole often pondered this conundrum. Alice never did. Then 'life' happened. Circumstances conspired to force everyone out of their ruts, along the way challenging the dynamic of Carole and Alice's friendship. How do Carole and Alice deal with the string of catastrophes that beset Alice? Can their friendhip survive or will it change forever?